THE COMPLETE TALES OF
SHERIFF HENRY, VOLUME 4

W. C. Tuttle

GALLOPING GOLD

THE COMPLETE TALES OF SHERIFF HENRY, VOLUME 4

W.C. TUTTLE

COVER BY

EMMETT WATSON

STEEGER BOOKS • 2020

TABLE OF CONTENTS

HIGH HEELS—AND HENRY

The smell of sheep wafts into cowmen's paradise!
And Sheriff Henry has a problem all the tricks
he learned in vaudeville can never solve

CHAPTER I

LEAD FOR A SHEEPMAN

JOHNNY "RUSTY" LEE had never been in a city larger than Tucson. All his twenty-three years had been spent in and around Wild Horse Valley, where he owned the TL Ranch, inherited from his father. Rusty was six feet tall, slender, but muscular, and as brown as an aborigine. His eyes were a peculiar green, which together with his copper-colored hair and tanned skin made a startling combination.

Rusty had admitted to himself that he was "a little bit leary" of this trip to Los Angeles. What on earth, he wondered, would cause Mary Brant to send him a telegram, which read:

COME AT ONCE IF YOU CAN AND WIRE ME IF COMING AND WHEN

Mary Brant was the daughter of King Brant, owner of thousands of sheep, and reputed worth millions. Rusty had met Mary in Tucson during a rodeo, and in spite of the fact that Rusty hated sheep, he fell deeply in love with Mary Brant. They had exchanged letters for about a year. Rusty had no idea that his love was reciprocated. In fact, he felt that Mary merely wrote to him for amusement.

Certainly no one in Wild Horse Valley knew that Rusty Lee was carrying on a correspondence with the daughter of King Brant, who had made the boast that some day he would sheep out Wild Horse Valley.

Brant's sheep outfit owned miles of the Black River Flats

country, which was across a mountain range and fifty miles away from the nearest point to Wild Horse. But there was always that threat of invasion, especially when a drought ruined the feed on Black River Flats. This was especially true right now. Rumor said that Brant would be obliged to sell out or secure new range.

Rusty was self-conscious and a trifle timid, as he got off the train in Los Angeles late that afternoon. Even wearing his Sunday best, cowboy boots and a nearly new sombrero, he felt out of place in the well-dressed throng, as they went down to the tunnel and came up the long ramp into the station.

Rusty's eyes swept the welcoming crowd on either side of the ramp, but was unable to see Mary Brant. Near the outer doorway a youngish man, wearing a chauffeur's uniform, stepped out and met Rusty.

"Pardon me, but are you Johnny Lee?" he asked.

"That's right," admitted Rusty.

"Miss Brant was unable to meet you. Follow me, please."

He led the way out to a parked limousine, placing Rusty's

HENRY
HARRISON
CONROY

battered suitcase on the seat beside him, and they rode away through the heavy, late-afternoon traffic. Rusty felt very small, but rather important, all alone in the back of that wonderful car. The illuminated windows and the mass of traffic amazed the young cowboy, as they threaded through miles of it.

In Beverly Hills they drew out of the traffic, where a road led up through a wooded cañon, twisting into the hills. They turned soon through a huge gateway, went up a wide, graveled drive-way and came to a stop in front of a huge, two-story mansion, almost hidden in the trees.

The chauffeur led Rusty into the house, where a wood-en-faced butler met them.

"Mr. Lee from Arizona," said the chauffeur quietly.

"Oh, yes," murmured the butler. "Miss Brant expects you, but has been unfortunately detained for a while. I can assure you that you are very welcome, sir."

"That's shore nice of yuh," said Rusty. "If yuh don't mind I'll wait a while and—"

"If you will pardon me, sir, your room is ready. The chauffeur will bring your bags. By the way, Mr. Brant always desires to have a guest register in his guest-book. Right over here, please."

He opened a huge book and offered a filled pen to Rusty, who was rather proud of his signature. It was sort of intricate, but well executed. The butler smothered a smile, as he led the way up an imposing stairway to a corner room on the upper floor.

The magnificence of the place awed Rusty.

"Shore cost plenty *dinero*," he observed.

"Beg pardon, sir?"

"A house like this shore cost plenty money."

"Oh yes, sir, a pretty penny, no doubt."

THE ROOM was almost too much for Rusty. He merely stood in the center of it, while the butler arranged the lights and the drapes. As the butler was inspecting the bathroom, the chauffeur brought in Rusty's lone piece of baggage.

"I am sure you will be comfortable, sir," said the butler. "Miss Brant will be back soon, and you will be notified. Is there anything more I can do for you?"

"I—I jist can't think of anything—not right now," replied Rusty.

"Thank you, sir."

As they closed the door behind them Rusty heard a sharp *click,* as though a bolt had been thrown. But he knew none could have been. He removed his coat, stretched his arms and looked the place over.

"My gosh, what a bunk-house!" he gasped. He walked over to the one window, which the butler had opened. The house had been built on the very edge of a deep, wooded cañon, and it was at least a hundred feet straight down to the brush tops. Further down the cañon he could see a curved portion of highway, where many cars were passing.

To his right, about twenty feet away, was the corner of a balcony, which ran along the upper front of the house. Apparently there was no roof on the balcony, because the corner post was only about a foot above the railing.

Rusty examined the bathroom. A sunken tub, an enclosed shower, all glass, gleaming tile and polished metal. And Rusty had been accustomed to taking his baths in a washtub.

"Lovely dove!" he exclaimed softly, as he sat down and rolled a cigarette. "Imagine livin' like this!"

He lighted his cigarette and went over to the window. He leaned out, watching the twinkling lights, which faded away in the distance, miles away.

"Like seein' a sky upside down," he told himself.

After finishing his cigarette he put on his coat, deciding to go downstairs. He glanced at himself in a door mirror, sighed and shook his head. "I don't fit here. I'll see Mary and then pull out for Arizona."

He walked over, twisted the knob—but the door resisted him. It was locked tight! He rubbed his chin thoughtfully, as he eyed the door. Rusty was not a little puzzled over this. As far as he knew, there was no earthly reason for locking him in a room.

"Must be a mistake," he muttered aloud. "Mebbe the latch was on, and they didn't notice it. Locked it by mistake. But doggone it, I don't believe they'd do a fool thing like that—either."

He tried the door again. Then he walked back to his chair, sat down to think things over. Queer situation… And suddenly it struck him that there were more queer angles to the thing. Mary had told him that her father knew nothing about their correspondence. If there was anything he could do for Mary personally, why would all the servants be let in on the knowledge that he was coming? She wanted him at once—why?

After thinking it over for several minutes Rusty stepped over, picked up his old valise and opened it. He pawed inside it for a moment and got slowly to his feet.

"Some son-of-a-buck stole my six-gun," he told the empty room.

Another search showed two shirts, several pairs of socks, an extra pair of pants, badly wrinkled, and a forty-foot lariat of spot-cord. Rusty, his forty-five Colt and his lariat were inseparable. But the gun was gone. Only a half-box of cartridges left—and the rope.

"I know danged well that somethin' is wrong now," he declared. "Any old time they steal yore gun and lock yuh in a room—somethin' must be wrong. And they put me in a room where it's a hundred feet to terry-firmy. I hope to tell yuh, they've got little Rusty caged."

HE WENT back to the window, where he rolled another cigarette. The cañon was only a dark void now. Cars flashed along the boulevard down there. Far off in the trees he could see the lights of another mansion. He looked over at the lighted corner of the balcony, and an idea formed quickly in his brain.

Going back to his valise he drew out the rope. Quickly he shook out a loop and went back to the window, where he dropped the loop outside. Estimating the distance, he swung the loop back, jerked it swiftly, and saw it sag away from the corner post. Swiftly he drew it up, paid out the loop and made another cast. This time the loop circled the post-top, and he drew the rope taut.

That rope looked too frail for what Rusty intended doing, but he had tested it well.

"If it'll stop a runnin' steer, it shore ought to hold me. Anyway, it's a chance. Probably batter my danged brains out against the side of the post, tryin' to be a circus actor. But Swan River Grush says I ain't got any brains; so I don't need to worry about batterin' 'em."

Going over to the bed he flung aside the silken cover, yanked out a fancy blanket, which he folded carefully and twisted around his body, under his arms. Sitting on the window-sill and taking up as much slack as possible, he tied the rope over the top of the blanket. It would cushion the jerk, when he came to the end of his swing.

With a prayer on his lips that the rope would hold, he slid over the edge as far to the left as possible, grasped the rope with both hands and shoved away from the wall.

It was a breath-taking swing, and it seemed as though he would sail forever, before the pendulum slowed and started back. He could see the whole front of the house now. Another long swing, in which he barely missed striking the corner under the balcony. But this time he did not go so high. He bumped the corner gently with a shoulder, as he came back, and it sent him spinning. However it served to shorten the upswing, and he was out of danger, as far as the corner of the house was concerned.

A few moments later he was hanging straight down from the corner of the balcony. He rested for a little time. He would have to go up hand-over-hand as swiftly as possible, because that rope was hardly a handful, and there was no chance to use his feet in the climb.

Wiping his moist palms on the blanket, he reached up, grasped the rope tightly in his two strong hands, and started up. It seemed a mile up that rope, before his left hand grasped over that balcony rail, and he sprawled over it to the floor. Swiftly he untied the rope. He tossed the blanket aside and coiled the rope.

There were potted palms on the balcony and cozy seats. About midway were wide doors, opening out from the house. Carefully, Rusty opened one of the doors, and stepped into a dimly-lighted hallway. Moving slowly he came to another door, which led to the hallway outside the room he had occupied. Thick carpets silenced his movements, as he went cautiously along to where he could see lights from the big room at the foot of the stairs.

Rusty could hear indistinct voices from down there; so he crawled the last twenty feet and sank down behind the ornate railing, peering between the posts. There were three men down there, seated around a table, apparently examining some papers. From his position Rusty could not see the men plainly, but could hear their conversation. One man was saying:

"The situation is as solid as a dollar, King. His signature was all we needed. That cowtown lawyer told us that Lee had a trick way of writing his name. All we have to do now is to rush the papers over to Scorpion Bend. I congratulate you on owning a key-ranch in Wild Horse Valley."

"And," added the other man, "you get a thousand acres of land for the bonus money you promised us."

RUSTY TWISTED around enough to get some idea of King Brant—a tall, gaunt, distinguished-looking man, gray-haired and slightly stooped.

"I still do not understand, gentlemen," said Brant. "You seem to have worked out details—and yet, I feel you have gone too far."

"Wait a minute, King. We told you we could put sheep into Wild Horse Valley. You gave us permission to work out a scheme, promising that you would give us ten thousand dollars for a workable plan—before June fifteenth?"

"That is true," agreed King Brant. "But I surely did not mean for you to commit criminal acts."

"Criminal acts! You had to have range for your sheep—thirty thousand head of them. Well, we've got it for you."

"And it is the only feasible plan," added the third man. "The deed is signed. Any man who has ever seen John Lee's signature would swear to the one on that deed. When it's on record, they can't keep you out of that valley. We've checked the whole county, and we know just how much land is actually owned by the cattle outfits. I tell you, your thirty thousand sheep will only be a beginning. You said you needed feed for that many. Well, you've got it."

"I can visualize that, gentlemen," replied King Brant, "but the fact still remains that your scheme is based on treachery, kidnaping and theft, not to mention forgery. When young Lee is released—"

"So that's worrying you, eh? Forget it. Lee merely drops out of sight. Naturally he never would go back to Wild Horse Valley. In order to make everything air-tight, we will have a man who resembles Lee buy passage to Australia, and under Lee's name."

"Of all the damn things I ever heard!" roared Brant. "Why, you must be joking. You told me you had persuaded Lee to sell out to me for twenty-five thousand dollars. Now I find that you have never consulted him in the matter. Somehow you decoyed him here—and now you talk of murdering him. I won't have it, I tell you! Bring the man here, and I'll make a deal with him. I'll pay you the ten thousand dollars—and then I never want to see either of you again."

"He might deal," said one of the men tensely. "Did you bring the money?"

"Certainly, I brought it. You told me—why—what on earth are you—"

A shot shook the room. King Brant shoved his chair back and jerked to his feet. Rusty Lee ducked his head instinctively, but drew closer to the railing.

King Brant was on the floor, and one man was bending over him. The other man stepped nearer the door and snapped out the bright lights, leaving only a rose-colored table lamp as illumination. Then he quickly swept up the papers.

"Finished?" he queried huskily.

"Right! Got the papers?"

"Everything. We've got to get out, before the police come. What about the cowpuncher upstairs?"

"Never mind him now. He probably don't even know he's locked in."

"What about that deal now—with Brant out of it?"

"What about it? Why, we've got the whole thing in our hands, if we work it right. Let's go. We'll tell Mike to wait five minutes and then phone the police."

They left the room, closing the door behind them.

NOT A little shaken, Rusty got to his feet and went down the stairs. He could have walked past the crumpled body and left the house, but curiosity prompted him to stop. The dim light flashed on metal, and he stopped to pick up a heavy automatic pistol, lying near the body. Apparently King Brant had drawn a gun, before the fatal bullet stopped his hand.

Somewhere a door opened, and Rusty heard muffled voices. Not realizing that he was in a dangerous situation if discovered there, he made no move to get away. He thought it might be the chauffeur or butler, and if it was, Rusty was going to pay them back for locking him up.

Then the door opened. There were two men and a woman, it seemed. The woman snapped on the lights. At sight of King Brant on the floor, with Rusty standing over him, a pistol gripped in his right hand, she cried out sharply.

The woman was Mary Brant. She came a little closer, bracing one hand against the polished top of the table. She swayed a little, and one of the men placed a hand on her shoulder. Rusty wanted to say something, but his throat grew tight, and he could only twist his lips. The butler came in, stopped short and stared at Rusty.

"You killed him?" whispered the man beside Mary.

"My God, it's Mr. Brant!" exclaimed the butler. "Miss Mary, you'd better go away. I'll phone the police and—"

Rusty's voice came suddenly.

"Stand still! One move out of you, and I'll cripple you for life. Who was here with King Brant?"

"My God, sir, I know of no one. I swear—"

"You lie, you pale-faced polecat!"

"As God is my judge, sir. You are the only person—"

"Michael, you will please call the police," said Mary weakly.

"All right," growled Rusty. "I reckon the deadwood is on me.

Don't move, any of you. Mike, for the price of a rusty pin, I'd shoot yore crooked heart out through yore ribs. Now—hold it!"

Rusty sidled past them, closed the door quietly, crossed the reception hall and went outside. There was a limousine at the bottom of the steps, the driver enjoying a cigarette. Rusty looked keenly at him, as he walked past the car, but it was not the man who had driven him from the station.

Unhurried, because he had no idea where he was going, Rusty went down the driveway and out onto the paved highway. A police car passed him. It was a long walk to the car tracks, but Rusty finally caught a street car, a dangerous move for him, because he knew that Mary had recognized him, and that the police must have his name and description.

In Los Angeles he boarded another car and got off near the Plaza. He had no idea where to go, nor what to do. He wandered down narrow Marchessault Street to Alameda, where a long freight train had halted.

He made his way over to the train. Through a few inches of open car door a voice drawled:

"Well, if you don't know your car number, buddy, this one is as good as another."

Without hesitation Rusty climbed into the car. Almost at once, the train jerked to a start. The man slid the door shut, leaving them in darkness.

"Keep it shut and the shacks won't bother us," said the man. "We'll be rattlin' steel pretty quick, and then we're safe."

"Where's this train goin'?" asked Rusty.

"East, I reckon. I don't know how far they'll drag this particular car. Mebbe San Berdoo. We'll have to wait and see. It ain't bad, riding at night. Daytime, it's hell down through Imperial. You heading for any place in particular?"

"Well, I'll tell yuh," drawled Rusty, "I'm supposed to be sailin' for Australia—but I done missed my boat."

CHAPTER II

SHEEPHERDER

A SLIGHTLY FACETIOUS police reporter wrote this story of the crime in one of the next morning's papers:

Apparently the murder tonight of King Brant depends on the apprehension of an alleged cowboy, whose description is as follows:

Six feet, one inch, to six feet, six inches tall; black, dark-brown or blond hair; weight, one hundred and fifty to two hundred and fifteen; age, twenty to forty. He was wearing a black, brown or gray suit. All of the witnesses agree that he wore a black, brown or light-tan sombrero, and that he spoke with a foreign accent—or not.

It is evident that King Brant expected to meet this man at the Brant residence in Beverly Hills tonight, because of the fact that just prior to closing time Mr. Brant drew twenty-five thousand dollars in currency from his bank, and as he did so he laughingly remarked to the bank manager that he had a deal on for some real estate and wanted to dazzle the seller.

The police are of the opinion that it was a frame-up to get King Brant to draw the money, and that the cowboy garb' was merely a disguise. Michael Finley, the Brant butler, who had been away for the day, and only returned a few minutes before the fatal shot was fired, said he had not known King Brant was at home.

Doctor Lawrence French and Thomas Healy, who were with Miss Brant when they discovered the murder, did not hear the shot fired. None of them recognized the murderer, who left the house, brandishing two guns and threatening to kill anyone who made a move. King Brant wore a shoulder-holster, but it was empty. Ballistic experts declare that the fatal bullet was fired from a revolver.

The police are seeking one vital clue—a missing page from

King Brant's guest-book. The last page of the register has been torn out, and it is very possible that the last name on that missing page is the signature of a murderer.

RUSTY LEE'S private car was switched off at Yuma next day, and Rusty went hunting a meal. In a little restaurant he overheard two frowsy individuals discussing a job, which one of them had acquired.

"I ain't never heard of no sheep outfit payin' a hundred a month," declared one of them, his mouth full of beans. "Yo're crazy."

"No, I ain't crazy either. Hundred a month and everything furnished."

"Aint no sheep outfit payin' that much money."

"Well, this one shore is, and we're pullin' out today."

"Where-at is this millionaire outfit?"

"Black River Flats."

Rusty pricked up his ears. That must be King Brant's outfit. A hundred a month did sound queer, when the average wage was thirty-five. Rusty walked over to the two men, grinning a little as they looked at him.

"I'm lookin' for a job," he told them, "and I heard yuh talkin' about somebody payin' a hundred a month."

"That's right, pardner. Didja ever herd sheep?"

"I'd herd rattlesnakes for a hundred a month," replied Rusty.

"All right. I dunno if they're filled up yet, but I'll be glad to take yuh over to the feller who's rustlin' the crew. Mebbe he needs yuh."

After their meal was finished Rusty went with the sheepherder to the depot, where the man in charge of the crew looked Rusty over critically. The sombrero and high-heeled boots puzzled him, because few cowboys ever seek jobs as sheepherders.

"Where you from?" he asked Rusty.

"Oregon," lied Rusty easily.

"Rather herd sheep than cattle?"

"A feller must eat," replied Rusty, "and nobody's offered me a job herdin' cows."

"Fair enough. Where's yore bed-roll?"

"Do I get the job?"

"I reckon yuh do. But yuh better get a pair of shoes. You won't walk far in them boots. Hundred a month and grub."

As Rusty lounged on the depot platform, waiting, he fell into talk with a frowsy individual beside him.

"I worked for that Brant outfit, before," confided the fellow.

"Good outfit to work for?" Rusty asked.

"Good as any. Nort Covelle is boss of the whole works, and jist between me and you I wouldn't trust him with a handful of sidewinders. They've got a big place outside Black River City. Thousands of sheep. Golly, I didn't know there was that many sheep on earth before I worked seven months over there, and when I got to blattin' like a sheep, I up and quit. But I could see right then that there's too damn many sheep for the grass they've got. Why, all of Black River Flats looks like a plowed field. Sheep shore do ruin a country."

"Did yuh ever wonder why they're payin' a hundred a month?" asked Rusty.

The frowsy man shook his head.

"I never count the teeth in a gift horse's mouth. They paid me thirty a month the last time. Mebbe they need men pretty bad now."

One of the men had a newspaper, and he came over to them.

"Take a look at that, will yuh?" he said, pointing at the headlines, which blared:

SHEEP KING MURDERED
BY COWBOY

Rusty's jaw tightened, as the man read the story aloud. Rusty's name was not mentioned. All the evidence was conflicting, and apparently he had not been implicated. The man read that Miss

Brant stated that she did not recognize the murderer. Rusty swallowed painfully, and wondered about it all.

" 'Michael Finley, the butler'—" read the fellow, and hesitated; "Mike Finley. Yea-a-ah, I thought that name was familiar. Why, he was that forger who served time in the Big House, and then got a job with Brant. It was in the papers at the time.

"He says he didn't even know that Brant was home that evenin'. Here it says that the cowboy got Brant to draw twenty-five thousand dollars out of the bank, shot him and took the money. Twenty-five thousand! My gosh, some fellers do have all the luck!"

The man who had hired Rusty came over to them then, and they showed him the paper.

"Yeah, I read it a while ago," he assured them. "But the job still goes. Our train'll be along in about ten minutes." He turned to Rusty. "What name are you usin'?" he asked.

"Why, I—" Rusty hesitated for a moment. "How many Smiths have yuh got already?"

"I've got a couple—Andrew and Frank."

"Make mine John," said Rusty. "Make it John H. Smith."

"What's the *H* for?"

"Betcha it's Henry," said the frowsy one.

"Is it?" asked the crew leader.

"Horseshoes," replied Rusty.

"Are yuh lucky?"

"Well, I ain't very smart, and I'm still out of jail; so I reckon it's luck."

"I gave my right name," said the man with the newspaper, after the boss went away. "I'd hate to have an assumed name on *my* tombstone."

"What *is* yore name?" asked Rusty.

"Frank Smith."

"Well," smiled Rusty, "after yo're dead it don't make any difference whether yore name was Minnow or Whale. Anyway, I ain't figurin' on goin' over to Black River City just to grab a tomb-stone."

"I dunno, pardner; but it's a cinch they ain't payin' a hundred dollars a month *to just herd sheep.*"

"Train comin'!" yelled the boss. "Grab your bed-rolls, boys!"

THE MEN were herded into a day-coach for the ten-hour ride to Black River City. A hard-bitted individual sank into a seat beside Rusty, and remarked:

"Yuh better git rid of them cowboy-boots, pardner."

"Why?" asked Rusty innocently.

"I'll tell yuh why," replied the man, as he filled his pipe. "As far as I can learn this Brant outfit is aimin' to shove sheep into Wild Horse Valley. You don't know Nort Covelle, do yuh?"

"No, I never seen him," replied Rusty.

"He's hell on wheels. If word ever gets to Wild Horse Valley that he's comin' with sheep, they'll meet us with bullets; and it just might be that Covelle will take a look at yore boots and—well, he might get an idea that you was spyin' on the sheep."

"I see," mused Rusty. "Well, he don't need to worry about me. All I'm lookin' for is that hundred a month."

"You'll earn it."

"Course," smiled Rusty, "I ain't never had any experience in herdin' sheep."

"Don't worry about that. There's twenty of us here that prob'ly won't never herd a damn sheep. You've used a rifle, I reckon. Well, that's about all you'll herd."

"I been wonderin'," said Rusty, "if King Brant gettin' killed would affect our jobs down here."

The other scratched his head reflectively. "I dunno what'll happen now," he answered. "But I've got a hunch that Nort Covelle will go ahead with the deal. I heard that he's goin' to marry Brant's daughter."

Rusty's lips tightened for a moment, but he said casually:

"We won't need to worry about our jobs, eh? What sort of a feller is Covelle?"

"Slick. I mean that's what yuh think, when yuh look at him. He's tall and kinda slender, but strong as a lion. Good-lookin' sort of a devil, too. His face is the color of ivory, and his hair and mustache are so black that they look painted. I reckon he's Italian. Don't cross him. If he gives yuh an order—do what he says. He's a killer, pardner."

"He's been with Brant a long time, eh?"

"About five years."

"I'll try and remember—about takin' orders," said Rusty.

"That's a good idea. And when we get to Black River City you'd be wise to get some shoes. It might save answerin' questions."

"It might be a good idea," smiled Rusty. "Yuh see, I'm about half out of answers."

CHAPTER III

HENRY'S ORDERS

HENRY HARRISON CONROY, Sheriff of Wild Horse Valley, sat at his office desk in Tonto City. Henry Harrison Conroy was not very tall, but he was very fat. His face was like a full moon—like a harvest moon, reddish and beaming—and on it grew one of the largest noses in captivity. The nose was redder than the face behind it, which gave the former decided prominence. Henry's eyes were small and squinty—but, as Judge Van Treece said, "Who would observe an eye, with a nose like that about?"

Nearly all of Henry's life had been spent on the stage, mostly in vaudeville, featuring that same nose. The decline of vaudeville, and the inheritance of the J Bar C Ranch in Wild Horse Valley, brought Henry Harrison Conroy directly from the footlights to a cattle country, where the inhabitants, exhibiting a sense of rough humor, elected Henry sheriff of the county. As Henry described it—Spats to Spurs.

"Judge" Van Treece, Henry's deputy, was sixty years of age, six feet, four inches tall, gaunt as a greyhound, with a long, lean face and deeply pouched eyes. Once a prominent lawyer, whisky had made him a derelict, and in order to match the humor of Wild Horse Valley, Henry had appointed Judge as his deputy. Oscar Johnson, nicknamed "The Vitrified Viking" by Judge, had been a horse wrangler on the J Bar C until Henry made him jailer. Oscar was a mighty Swede with faded blond hair, a button-like nose and small blue eyes.

Judge Van Treece tilted back in a chair against the wall, smoking a vile-smelling cob pipe, while Oscar hunched on a cot, tinkering with a sawed-off shotgun which he had taken apart.

"Ay know das ha'ar Yohnny Lee," remarked Oscar.

"Yes?" queried Henry.

"Yah, su-ure. He's got a ranch between here and Scorpion Bend."

"I know the place," said Judge. "It is the TL Ranch. I knew his father, before he died."

"That's a good time to know a man," said Henry. He sighed and picked up again a recently arrived telegram, sent by the Los Angeles Police Department, which read:

ARREST AND HOLD JOHN LEE SCORPION BEND ON CHARGE OF MURDER STOP ADVISE US AT ONCE

"His name is Rosty," said Oscar blandly.

"Whose name?" asked Henry.

"Yohnny."

"Rusty," said Judge. "I wish we knew more about it, Henry. I should hate to ride way up there unless we knew Lee was home."

Henry sighed deeply. "At least they might have told me who was murdered and when. I should like to be able to talk intelligently with Mr. Lee about the matter. Suppose I should walk up to him and say:

" 'Mr. Lee, I arrest you for murder,' and he would say, 'Mr. Conroy, who did I murder?' You can see the situation, Judge. I might say:

" 'John Doe,' and he would say, 'Where and when?' I could say, 'You shot him in Los Angeles, but I don't know when.' "

"Yust vat did he kill him *with?*" queried Oscar.

"There you are!" snorted Judge. "The Viking makes an addition."

SOMEONE WAS riding up to the front of the office, and they heard the creak of leather as the man dismounted. Feet shuffled across the sidewalk, and Quincy R. Adams, a Scorpion Bend lawyer, limped into the office.

Quincy Adams was built from the physical specifications of a sandhill crane. He was about forty years of age, almost entirely bald, and addicted to baggy, black clothes, stiff-bosom shirts, barrel cuffs, but no collar. On his feet he habitually wore gaiter shoes, in which the elastic sides bulged loosely.

Just now Quincy did not appear to be in the best of physical condition. One eye was entirely closed, one side of his chin was purple and swollen, a front tooth was missing, and he limped painfully.

"Quincy, I am surprised!" exclaimed Henry.

"Yeth?" queried Quincy, a trace of sarcasm in his lisp.

"Yumpin' Yudas!" exclaimed Oscar softly, eyeing the lawyer.

"I demand the arretht of Thwan River Gruth, on a charge of athault," stated the lawyer. "Damn thith tooth!"

"Swan River Grush?" queried Judge. "Why, he is the partner of Rusty Lee."

"Yeth, thir. He athaulted me."

"Did you," propounded Henry, "have this lisp, before you met him?"

"No, thir! He knocked the tooth out himthelf."

"He's a tough yigger," declared Oscar.

"Well, Quincy, what caused the trouble between you and Swan River?" asked Henry curiously.

With many a lisp Quincy explained that some time ago a man came to him, asking him to act as their agent in acquiring the TL Ranch. He made out the necessary papers and sent them to Los Angeles, where they were signed by Rusty Lee and the buyer. The papers had been sent back to Quincy for filing, with instructions to notify Lee that the buyer wanted immediate possession. Quincy had gone to the TL Ranch to so notify Lee, who was not there; so he explained the situation to Swan River Grush, who told Quincy he was a liar and a crook, and then proceeded to chastise the lawyer and send him home.

"This plot," observed Henry, "gets thicker every inch of the way. Who did Lee sell the place to, Quincy?"

"The man's name ith K.G. Brant."

"And what was the consideration?"

"Wait a minute!" blurred Judge. The front legs of his chair struck the floor with a bang, and he jerked to his feet, facing the lawyer.

"What did you say the name was?" he asked.

"K.G. Brant."

"You triple-distilled damn fool, you!" roared Judge. "K.G. Brant! King Brant, the sheep king from Black River Flats!"

"He—he didn't thay," faltered Quincy.

"Just a moment," begged Henry calmly. "Quincy, you sold the TL Ranch to a man named Brant, who purchased said ranch from Johnny Lee, who is known as Rusty. Am I right—so far?"

"Yeth thir."

"How much did Brant pay for this ranch?"

"Twenty-five thouthand dollars."

"The deed is all signed, sealed and delivered, eh?"

"Yeth, thir, it ith."

"But, my gosh, Henry!" expostulated Judge. "King Brant—

will you listen to me? That TL Ranch reaches back to the main divide. If King Brant has a way to move sheep over that divide— all hell can't keep them from ruining Wild Horse Valley! Your own ranch, sir! Wait a moment, Quincy. What did Swan River Grush say about such a sale? Did he know what Rusty Lee had done?"

"I told him," replied Quincy Adams wearily. "I gueth it wath news."

"Rusty Lee was not home?" queried Henry.

"I did not thee him. I deman' the arretht of Thwan River—"

"Arrest him!" exploded Judge. "Quincy, you damn fool! When Wild Horse Valley finds out what you've done, they'll hang you to the tallest tree available. You sold a key-ranch to a sheep king; and may God have mercy on your soul, sir."

Quincy Adams stumbled outside and untied his horse. Judge paced the office, growling under his breath, while Henry watched him thoughtfully. Finally he turned to Henry.

"We must alarm the valley," he said. "We must sound the tocsin."

"True," nodded Henry gravely. "Oscar, will you sound the tocsin?"

Oscar, who had repaired and reloaded the shotgun, pumped a cartridge into the chamber, and apparently forgot to keep his finger off the trigger. The roar and concussion of the heavy explosion deafened them for a moment, while a handful of splinters flew from the threshold.

"Yust like Ay have alvays said," commented Oscar, "you can't trust von of dese damn pompgons."

Judge, white-faced and shaking, glared at Oscar.

"I said 'tocsin,' Oscar," reminded Henry. "Not shotgun."

"Yah, su-ure, Hanry."

"That Vitrified Viking hasn't the slightest idea what I meant," groaned Judge.

"Neither have I," said Henry. "He did his best, I believe. I agree with you that something must be done at once, Judge. The stage for Scorpion Bend is due to leave in a few minutes, and I believe you should go up there. I shall go to the ranch and tell Danny Regan, who will spread the alarm in this end of the county. Under the circumstance, I am very much afraid that Rusty Lee did not come back to Wild Horse Valley."

"This is going to mean war, Henry," said Judge nervously. "Wild Horse Valley will fight to the last man."

"There will still be the two of us, Judge," corrected Henry.

"Three," corrected Oscar blandly. "Ay am ha'al of a good man, too."

"Put down that damn shotgun, and saddle the horses!" snapped Henry. "I would as soon be shot by a sheepherder as by you."

FOR THREE days Rusty Lee and the sheepherding crew loafed around Black River City, eating free meals and sleeping at Brant's big ranch, three miles from the town. No one gave them any information, but it was rumored that Nort Covelle was detained in Los Angeles, because of the funeral of King Brant.

More than a hundred stock cars were spotted on the siding tracks near the huge loading pens, indicating that sheep were to be transported by rail. Rusty was unable to figure out just how this was to be done. Scorpion Bend was the only railroad point in Wild Horse Valley.

Rusty had about made up his mind to acquire a horse and try to get over the divide to Wild Horse Valley, when a newspaper story apprised him of the fact that there was a murder charge against him. The missing page of the guest register had been found—and Rusty's name was the last signature on the page. The police of all the Coast cities were looking for him, and the officers of Wild Horse Valley had been notified to arrest and hold him for murder.

The newspaper story also said that Rusty came to Los Angeles to sell his ranch to Brant, and that, during an argument, Rusty had shot Brant. There was no theft charge against Rusty, because the evidence showed that Brant had paid him the twenty-five thousand dollars. James Small, attorney for King Brant, testified that earlier in the evening he had been at Brant's home, where he witnessed the transaction, and later mailed the papers to Quincy Adams, a Scorpion Bend lawyer, for recording. He said that at that time John Lee and King Brant were drinking together, and were very friendly. He said that the reason Michael Finley, the butler, did not see either King Brant or John Lee was because the butler had taken the afternoon off, and when he returned to work, Brant and Lee were probably in the garden.

The frame-up was plain enough to Rusty now. Someone had acquired the services of Quincy Adams to act as their agent, telling him that the deal was all agreed on between Brant and John Lee, possibly paying the Scorpion Bend lawyer a nice fee for handling the papers, and for keeping his mouth shut.

The decoy message had brought Rusty to Los Angeles, and the signature on the guest register was their way of getting Rusty's signature to forge on the papers. They intended later to put Rusty out of the way. It was evident that King Brant had offered the two men a bonus of ten thousand dollars for a workable scheme to put sheep in the valley.

When King Brant balked at murder they killed him, took the twenty-five thousand dollars—and through no fault of theirs, the evidence pointed straight at Rusty. Evidently Michael Finley was the one who had forged Rusty's name to the papers, and probably also forged King Brant's name, after Brant was murdered.

James Small, Brant's attorney, had lied to the reporters; so Rusty decided that Small was one of the two men who had killed Brant.

"But that don't help me any right now," he told himself. "Every bit of evidence is against me. My best bet is to stay right here, 'cause a sheep camp is the last place on earth they'd ever expect to find me."

RUSTY BOUGHT a pair of heavy shoes, and hid his boots

under his bunk. At a hardware store he traded the automatic he had picked up in Brant's house for a second-hand Colt .45. He quit shaving, and acquired an old felt hat, which flopped low over his face.

A big, burly, tobacco-chewing ruffian, who answered to the name of Butch, was in charge of the crew while Covelle was away. At first he paid no attention to Rusty; but during an impromptu shooting match at the ranch he saw Rusty, shooting a revolver, bounce a tin can across the yard, blasting it to ribbons.

"Purty damn good!" he declared heartily. "Good's I've ever seen. I'll have to tell Covelle about that shootin'."

"Is he a good shot?" queried Rusty.

"I hope to tell yuh, Kid. He can split a playin'-card at fifteen feet."

Rusty grinned slowly. "What's the matter with his playin'-cards?"

"Matter with 'em?"

"Yeah. Does he have to sneak up on 'em?"

Butch spat dryly, shoved his hands deep in his pockets and narrowed his eyes, as he looked at Rusty.

"I'll tell yuh somethin' for yore own good, Kid," he said. "Don't try to be smart with Covelle—he won't take it."

Rusty laughed at Butch. "Ever since we left Yuma I've had that dinned in my ears," he said. "Look out for Covelle! Who the heck is this jigger, and what makes him so tough? I don't see any tombstones around here."

"Mebbe they don't git a decent burial," suggested Butch. "Anyway, tombstones cost money."

"You ain't tryin' to scare me, are yuh?" asked Rusty.

"It ain't none of my business what yuh do," replied Butch. "As long as yuh do yore work, obey orders and don't cross Covelle, you'll be all right. If yuh don't play the game *his* way—well, jist remember that Butch warned yuh."

Later that afternoon one of the men brought a telegram to Butch. At supper Butch whispered to Rusty:

"After supper you harness the sorrel team to the spring wagon. Covelle will be in on that nine o'clock train, and we'll meet him."

Butch drove the team to Black River City. Butch was a thirsty soul. Rusty declined to partake, but Butch was mildly drunk when the train arrived. There were three men and a woman got off the train, and Rusty gasped with dismay when he recognized Mary Brant and Michael Finley. The other two were Nort Covelle and James Small, the attorney.

Luckily for Rusty the depot was badly lighted, and he kept in the background, his slouch hat well down over his eyes, moving in to get the baggage as they walked toward the wagon.

"Miss Brant is going to the hotel, Butch," informed Covelle. "The accommodations at the ranch might not be any too good now. Small and Mike will go out to the ranch with us. You take her baggage clown to the hotel, and I'll walk down with her."

Rusty prayed all the way to the hotel that no one would suggest that he take Mary's baggage into the hotel. Apparently his prayer was answered, because Butch did the honors. Rusty was due for another shock, when he looked through the windows of the hotel and saw Quincy Adams, talking with Nort Covelle. He drew back quickly, as Butch came out, and the other two men followed.

As they climbed into the wagon Rusty said to Butch:

"No use crowdin' in there. Suppose I come in later, Butch."

"Shore, that's all right. Some of the boys will be in and you can ride back with one of 'em."

With a sigh of thanksgiving, Rusty watched the wagon roll away in the darkness. He was safe for the moment—but what of tomorrow? Mary Brant, Michael Finley and Quincy Adams were sure to recognize him on sight.

Rusty, of course, did not know that Quincy Adams was a fugitive from Wild Horse Valley, where the enraged cattlemen would have lynched him for his part in selling the TL Ranch to the sheep interests. But in the wagon on their way to the ranch, Nort Covelle, James Small, Butch and Michael Finley were finding it out, as Quincy Adams poured out his tale of woe.

"So you had to go right to that half-witted sheriff and spill the whole story, eh?" snarled Covelle. "Didn't you take my money and swear you'd say nothing until after everything was settled?"

"Well, I didn't know what it meant to Wild Horse Valley," replied Adams. "You never told me it was *sheep*."

"You didn't need to know what it 'was. It wasn't any of your business, you blabbing fool. You've done your best to ruin the whole deal. I suppose the whole valley is up in arms by this time. Is the deed recorded?"

"Yes, it is recorded."

"Well, why did you come over here? I'm through with you."

"I came to get my money. You owe me twelve hundred and fifty dollars, plus the recording fees."

Nort Covelle's laugh was like the sound of a band-saw on a sand-soaked log.

"All right, Adams," he said. "You'll get yore pay."

CHAPTER IV

RECOGNIZED

RUSTY DIDN'T KNOW what to do next. The sensible move for him would have been to put as many miles as possible between himself and the State of Arizona. If he stayed in Black River City it would only postpone the recognition, and if he went back to the ranch, Michael Finley or Quincy Adams would recognize him in the morning. He might appropriate a horse at the ranch and head for Wild Horse Valley, where they probably would hang him on sight as a traitor.

"The story I could tell them would be awful thin for a mad

bunch of cowpunchers to believe," he told himself. "I've shore got myself into a tight corner."

None of the men came in from the ranch; so Rusty finally decided to walk out there, and trust to blind luck to see him through. When he got there he saw that there was a light in the main ranch house, but the barracks-like bunk-house was in darkness. Rusty had been bunking in a small shack, in which there were only two bunks. Thus far he had been the only occupant.

He went in, scratched a match and lighted a lamp. His back was to the bunks, and as he turned he saw Michael Finley sitting up in the extra bunk, staring at him.

For several moments they looked at each other. Rusty's hat was in his left hand, and the lamplight illuminated his hair. He saw the recognition in Finley's eyes, saw his hand moving slowly under the blanket. Finley's thin lips moved jerkily.

"So you came here, eh?" he whispered.

Suddenly he jerked his hand from under the blanket, and the lamplight flashed on a six-shooter in his hand. But the moving hand under the blanket had warned Rusty, and as Finley's gun flashed in the light, Rusty's Colt flamed past the lamp.

The concussion of the heavy explosion shook the little shack, and the light nearly went out. Rusty took one close look, blew out the lamp, stepped outside and darted around the shack. He ran swiftly away. Someone threw open a door at the house, calling loudly, asking what had happened. But Rusty kept on going, circling back toward the road. Less than half a mile from the house, he sat down beside the road, panting heavily.

With a section of handkerchief he quickly cleaned the barrel of his six-shooter and replaced the used cartridge. He could see lights around the house, as someone went from place to place with a lantern. He saw it bobbing down to the stable. Rusty was cool and collected now after his run.

He had been there about ten minutes, when he heard riders coming from the ranch. Getting to his feet he came on, walking slowly. The riders met him, asked who he was, and Rusty replied. The riders were Butch and another of the men, the one called Len.

"It's a damn long walk," declared Rusty wearily, "but there didn't seem to be any other way to get here, Butch."

"That's right," agreed Butch. "Yuh didn't meet anybody, didja?"

"Met one feller on a horse a little while ago. I dunno who he was, but he was shore in a hurry. I yelled at him, thinkin' it was one of our gang, but he didn't stop."

"That's jist what I figured!" exclaimed Butch. "I told Covelle I'd bet that some feller in Black River seen Finley and follered us out here."

"What about?" asked Rusty.

"One of the fellers that came on the train t'night got his lights blowed out at the ranch a few minutes ago."

"Killed?"

"Deader'n a last year's bird's-nest. Must have rec'nized the feller, too—'cause he had his gun drawed when the bullet hit him."

"In yore shack, too," added Len. "Lucky thing yuh wasn't there—mebbe he'd have got both of yuh."

"Yea-a-ah, that's right," agreed Rusty.

THEY RODE slowly back to the ranch, while Rusty walked beside Butch. As they stabled the horses Butch drew Rusty aside.

"Are yuh pretty good on keepin' yore mouth shut?" he asked.

"I've always figured I was pretty fair at it," replied Rusty.

"All right. If anybody asks yuh—only three men rode back from town with me tonight—and the dead man is one of 'em. The other two was Covelle and Small. Can yuh remember that?"

"I've always had trouble with figures," said Rusty, "but three has always been a favorite with me. I'll remember."

"Good! I told Covelle you was to be trusted. Unless yuh crave to sleep in the same room with a corpse, you can bunk in the house with me tonight."

"Suits me fine," replied Rusty. With both Finley and Quincy Adams removed, there was no one left at the ranch to recognize him.

"Yuh didn't happen to know that *fourth* feller, didja?" asked Butch.

"There wasn't any fourth feller," replied Rusty. "Can't yuh count?"

"Excuse me all to hell," chuckled Butch. "I'll have to tell Covelle."

The inference was plain enough. They had killed Quincy Adams and disposed of the body. Rusty had no twinges of conscience over the shooting of Michael Finley. It was his life or Finley's—and Finley had been too slow with his gun. No doubt Finley had been in the plot to murder Rusty in Los Angeles; so Rusty owed him something.

They went into the living-room of the ranch house. Nort Covelle and James Small were seated beside a table, on which were glasses and a whisky bottle. Nort Covelle was just what Rusty had been told—slick. Narrow, black eyes studied Rusty, as he and Butch stood near the table. Covelle's complexion was like old ivory, his hair as black as the proverbial raven's wing. His hands were long and muscular.

James Small was below medium height, sallow, his sandy hair thin on top. He paid no attention to Rusty, but poured a drink for himself.

"This is the Kid I told yuh about, Nort," said Butch. "Me and Len met him out about half a mile, walkin' to the ranch. He said a feller passed him, ridin' like hell toward town, a while ago."

Covelle said nothing, but his keen eyes searched Rusty's face.

"Have a drink?" he asked coldly.

"I don't drink," replied Rusty.

Covelle's eyes shifted to Rusty's holstered gun.

"Do you mind if I look at that gun?" he asked.

Rusty flipped the gun loose, spun it on his finger and handed it, butt first, to Covelle. Covelle smiled thinly as he examined the loaded cylinder. Then he lifted the muzzle to his nose and sniffed.

Rusty had done a good job of cleaning. Covelle handed back the gun, leaned back in his chair and said: "Butch says you can shoot, Kid."

"I never got so good that I'd brag about it."

Covelle shrugged his shoulders. "Well, if you won't drink—go to bed. Small and I have business to discuss. Pleasant dreams. By the way, Butch, you better send one of the boys after the sheriff. He would likely be interested in the party out in the bunk-house. It's a nuisance, but we must conform with the law in all things."

"That's right," laughed Butch. "We must be law-abidin' at all times. I'll send Len."

Butch opened a door and took Rusty into the bedroom, which was just off the main room. Then he went to give orders to Len. Rusty was undressed when Butch came back.

"I'm ridin' to town with Len," he told Rusty. "He thinks I can tell it to the sheriff better'n he can."

"I'll bet yuh can," grinned Rusty.

Flattered a little, Butch laughed and picked up his hat.

"I'll see yuh later, Kid. I think you made an impression on Covelle."

HE HEARD Butch leave the house. From the main room came the murmur of voices. Rusty wanted to hear what was being said in there, but decided not to take chances. After blowing out the lamp, he rolled into bed.

His decision proved a wise one. He had only been in bed about ten minutes when, without warning, his door was suddenly yanked open. Covelle stood there, his back to the light. Rusty merely turned over, creaking the bedsprings. Slowly Covelle closed the door. Rusty heard him laugh, as he went back to the table in the other room.

Quietly Rusty got out of bed, then, and went to the door. Peering through the key-hole he could see the two men seated at the table, looking over some papers. By pressing an ear against the thin panel of the door, he could hear what was being said. Small's voice was high-pitched.

"I tell you, I didn't dare make it more. We must be careful. No one would suspect anything, if he left us each twenty-five thousand. That five thousand dollar bequest, left to Michael Finley for faithful services, was all right. Mike wanted more, of course. Still, the poor devil won't even need the five thousand—now."

"I'm not kicking, Jim," laughed Covelle. "But what a snag we'd have run against if Mike's enemy had found him before this document could have been created. I figure it's all for the best. Mike would have caused trouble, because he wanted a big split. Well, he's out—now. He's probably forging a pass to get him past the pearly gates right now at this minute."

They both laughed and poured another drink.

"What about Mary?" asked Small.

"What can she do?" queried Covelle. "She says she is going to sell the sheep—close everything out. By the terms of this will she can't do it. She must continue in the sheep business, with me as general manager, and without interference. Small, what losses we can show! That calls for another drink."

"You are still going to try and marry her, aren't you?"

"Try it? Why, I'm going to marry her—of course. Here's luck."

"That damned Quincy Adams worries me a little, Nort. Suppose anyone else saw him start out with us. They might—"

"No one saw him. The hotel clerk had gone to the room with Mary. Only our own gang—"

"Do you trust that new man—the Kid?"

"Butch says he's all right. If he isn't, I'll soon find it out. They don't fool Covelle—not long. I'll trap him if he isn't right."

"But what about moving the sheep—now that Wild Horse Valley knows a few things?"

"We'll wait. I'll send a man in there. Now that Brant is out of the game, we haven't any time limit, Jim. Let's have another, and then go to bed. It has been an interesting evening."

"Interestin' is the right word," Rusty told himself, as he went cautiously to bed. "I'll have to smell all bait from now on."

CHAPTER V

THE VANISHED TESTAMENT

THE SHERIFF AND coroner came out next morning. The sheriff was a tall, gangling, tobacco-chewing hill-billy, who gazed sourly upon the remains of Michael Finley, as he questioned Nort Covelle.

"I don't quite *sabe* it," he declared. "Yuh say this feller was workin' as a butler for King Brant? Huh? Who'd want to go gunnin' fer *him?*"

"This man was formerly a convict, who served a term in the penitentiary in this state for forgery, Sheriff," explained Covelle.

"Oh, yeah! Well, that's different. Prob'ly had enemies."

"So it seems," murmured Covelle dryly.

They placed the mortal remains of Michael Finley in a wagon and the sheriff and coroner took them back to Black River City.

"Not very bright," remarked James Small as the wagon rattled away.

"The sheriff?" queried Covelle. "No, he isn't—but he's smart enough to know who supports the county. We never have to worry about *him.*"

Rusty, meanwhile, had been managing to keep pretty much within hearing and seeing distance of the pair, the while certain plans matured within his mind. Now he heard Covelle order Butch to hitch up the buckboard team for him and Small, as they were going to Black River City. And as Covelle and Small walked down toward the big stables, Rusty went into the house.

There was no one else in there, except "Salt-risin'" Reed, the ranch cook, who was in the kitchen.

On the table of the main room was James Small's leather brief-case. Rusty glanced at it closely and noticed that it was unlocked. He walked to a window and looked out. Covelle and Small were leaning on the corral fence, talking. Rusty went quickly back to the table, and in a few moments he went outside again and over to the bunk-house.

Rusty watched closely as Small came out later, carrying his brief-case, and got into the buckboard. Rusty wasn't exactly sure that the unlocked brief-case might not have been a trap, but he was willing to take that chance.

"You shore stacked up pretty good with Covelle," Butch told him.

"It's a good thing to stand in right with the boss," smiled Rusty.

"Yo're danged right. He was talkin' about sendin' a man over to Wild Horse Valley to do a little spyin' for us, and he wondered if you wouldn't be the right one to do it. We're kinda workin' in the dark, and we've got to have some information before we can go ahead and do anything. Everything is set, except that we don't want to move in against a lot of hot lead."

"That's right," agreed Rusty. "But I don't hanker for any spy job. I hired out to herd sheep—not to stretch rope."

"Well, mebbe yo're right. But if Covelle asks yuh to do it—I'd do it, if I was you."

Rusty laughed shortly. "Listen, Butch. I sold my services— not my life. Neither Covelle nor any other man can force me to do anything I don't want to do. You may be afraid of Covelle, but I'm not, and you can paste that in yore hat. To me, he's just another boss shepherd."

"Yea-a-ah?" drawled Butch. "You don't know him—yet."

"Mebbe I'll stick around and get acquainted," grinned Rusty.

NORT COVELLE and James Small found Mary Brant in the lobby of the dingy little hotel, writing a letter.

"I'm glad you came," she told them, as she folded the letter and placed it in an envelope. "What in the world happened to Michael?"

"Terrible, wasn't it!" exclaimed Covelle. "Someone shot poor Mike last night. We haven't the slightest idea who did it, Mary. We heard the shot, and ran out there, but it was too late."

"I heard them talking about it when I came down to breakfast. I—with things like that happening, it makes me feel that I ought to get out to the ranch right away."

"Mary, I want to talk about that with you," said Covelle. "There is nothing you can do at the ranch. Why stay in this country and be uncomfortable, when there is no need of it?"

"I thought we threshed that all out before we came here," said Mary firmly. "I told you that I was going to come here and run the business. Dad would want me to," she added wistfully. "I believe my first move would be to sell all the sheep. Dad and I have talked it over several times. The range is all gone here."

"Of course," said Small, "you haven't any idea what is covered in your father's will. I believe he has made certain provisions which must be carried out. The will was drawn here, and with his interests centering right here, the will should be probated here, Miss Brant. I have the will with me, and suppose we go over to Judge Myers' office and have it opened. We could have the judge read it."

"All right," nodded Mary. "But as far as dad's will is concerned, I believe I know what it contains. However, it must be probated."

They went to the old frame courthouse, where they found Judge Myers, a tall, hard-faced, hard-eyed old man, who greeted them curtly, until he was introduced to Mary Brant.

"Sorry about your father," he said then. "I knew him pretty well. Fine man. Heard you had a man for breakfast this morning, Covelle."

Mary shuddered at the calloused expression. Covelle nodded soberly.

"You knew him, didn't you, Judge?"

"Ought to. I sent him to the penitentiary. What can I do for you?"

Covelle explained about King Brant's will.

"Miss Brant wishes to take charge of her father's interests," he told the judge, "but before she does so we must discover just what provisions King Brant left in his will."

"I believe that would be a good idea," nodded the judge dryly.

James Small unlocked his brief-case, rested it on his knees and began separating the number of legal papers. Twice he went through the contents, a puzzled frown on his face. Then he looked up slowly.

"The will is missing," he said shakily.

"Missing?" gasped Covelle. "Why, Jim!"

"You mean—you've lost my father's will?" queried Mary.

"The will is not in this case," replied Small. "Where on earth is it? Why—why, I'm sure—"

"When did you see it last?" asked Covelle anxiously.

"Last night. I—I had some papers out… yes, I'm sure it was there."

"Perhaps you left it out last night," suggested Mary hopefully.

"No, I—I'm sure I didn't. Still, it is possible."

Covelle got quickly to his feet.

"We will leave Mary at the hotel and go back to the ranch at once. Possibly… when you opened the case last night…."

"Yes, I believe that must be what happened. Judge, I'm sorry we troubled you, but—"

"That's all right," replied the judge. "Come back, when you find it. I'm very glad to have met you, Miss Brant."

"Thank you, Judge; you are very kind."

"No, I'm not. They say I'm the meanest old scoundrel that ever sent an innocent man to prison. Ask anybody; they'll all tell you that I'm meaner and harder-headed than any ram in the Brant herds."

"I have my own opinions, Judge," smiled Mary.

"Well, your father was that way; and I liked him. Good day."

COVELLE AND Small left Mary at the hotel, and drove out of town. Covelle was blazing with suppressed wrath, as he saw their carefully planned scheme falling to pieces.

"I don't see—" began Small weakly.

"Of course you don't see!" snapped Covelle. "Somebody stole that will!"

"The deed to the TL Ranch is gone, too," groaned Small.

"It is? Well, damn the deed! But if we can't find that will, we're sunk, Jim! Without that will that girl will inherit everything, and we'll be left holding the sack."

"I realize that, Nort. But who on earth would steal that will? Who would know anything about that will being in my case? It isn't reasonable, I tell you. It doesn't make sense."

"Sense or not, it is gone, Jim; and it's up to us to recover it."

"How on earth can we recover it, if it's stolen? I still don't believe it is stolen, though. It wouldn't interest anyone at the ranch. People don't steal merely to be stealing something."

"Your argument is sound," growled Covelle, "but the fact remains that the papers are gone. Where they went—who knows? But if I find out who got them, I'll shoot their heart out. Good Lord, I've built this deal up, step by step, until we've got a fortune in sight—and I won't let anybody block me now."

"I think we'd better go calmly," said Small. "We can't accuse anybody just now. I suggest that we say nothing until we have some idea what move to make. If anyone at the ranch took the papers, the papers are likely still there. No use making a big commotion, Nort."

"I guess you're right, Jim; we'll take it easy—until we find out."

CHAPTER VI

TRAPPED

WHEN COVELLE AND Small drove into the ranch yard after their abortive trip to town, Rusty Lee and Butch were at the stable. Both men had calmed down, and there was no indication that they were worried about anything. Small had remembered leaving the brief-case on the table in the main room that morning. Covelle went into the kitchen, where Salt-risin' was baking bread.

"After the sheriff took that body away," said Covelle, "Small and I were down at the stable, while Butch harnessed the team. Did you see anybody come into the house at that time?"

The old cook wiped his hands on his flour-sack apron and squinted thoughtfully for several moments.

"No, I didn't see anybody," he answered. "Didja lose somethin'?"

"Yes, I lost something."

"Well, what can yuh expect, with a crew of loafin' shepherds around here? They'd steal the sleeves out of a vest. You ort to have more sense than to leave anything val'able layin' around."

Covelle scowled, leaning against the doorway.

"And another thing," said the cook belligerently, "I want yuh to understand that I ain't no danged sentry, guardin' the door; I'm the cook. Forty shepherds could go in and out of the house when I'm busy and I'd never see 'em. I'm a worker—not a danged loafer."

Covelle went back to the main room to talk with Small, who had searched the house.

"Blank wall," he told Small. "The cook didn't see anyone. But I'm sure that is when it happened. Butch is eliminated, because he was at the stable. The cook could have done it. And there's a dozen herders, any one of whom could have been in here."

"No sneak thief did it," declared Small. "Those papers aren't worth a dime to anyone except us. I tell you, Nort, they were taken by someone interested in our deal—someone who wants to hold us up for a share."

Covelle sat down, pondering the entire matter. "I hope you're right, Jim," he answered thoughtfully. "I know how to deal with that kind. We'll wait and see how much they want."

But after a moment he shook his head.

"No good, Jim," he said. "There were only three people who knew of that will—you and Mike Finley and myself. There's only two now."

"Perhaps Mike told somebody else," suggested Small. "I never did trust Mike. He was getting less than any of us, and he might have schemed to have another party hold us up, you know."

"You might be right, at that! Possibly the party who shot him. Got Mike out of the way, came back and stole the will…. But he couldn't prove it was a forgery. Damn it, he can't blackmail us! We could throw him in jail for stealing a legitimate will."

"Let's not talk about throwing anyone in jail," said Small. "What are you going to do about sending a man to Wild Horse Valley?"

"I don't know. Wait a minute." Covelle got to his feet again. "That damn Kid slept with Butch last night. Maybe he—by heaven, I believe that's the answer. I'll have him in here—and we'll see what he has to say for himself."

He went to the door.

BUTCH CALLED Rusty from the bunk-house a moment later.

"Covelle wants to see you," he said. "I reckon it's about goin' over to Wild Horse Valley."

"He can save his breath," growled Rusty. He followed Butch into the main room of the ranch house, found Covelle and

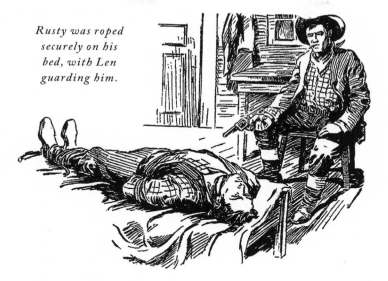

Rusty was roped securely on his bed, with Len guarding him.

Small sitting at the table. Rusty's holster was empty, but he was wearing a coat.

Rusty stopped near the table, looking questioningly at Covelle, who eyed him narrowly.

"Yuh wanted to see me about somethin'?" queried Rusty.

"Yes, I wanted to ask you a question," replied Covelle. He shifted in his chair, his right hand slid under his coat, and came out holding a cocked automatic. With an elbow braced on the arm of the chair, the muzzle of the gun covered Rusty's mid-section.

Rusty's eyes merely flickered and his lips tightened a little.

"I wanted to ask you a question," repeated Covelle.

"You seem to be in a fine position to get an answer," said Rusty. "What do yuh want to know—*that bad?*"

"I want to know what you did with the papers you stole from Jim Small's brief-case this morning?"

A slight scowl creased between Rusty's eyes.

"Yo're talkin' riddles, Covelle," he said calmly.

"Am I? It happens that you were seen coming into this room,

just before the papers were missing. The case was on this table, and you took two papers from it. Where are they?"

Rusty thought swiftly. He was sure that no one had seen him come into that room. Covelle was bluffing.

"I don't remember comin' in here at any time today," he said. "I might have come in here, goin' through to the bedroom, but I don't remember it. So what's the idea of pullin' a gun on me and accusin' me of stealin' some kinda papers? Or is this yore idea of a joke?"

"So you think you can get away with it, eh?" sneered Covelle. But he was half convinced. His muscles relaxed, and he dangled the gun beside the arm of his chair.

Rusty sighed, shrugged his shoulders—and with a motion almost too fast to follow, he drew his gun from under his coat, the muzzle only a few short feet from Covelle's nose.

It was Covelle's turn to be amazed. Small gasped audibly, while Butch swore softly, as though to himself.

"Let that gun drop on the rug," said Rusty.

The gun thudded to the Navajo rug, and Covelle lifted his hand to the arm of the chair.

"The empty holster fooled yuh, eh?" smiled Rusty. "You'll learn. Well, what's all the trouble about? Yuh know I hate to have a man point a gun at me and call me a thief. It don't give me a chance to talk back. Well, go ahead and tell me what I stole."

Covelle's grin was a sour grimace.

"I was just trying you out, Kid. Before I trust a man I want to find out what's inside him. You stood the test pretty well."

"So that was it, eh? Testin' me out. Well, I think yo're pretty much of a fool, testin' a man thataway. I came dang near blastin' yuh, instead of orderin' yuh to drop that gun. Next time you better be careful who yuh test; yuh might not live through it."

"It was a fool trick," admitted Covelle. "You're all right, Kid. Now, how about going to Wild Horse Valley for me, and looking over the situation. You could drift into Scorpion Bend, looking like a cowboy out of work, and find out, how things stand. You'll be well paid."

Rusty holstered his gun and sat on a corner of the table.

"I dunno much about yore deal, Covelle," he said, "but I do know what would happen to a sheep spy if he was discovered in a cow country. There's a lot of ropes on a cow range. Yore pay wouldn't do me much good, if they found out what I was doin' over there."

"I guess you're right," agreed Covelle. "It would require a man with nerve. Well, that's all, Kid."

After Rusty left the room, Covelle laughed shortly. "He's got plenty of nerve," he said, "but I still think he got the papers."

"If I knew what papers…" suggested Butch.

"The will of King Brant and the deed to the TL Ranch," Covelle told him. "They were stolen from Small's brief-case this morning, while you were hitching up the buggy team for me. Find 'em, and I'll give you a thousand cold dollars, Butch."

"My gosh!" gasped Butch. "A thousand? What wouldn't I do for that much money! But what good would them papers be to that feller?"

"No good. There isn't a thing of value in them, except to us. The only thing he could do would be to force us to pay well for their return."

"Personally," said James Small, "I think you're barking up the wrong tree. Find the man who killed Mike Finley—and you'll have the man who stole the papers."

"Well, I'll do my best," promised Butch.

THAT AFTERNOON, Rusty saw Len ride in with the mail and take it to the house. Butch had been talking to Rusty about the stolen papers.

"I dunno what the value of the blamed things are," said Butch, "but I'll betcha Covelle would pay heavy to get 'em back. A feller would have to work out some scheme, keepin' himself in the clear, of course. He offered me a cold thousand to get 'em back, but I'm tellin' you I'd make him come through with a hell of a lot more than that."

"I wish I could help yuh, Butch," replied Rusty earnestly.

"Yeah, I wish yuh could," nodded Butch, and went up to the house.

When Rusty had purloined the papers he was at a loss for a hiding-place. His sleeping quarters offered no safe place of concealment, until he noticed that there was a space between the ceiling and the wall. There was no time for finding anything better, but if he put them up there they would fall down inside the outer and inner wall. Hearing voices outside, and fearing discovery, he had dropped them inside the walls, where he did not think anyone would ever find them.

Now he saw Covelle, Butch and Len come from the house. Covelle came down where Rusty was standing beside the corral, while Butch and Len went over to the stable. Covelle seemed in good spirits.

"Well, I think we'll be going into action soon, Kid," he said.

"That's fine," replied Rusty. "Gettin' all set, eh?"

"Just about. I'm going to need a right-hand man on this job, and you might fill the bill. You've got plenty nerve—and that's what it will take."

"Well, that's fine," smiled Rusty. Butch and Len were coming over from the stable.

"I was just telling the Kid that we're about to see action," said Covelle.

"That's right," nodded Butch. "Plenty action—right now!"

As he finished Butch flung both of his powerful arms around Rusty, pinning his arms to his sides, while Len deftly removed Rusty's gun from his holster. Taken by surprise, Rusty did not offer any resistance for a moment. He was powerless to use his arms, but his feet were free, and he proceeded to drive his toe against Butch's shins.

With a howl of agony Butch released him. Len grabbed Rusty by the right arm, and at the same time Covelle slashed

Rusty over the head with the barrel of his automatic. That was the last he knew for a while.

RUSTY'S RETURN to consciousness was very painful. Half-blinded by a splitting headache and roped securely, he found himself lying on his bed in the ranch house. Sitting in a chair near the door was Len.

"Woke up, eh?" Len said. "I was scared he killed yuh, Kid."

Rusty was too miserable to answer. It was several minutes before he could remember what had happened; and even then he did not know why they had attacked him.

"Yuh been out danged near an hour," informed Len. He gave Rusty a drink of water, revived him a little.

"What happened, Len?" whispered Rusty.

"Covelle got a Scorpion Bend paper and it had yore description."

Rusty groaned softly.

"They found the papers yuh stole and cached in the wall," informed Len. "Covelle is a hard feller to fool."

"What's goin' to happen to me, Len?"

"Hell, I dunno. Covelle don't even know. I reckon it all depends on how things turn out for him. Mebbe he'll turn yuh over to the sheriff. Yo're wanted for murder, yuh know."

Rusty laughed painfully. "Covelle's too wise to do that, Len."

"Too wise?"

"Covelle don't want to hang himself—and the rest of you fellers; and that's what's goin' to happen. I'm sorry, Len—but you've been marked down, too."

Len got out of his chair and came over to the bed, staring down at Rusty.

"I don't quite git that," he said. "I ain't done anything that they could hang me for, Kid."

"Yo're one of Covelle's right-hand men—and Covelle is a murderer. Do yuh think the law is goin' to excuse you, jist 'cause yuh didn't pull the trigger?"

Len was not very bright, but he had imagination. Even in his painful condition Rusty could see this, and he pressed his advantage.

"You don't think I came over here on my own, do yuh, Len?" he asked. "I'm no fool. Every move of this outfit is bein' watched. I can tell yuh who killed Michael Finley—and why. I know who murdered King Brant—and it wasn't me. Didn't you know that a man was murdered the night Covelle and Small came here— another man besides Finley?"

"Hell, I didn't know anything about that!" whispered Len. "Who was it?"

"Quincy Adams, a lawyer from Scorpion Bend."

"But—but I didn't have anything to do with that, Kid. I didn't even know...."

"The law won't believe yuh, Len. I'm the only one who knows that you didn't have a hand in the killin'. With me out of the way—yo're sunk, when the bust-up happens—and it ain't far off."

"Well, what the hell!" exclaimed Len huskily. He went to the door, looking very scared, and walked out through the house. In a few minutes he came back.

"I'm lightin' a shuck out of here, Kid," he said. "There's plenty horses in the stable. I'm headin' south. Got friends in Mexico. I'll cut the ropes off yuh. Kinda make it look like I didn't do it, 'cause I could have untied the knots. Yore gun's on the table out there. You know now that I didn't have no hand in any killin', don'tcha, Kit?"

"Shore," agreed Rusty. "I've knowed it all the time. But I'm the only one who could swear it in court, Len."

Old Salt-risin' Reed was sitting outside the kitchen door- way, peeling potatoes. When he saw Rusty and Len leave the house and go to the stable, his eyebrows merely lifted slightly. He knew that Rusty was a prisoner and that Len had been left there to guard him. But the guard was still *with* the prisoner— and anyhow, it was none of Salt-risin's business.

Quickly the two selected horses and saddles. Rusty took a snake-headed sorrel gelding, which had a local reputation for speed and endurance. Outside the stable, Rusty and Len shook hands.

There was nothing to be said. Len's one big desire was to cross the Border as quickly as possible. He waved at Salt-risin' as he spurred away from the ranch, and the old cook lifted his hand in an indifferent salute.

Rusty wasn't sure just what would be his best move. He watched the receding horse and rider, heading for Mexico, and wondered if that wasn't the best direction for him to go. The law knew now that he was in the Black River Flats. In Mexico he would be safe, at least for a while.

"I reckon Swan River was right when he said I didn't have any brains," Rusty told himself. "But they've stolen my ranch and tagged me with a murder—and brains, or no brains, I'm not goin' to run away and let 'em have clear sailin'. C'mon, bronc, we're headin' straight for a hangman's loop."

CHAPTER VII

OSCAR ANSWERS

MARY BRANT SAT in Judge Myers' office, listening in amazement to the reading of her father's will. Her father had often told her that she would inherit everything he owned; and they had talked about the disposition of the vast number of sheep. But this will, drawn only a few months ago, gave Nort Covelle absolute charge of the sheep interests, without hindrance, for a period of five years. James Small was named executor of the will. It also specified that Covelle and Small were to receive twenty-five thousand dollars in cash, and an additional five thousand in cash was to be given Michael Finley, for faithful services.

Judge Myers finished the reading, placed the will on his desk and cleared his throat raspingly.

"I—I don't know what to say," faltered Mary. "It isn't... like Dad told me. The sheep were to be sold and... I don't see...."

"I don't believe he ever had any idea of selling out," said Covelle. "We talked this over several times together. He made big money out of sheep; so there was no reason—"

"With his range all gone?" queried Mary.

Covelle smiled slowly. "But, my dear, we'll have new range. In fact, a better range than this ever was."

"I believe," said Small, "that King Brant considered it all very carefully, before he dictated this will. He was a shrewd business man; a man with a very keen mind."

"I suppose there's nothing left to say," sighed Mary. "If those were Dad's wishes, I suppose we must abide by them."

Judge Myers cleared his throat again, as he folded up the document and handed it back to James Small.

"Unquestionably the last will and testament of King Brant," he said, "but it reads as though the man anticipated an early demise."

"What do you mean, Judge?" queried Small quickly.

"I talked with King Brant only a few weeks ago," replied the judge. "At that time he told me that he was going to market every head of sheep that he owned; that he was tired of fighting for rangeland. We talked of the difficulty of marketing so many sheep, and he said he would close out, regardless of a heavy loss."

"But what has that to do with this will, Judge?"

"Merely that after making that decision he would go ahead, draw up a will, in which he gives one man absolute charge of the sheep for a period of five years."

"Men have been known to change their minds, Judge."

"Apparently," remarked the judge dryly.

Nort Covelle and James Small walked back to the hotel—with Mary. Neither of the men noticed that one of the ranch horses was tied to the hitch-rack in front of the hardware store, where Rusty had left it.

"I believe I shall go back home," Mary told them, as they stopped in front of the hotel. "There doesn't seem any reason for me to stay here any longer."

"It's a wise decision, Mary," said Covelle. "Don't worry about anything, as far as the sheep are concerned. Will you leave tonight?"

"There is a train about midnight," replied Mary. "I believe I'll take that one."

"That's fine. I will be in this evening, Mary."

They watched her go up the stairs. Covelle was jubilant. Everything was working out to suit him at last.

"That damn judge is suspicious," declared Small.

"Let him have his suspicions," laughed Covelle. "Jim, we're set to make a stake. Now—about Rusty Lee. I believe our best bet is to have the sheriff come out and get him. Once in jail, with a murder charge against him, we won't have him to worry about."

"Yes, I believe that's the best move."

Down at the sheriff's office they found Dick Heppner, the deputy, sprawled in a chair, reading a book.

"Lookin' for Dud Miles?" queried the deputy. "Mebbe he's at home. His place is that house out there, straight back of the hotel—used to be painted white. Dud batches out there."

They thanked the deputy and went back up the street.

RUSTY HAD entered the second floor of the hotel, via the back stairs, and was waiting in the hallway as Mary came up. She paid no attention to him, as she unlocked her door, but he was right behind her when she entered the room.

Mary gave a little cry of fright, as this disreputable-looking person closed the door and stood there facing her. Rusty had not shaved since before he reached Los Angeles. Now he removed the battered hat. Mary stepped back, staring at him.

"You?" she gasped.

"Yeah, it's me," agreed Rusty quietly. Now that he was with her, he hardly knew where to begin a conversation.

"What do you want?" she asked tensely.

"I want to talk with you," he replied. "I can't stay long, 'cause they'll be on my trail mighty soon. Mebbe they'll get me—cold. But before the shootin' starts, I want you to know that yore father's will was forged. I stole it from Small and hid it. But they got me today, and managed to find the will.

"They sent me a telegram, signin' yore name to it. At yore home they locked me in a room, intendin' to murder me. They had my signature on that guest book; so they forged a deed to my ranch. Then they shot yore father. I got loose and was down there, when you came. I couldn't prove that I—Mary, you don't believe my story?"

"Who do you mean by 'they'?" she asked.

"I don't know who killed him, Mary. Small was one of them. Mike Finley forged the papers. Mary, you've got to believe me. The time is so short that I can't argue the case with yuh. Don't let Covelle get away with this deal. Mary, he's a killer."

"Did—did Covelle kill Mike Finley?" she asked weakly.

"He did not—I killed him myself. Finley swore that he never seen me, until he came into that room where yore father was dead. He lied, Mary. Finley and yore chauffeur locked me in that room in yore house. When Finley saw me out at the ranch, he drew a gun—but I got him."

"Why do you call Covelle a killer?" she asked huskily.

"Because he has murdered a man here, since you came. The man was a lawyer from Scorpion Bend. Covelle is as dangerous as a rattler, Mary. He'd kill you, if it would serve his end. Don't trust him. Don't trust Small, either. You've got to believe me, Mary."

Mary sank down in a chair, weak and helpless.

"I—I don't know what to believe," she said wearily.

Rusty, knowing it was useless now to say any more, walked

past her and went to a front window, where he looked out onto the main street.

ON THE way back from the sheriff's office Covelle and Small were joined by Butch, who knew where the sheriff lived. They found Dud Miles, the hill-billy sheriff, cooking a meal. Covelle explained that they had Rusty Lee tied up at the ranch house.

"Well, dog my cats!" exclaimed the sheriff. "That's shore nice of yuh, Mister Covelle. It ain't often we grabs off a famous killer as easy as that. I'll be right with yuh, in two shakes of a dead lamb's tail. How'd yuh ever discover the son-of-a-gun?"

"Read his description in the Scorpion Bend newspaper," laughed Covelle. "It was easy—when we knew what he looked like."

A passenger train whistled for Black River City, as the four men walked back to the street. They crossed and went to a hitch-rack in front of a big saloon. Dick Heppner, the deputy, coming from the office, joined them.

"Saddle up our horses, Dick," the sheriff said. "We're goin' out to Brant's ranch to git Rusty Lee, that murderer. Mister Covelle's got him all tied up out there for us."

"Yeah?" queried the deputy. "Rusty Lee? Is he that feller with the kinda copper-colored hair that's been out there several days?"

"Yes, that's the man," replied Covelle.

"Tied up, yuh say?"

"Hell, yeah," snorted the sheriff. "Git them horses, Dick."

"I'll git the horses all right, Dud. But if it's the same copper-head I mean, he come to town a while ago. I seen him standin' in front of the hardware store over there."

"Impossible!" exclaimed Covelle.

"Wore an old brown hat that hung down all the way around?" asked the deputy.

"That is what he wore," said Small. "But—"

"Packs a bone-handled Colt six-gun in a holster?"

"Yes!" exclaimed Covelle. "Did this man—"

"He shore did!"

"Wait a minute!" snapped Covelle. "Take it easy. If he got away from Len and came here, he's gone up in the hotel to find Mary. We've got to get him—and get him cold. Don't move quick. Wait! Dick, you stroll over to the front of the hotel and watch that side. Butch, you cut through the alley and go back of the hotel. There are steps down from the second story. Get in close—so he can't see you until he's on his way down. Sheriff, you and I will go into the hotel after him. Small, you keep out of it. Go in the saloon. Remember that this man is wanted for murder—*and stop him.*"

Rusty, watching from the front window, saw the men talking, and saw them separate. He knew they were coming for him. There was a possibility, though, that no one knew which horse was the one he had ridden into town. Mary did not look up, as he stepped past her and went to the door.

"The coyotes are circlin' me," he told her, "so I've got to get goin'. Believe what I told yuh, Mary, 'cause it's true."

HE SLIPPED into the hallway and carefully closed the door. There were voices in the little hotel office, as Rusty went quickly down to the short hallway which led to the balcony at the rear. Rusty knew that someone would be on guard out there. He crouched low and went to the railing.

Down below him, hunkered in the angle between the wall and the stairway was Butch, gun in hand.

There were several chairs on the balcony. The nearest was a huge, home-made one, built of heavy pieces of gum-wood, with a seat and back made of untanned rawhide. It would weigh fifty pounds, at least.

Without making a sound Rusty lifted it clear of the railing, drew it in close to the wall, straight above Butch's head—and let it drop.

There was no chance for Butch to dodge. He was leaning forward, listening, when that huge contraption crashed down on his head. It drove him flat on the ground, his head and shoulders still inside the lower part of the chair. He didn't move.

Running swiftly down the stairs, Rusty stopped and picked up Butch's gun, which had fallen several feet away. Then he ran swiftly around to the rear of the hardware store, where he entered through an open doorway. Only the proprietor was in there, arranging some goods. He glanced at Rusty.

"Howdy. How'd your new gun work?"

"Pretty good," smiled Rusty. "I reckon I got the best of the deal."

"Well, mebbe you did, but I'm satisfied. How is everything?"

"Kinda slow," said Rusty, as he moved slowly toward the front of the store, stopping to examine goods in the show-cases.

At the front door he stopped. Not over twenty feet away was that sorrel.

A twitch of the tie-rope, into that saddle—and they would have trouble in overtaking him. But to reach the horse and mount without inviting disaster....

He opened the door and stepped outside. The doorway was deeply recessed. There was no one watching from across the street. Rusty leaned out and looked up the street, past the sheriff's office, to where Dick Heppner, the deputy, was watching through the hotel window. As he turned more toward the door of the hotel, Rusty went swiftly to his horse, yanked loose the tie-rope and vaulted into the saddle.

At that moment Dick Heppner turned and saw him.

"There he goes!" yelled the deputy, and fired at Rusty. The bullet was wide of the mark. He fired again and again.

Rusty whirled the sorrel and spurred viciously away. But the horse had barely gotten under way, when he felt the animal go out of stride. A moment later it went down, flinging Rusty into a sliding fall. A bullet had broken its hind leg.

Rusty came to his feet, gun in hand. Heppner was running toward him, holding his gun high, when Rusty fired. Heppner's left leg crumpled, and he fell headlong, flinging his gun far down the sidewalk. Rusty did not hesitate, but sprang across the side-walk, racing in behind the buildings.

The shooting brought people into the street, but Heppner, howling with pain, was the only one who had any idea which way Rusty had gone. Covelle and the sheriff had found that Rusty was not in the hotel, and they had just discovered the unconscious Butch, when the shooting brought them back to the main street again. They ran up to the deputy and asked him as to Rusty's whereabouts.

The bullet had struck Heppner's shin bone, shattering it, but the rest of the leg was not injured, except for the bullet-cut. He had rasped his chin and palms on the wooden sidewalk, filling them with slivers; and he was now too miserable to care where Rusty had gone. As a matter of fact, he didn't know exactly where he had gone.

COVELLE WAS white with rage as he questioned Heppner. A crowd was collecting about them.

"Lee crashed a heavy chair down on Butch's head," Covelle told the crowd. "He's as cold as a frozen herring. I guess Lee got his gun, too. Watch the horses along the street; he may try to steal one. That's his only chance to get out of town. I'd like to know how in hell he ever got loose at the ranch."

"Das ha'ar Yohnny Lee is a tough yigger," declared someone in the crowd.

Covelle turned quickly and looked at the stranger. He seemed to know Rusty Lee. The big Swede smiled a little as he blinked back at Covelle.

"Who in the devil are you?" growled Covelle.

"Ay yust coom in on de train."

"I didn't ask you *how* you came here," reminded Covelle.

"Oh, Ay yust vanted to explain that Ay didn't valk in."

"Do you know this Rusty Lee?" asked the sheriff.

"Will somebody get me a doctor?" asked Heppner.

"Yah—su-re," replied the Swede. "Ay know him."

"Who are you?" asked the sheriff, ignoring his suffering deputy.

"Me?" queried the other blandly. "Ay am Oscar Yohnson, de yailer from Tonto City."

"The jailer from Tonto City," parroted the sheriff. "Well, what the devil d'you want here?"

"Va'al," said Oscar, "Ay told Hanry ven ve left home that dese damn ship-horders better not get smort vit me."

Covelle stepped in and put a hand on Oscar's sleeve.

"Listen, Swede, we don't need any jailers from Tonto City. This is Black River City—remember."

"Yah, su-ure. Ay told Hanry—"

"You don't need to tell us what you told Henry," interrupted Covelle. "Just keep on moving, and it will suit us fine."

"Ay am cattle-man," declared Oscar, "and Ay don't take orders from any ship-horder."

"Well, the nerve of the square-head!" exclaimed a sheep-herder.

"Who's a square-head?" asked Oscar innocently.

"I believe the consensus of opinion is that you are," smiled Covelle.

Oscar's grin widened.

"Is dat your opinion, too, faller?"

"Yes, I believe it is, Swede," replied Covelle.

The next movement of the smiling giant was unexpected. With a wide grin on his face, his huge left paw shot out, gathered tightly in Covelle's collar, yanking the sheep boss close. Oscar's right hand groped into Covelle's bosom. There was a heave, the snapping of leather straps, and Oscar's right hand came away, gripping Covelle's shoulder holster and gun. He tossed it behind him. Then, with a heave and flip of his big arms, he flung Covelle ten feet away. The sheep boss landed in a sitting position, nearly knocked out.

Without even taking a deep breath, Oscar turned to the amazed sheriff and said:

"Ven you are not too busy, de Shoriff of Tonto City is down at your hoose, vaiting to talk vit you."

"By the great horn-spoon!" gasped the sheriff.

"Ay don't know anyt'ing about a horn-spoon," said Oscar. "Ve don't use 'em."

Then Oscar turned on his heel and walked away, not even looking back. Covelle got to his feet, humiliated, slightly injured, and very mad.

"I'll betcha," said a sheepherder, "that Swede don't know his own strength. Why, he tore that holster off as easy as I'd tear a button off my shirt."

Oscar Johnson continued on his way, slowing up to gaze into store windows.

"Well," said James Small anxiously, "all the time we're wasting in—er—horse-play, Rusty Lee is making good his escape."

"Is somebody goin' to git me a doctor?" asked Heppner peevishly.

"Right away, Dick," promised the sheriff. "One of you fellers get a doctor for Dick, will yuh? I've got a job on my hands."

Covelle straightened his clothes and picked up his shoulder holster and gun. The straps were ruined.

"I'd like to bend this gun over the cranium of that Swede," he said bitterly.

"You would very likely ruin the gun," Small answered soberly.

"What's to be done?" asked the sheriff. "While all this has been goin' on Lee has had plenty time to get out of reach."

"Watch the hitch-racks and the depot," ordered Covelle, regaining some of his composure again. "I'm sure he won't try to walk out of the country. We'd better examine Butch; he may be dead...."

Butch wasn't dead, but he was still there, holding his head in his hands. His shoulders and head had taken the brunt of that falling chair, which had left plenty of marks in the way of bruises and swellings. They finally made him understand what had happened, and wanted him to go and see a doctor, but Butch refused.

"I'm goin' out to the ranch and kill Len for lettin' that damn murderer loose," he declared. "I should have stayed with him myself."

"You will stay right here and help us capture him," declared Covelle. "Len can wait until we go out there."

CHAPTER VIII

HENRY'S WARNING

RUSTY LEE LEFT the scene of his shooting scrape as swiftly as possible. Skirting the rear of the buildings, he darted through a long shed, passed by several shacks and stopped near the corner of a fence, which surrounded a small cottage. Crouching beside the fence, he watched for the pursuit to form and follow him.

Beyond the house was open country, where there was not enough cover to conceal a cottontail rabbit. Rusty crouched there for a minute or more, before vaulting the fence and going over to the rear of the house. Since leaving the main street he had not seen a person. If he could find a place to hide he could wait until dark, and take a chance of getting safely out of the country.

Quietly he walked around the house—and ran face to face with Henry Harrison Conroy, the Sheriff of Tonto City.

Henry was not wearing the garb of an Arizona sheriff. In fact, Henry was resplendent in a light, fawn-colored suit, fancy vest, tan Oxfords, and on his head he jauntily wore a tan-colored derby hat. In his gloved hands he carried a gold-headed cane.

Rusty's gun centered on Henry's lower vest button, as they stopped and stared at each other for several moments. Then Rusty gasped:

"Lovely dove! The sheriff—himself!"

Henry pursed his lips and nodded jerkily.

"None other," he said quietly. "And if I am not mistaken in my own written description, you are Johnny Lee, erstwhile cattleman of Wild Horse Valley, but now a fugitive from justice."

"Injustice, Sheriff," corrected Rusty coldly.

Henry sighed audibly. "There may be a modicum of truth in your correction, sir," he admitted. "However, not having any scales of justice with me, I am at a loss to—well, strike any balance whatever. I came here to wait for the sheriff. Having sent my emissary—the Vitrified Viking—to notify said sheriff of my presence, I—er—Lee, what the devil was all the shootin' about, anyway?"

Rusty grinned slowly. "The deputy sheriff shot my horse; so I shot the deputy sheriff. I don't believe he got hurt above the knees."

"I see," nodded Henry. "After turning traitor to the cattlemen, you then proceed to invade the sheep country and—er—shoot their officers below the knees. As our English cousins would say, 'Ripping sport, eh, what?'"

"This is the first one I've shot," replied Rusty soberly.

"Tck, tck, tck! Well, I suppose one must start sometime, mustn't one? And what are you doing here—waiting to waylay the sheriff, and make it a clean sweep? Or are you gunning especially for me? I haven't any gun with me, if that will cause less pressure on that trigger. Really, I have no intention of attacking you, Lee. This cane is not exactly a lethal weapon—at least, not in my hands. My only experience in fencing was while playing *The Count of Monte Cristo.* On the first parry the hilt came off my sword; so I was obliged to run my opponent through with the hilt. It brought down the house."

"Is this the sheriff's home?" asked Rusty, grinning.

"So I was told by the agent at the depot."

"I shore picked a swell place to hide," laughed Rusty. "But what are you doin' over here, Sheriff?"

"I," REPLIED Henry soberly, "am a dove of peace. I came here to see if—well, if we cannot work out a reciprocity agreement, between the cattlemen and the sheepmen. For instance, we will agree not to bring cattle over here, if they will agree not to attempt to take sheep over to Wild Horse Valley.

"In other words, I am prepared to point out to them the impossibility of ever bringing sheep into our valley, in spite of the fact that they have acquired the TL Ranch. They may have and hold said thousand acres—but to populate it with sheep—never! We will ring that rim with steel, and the rivers will run with a crimson tide, before we—well, we'll shoot hell out of a lot of shepherds, before they spot a woolly on the TL."

"That's a good-lookin' suit you've got," said Rusty.

"It should be," replied Henry. "I paid a hundred and fifty dollars for it three years ago. Little tight across the shoulders and at the waistline, and it may be a trifle out of style; but I believe it is very impressive. But what are you intending to do, Lee?"

"Quien sabe?" replied Rusty soberly. "What would you do, if you were in my boots? The law wants me for murder, Wild Horse Valley wants to hang me as a traitor, and Black River City wants to lynch me for shooting a deputy sheriff in the leg."

"What would I do?" queried Henry seriously. "Why, I would probably shiver myself down to about a hundred and forty pounds, and walk off in perfect disguise. Why did you do it all, Lee?"

"The queer angle about the whole thing," replied Rusty, "is the fact that I didn't. Of course, I shot the deputy in the leg. But he shot my horse and was shootin' at me."

"Justifiable—er—legicide, I suppose. You say you did not murder King Brant?"

"No. I never sold the TL Ranch, either—but I can't prove it."

"Interesting," murmured Henry. "Your signature has been identified."

"Forgery."

"Indeed. Who was the forger?"

"A man named Michael Finley, who worked as a butler for Brant."

"That is interesting. Where is Mr. Finley at present?"

"I reckon he's permanent," said Rusty. "They either buried him here or shipped his remains. I never did hear what they done with him."

"Ah, yes—I see. Someone—er—objected to further imitations, eh?"

"Yeah, that's right," nodded Rusty soberly. "I liked the idea of writin' *my own* signatures."

"Well, bless my soul!" exclaimed Henry, and looked askance at the cocked gun, which Rusty still held in his right hand.

"And still," continued Henry, "I would be the last person on earth to contend that private signatures should be—er—and your signature was, or is, rather involved. It seems perfect on that deed."

"They got me to sign that guest register," said Rusty.

"I see-e-e," murmured Henry. "I read about that missing page, which later was recovered, bearing your signature. Yes, I can see where a forgery would be possible. But I find you in a sheep country, Lee."

"I've been workin' for the Brant outfit," said Rusty. "I reckon I lost my job today. They found my description in a Scorpion Bend paper; so they jumped me, tied me up. They had some more crooked business to attend to, before turnin' me over to their sheriff—but I talked faster than the man they left to guard me, and came here to mix into their deal. Somebody told them I was in town; so they had me corralled in the hotel, until I dropped a rockin'-chair off the upstairs porch and cooled off their rear guard."

"Bless my soul!" exclaimed Henry. "But Swan River said you were very resourceful."

"He said I was crazy."

"Well, he said you were resourceful—in a crazy way."

"Yeah, I reckon—" began Rusty. Then he heard voices near the front of the house.

Slanting in against the wall of the house was a cellar door, unlocked. It was the best possible hiding-place. Rusty stepped over, lifted the door and looked back at Henry, who was indifferently brushing some dust off the back of his left glove. A moment later Rusty was out of sight, the door back in place.

HENRY SIGHED, turned and walked to the front corner, where he saw Dud Miles, the sheriff, and Nort Covelle. Both men were leading horses. They had tied these to the fence before they noticed Henry Harrison Conroy.

The sheriff swore under his breath, while Covelle's thin lips twisted in amusement at sight of the sartorially perfect sheriff from Tonto City. Henry twirled his cane and squinted at the two men.

"Yo're Conroy, eh?" growled the sheriff.

"At your service, sir," replied Henry, bowing a trifle.

The sheriff scowled darkly.

"Services, hell! I don't want yore services. I'm huntin' a murderer."

"Really?"

"Yeah, really! What the devil do youn want here, anyway?"

"Well, I at least expected courtesy," replied Henry stiffly.

"Can yuh beat that, Covelle?" sneered the sheriff.

"You are Mr. Covelle?" queried Henry.

"I am," replied Covelle.

"Perhaps it is fortunate that I am able to meet you, sir," said Henry. "It will afford us a chance to talk over matters."

"We ain't got any time to talk," declared the sheriff. "That damn Rusty Lee shot my deputy through the leg and mighty near killed one of Covelle's men with a chair. Do yuh think we're goin' to waste a lot of time talkin' to you? If yuh do, yo're crazy."

"Just what did you wish to talk about?" asked Covelle curiously.

"Speaking bluntly," replied Henry, "I wish to talk about the possibility of Wild Horse Valley buying back the TL Ranch."

"I am very much afraid you are wasting your time and mine," said Covelle. "The TL Ranch is not for sale."

"I trust you understand that it will never be possible for you to put sheep on that ranch," said Henry coldly.

"Has anyone ever told you that it was our intention to put sheep on the TL Ranch, Mr. Conroy?"

"That is our impression, Mr. Covelle. I wish to warn you against such an attempt. Wild Horse Valley is armed and—"

"What in hell's the use of arguin'?" interrupted the sheriff. "We've got to catch a murderer."

"I am sure that would not be difficult," said Henry.

"What do you mean?" asked Covelle sharply.

"From what I have heard," replied Henry, "there are unlimited possibilities of catching a murderer in the Black River Flats."

Covelle's eyes blazed for a moment, but he held his temper.

"If you don't mind, Mr. Conroy, we will bid you good-day," he said coldly. "Your warning is interesting, I am sure."

Henry bowed and walked out to the little gate, where he turned and went up toward the main street.

"Of all the damn fools!" snorted the sheriff angrily.

"Wait a minute," said Covelle. "Don't misrate that party, Dud. He has proved that he's not anybody's fool. Several bad boys have found out to their sorrow that he isn't a fool—but too late to do anything about it."

"Damn red-nosed dude!"

"All right. But where in the devil did Rusty Lee go? Heppner doesn't know which way he went, but I'm sure he went this way, because his horse fell on this side of the street. He wouldn't *cross* the street."

"He can't git away," declared the sheriff. "Everybody in town is on the search for him. I'd like to know what he done to Len.

We'll know pretty soon. Now what was it yuh wanted to talk with me about?"

"We'll talk about it in the house, Dud."

CHAPTER IX

OUT OF THE FRYING PAN—

RUSTY LEE FOUND himself in almost total darkness in the sheriff's root-cellar. There was a strong odor of decayed vegetables and mouldy boards. The place was about ten by twelve feet, and barely high enough for Rusty to stand erect. At one corner was a rickety stairway under a trap-door, which apparently opened into the sheriff's kitchen. Daylight came through the cracks around the door.

Rusty heard Covelle and the sheriff enter the house, and their footsteps sounded on the board floor over his head. He heard the rattle of chairs, as they sat down, and muffled conversation.

By standing part way up the steps and listening closely, Rusty was able to catch some of the words, but not all. Covelle was telling the sheriff something about Mary and the will of King Brant. He heard the sheriff say: "Well, what in hell can *she* do?"

He could not hear Covelle's low-toned explanation, except for a word here and there, after which the sheriff said:

"Then she knows the will was forged, eh?"

"Lee was in her room, telling her. She can cause plenty trouble, if she gets a chance. Hold up probating the will, cause investigations and all that. Mike Finley was known as a forger. The law might…"Covelle lowered his voice again, talking for several minutes.

"Yeah, I can see that," admitted the sheriff. "But what can you do…?"

Rusty strained his ears, but Covelle was speaking too quietly. He heard Mary's name mentioned. There was something about tickets, a midnight train, and something about several witnesses. Covelle assured the sheriff that he would be well paid, and in no danger. Apparently the sheriff was a willing soul, because he said:

"Why, shore yuh can. Hell, any of 'em are lookin' for a chance to make money. I'll help yuh git one."

"Well, that's settled," said Covelle. "Let's go and see if anybody has found that damn red-head."

Rusty sat down on the steps and tried to puzzle out what Covelle wanted the sheriff to do. It was something concerning Mary Brant, who had, no doubt, told Covelle that she knew the will was forged. It thrilled Rusty to feel that Mary believed him. Evidently the whole town was searching for him by this time. However, the last place they would look for him would be in the sheriff's root-cellar; so he decided to wait there until after dark.

HENRY HARRISON CONROY left the sheriff's home and walked back to the main street, where he halted in front of the hotel. From a saloon across the street came the sounds of a commotion, loud voices and the thudding of blows. Henry had started across the street, when out of the saloon doorway came two tumbling figures, locked in each other's arms. Behind them surged a yelling crowd of men and dance-hall girls.

Out in the dust of the street the two huge combatants pulled apart and got to their feet. One was Oscar Johnson, his shirt almost torn off, his blond hair flying. The other man crouched for a moment and then charged to battle, fists swinging. Oscar side-stepped clumsily, hooked wickedly with his powerful right fist to the jaw of his charging antagonist—and the fight was over.

Then Oscar whirled, facing the crowd in front of the saloon.

"Oll right!" he yelled. "Who is de next lucky faller?"

Oscar's vanquished enemy sat up, caressing his jaw, his eyes blank.

"Oscar, are you fighting again?" queried Henry. Oscar turned, looked at Henry Conroy, and a wide grin split his sober face.

"Oh, hallo dere," he said brightly. He pointed at his late antagonist and said:

"Hanry, Ay vould like to have you meet Olaf."

"Olaf?" queried Henry.

"Yah—su-ure. You remember Olaf? He tried to steal Yosephine from me von time."

Josephine, who happened to be Oscar's heart's desire, was a maid in the Tonto Hotel, at Tonto City.

"Olaf," explained Oscar brightly, "is de champion fighter hare."

"I see," murmured Henry, "So you had to fight him, eh?"

"Yah, su-ure. He insolted me."

"He insulted you? How?"

"Va'al, he says, 'Yentlemen, Ay vant you to meet my old friend, Oscar Yohnson.'"

"Well, my goodness, I do not see where that was an insult, Oscar."

"Ay am not so damn old."

"Not over six," murmured Henry. "I believe we had better buy you a new shirt, Oscar."

Oscar meekly followed him to a general store, where they managed to find a shirt large enough for Oscar.

"You stay with me for the remainder of our visit here," ordered Henry. "The next thing you know a lot of these sheepherders will gang up on you."

"Ay vould lofe it," grinned Oscar. They walked up to the front of the hotel, where several men had gathered. These looked askance at Henry's clothes, but grinned openly.

Nort Covelle and the sheriff were coming down the street. Evidently this group of men had been searching for Rusty Lee. A man rode in and dismounted, and as the sheriff came up to them he said:

"Len cut the ropes and turned Lee loose. The cook out there said he seen 'em leave the ranch, and he said that Len rode south toward Mexico."

Covelle swore bitterly. He could figure no reason for Len doing such a thing.

"We've searched the whole damn town, Dud," reported one of the men.

"He's got to be here," declared Covelle.

"If he is, I dunno where he can be. A couple of the boys are watchin' the depot, and we've got the hitch-racks covered. But that won't stop him from walkin' away. I reckon we've done all we can."

Covelle turned to the sheriff.

"Well," he said, "I guess he has made a fool of you, Dud."

"You mean 'us' don'tcha?" queried the sheriff. "You gave orders to the rest of us, when Lee was at the hotel, if yuh remember. I'd have spotted his horse, and got him, before he got started."

COVELLE COLORED angrily, but made no reply. He shot a malevolent glance at Oscar Johnson and Henry Conroy, who were interested listeners to the conversation. At that moment Henry glanced through the hotel window and saw Mary Brant, who was anxiously looking at the group outside.

"I'll buy a drink," offered Covelle to the men, and they went across the street, leaving Henry and Oscar. Henry stepped into the hotel.

"I'm sure they didn't find him, Miss Brant," the hotel proprietor was just telling her.

"Thank you very much," said Mary quietly. She turned to look at Henry.

"You are Miss Brant?" queried Henry.

"Yes, I am Mary Brant. Did you wish to see me?"

"Well, my dear lady," smiled Henry, "the pleasure is unexpected, I can assure you. I am Henry Harrison Conroy, the Sheriff from Tonto City. I came here to talk with the local sheriff, hoping that we might work out some plan to avert bloodshed between the sheepmen of this country and the cattlemen of Wild Horse Valley. I would like to say that I am very sorry about your father, Miss Brant."

"Thank you," murmured Mary. "But I am afraid that—" She hesitated for a moment, then went on: "You see, my father's will specified that Nort Covelle has entire charge of the sheep for a period of five years."

"How remarkable!" exclaimed Henry quietly.

"Yes—isn't it," said Mary.

Henry pursed his lips thoughtfully. "I understand," he said, "that your father, before his death acquired the TL Ranch, belonging to Johnny Lee, with the intention of using it as a base of operations in Wild Horse Valley. We also understand that you assisted in negotiating the sale of this property."

Mary flushed.

"That isn't true," she said. "I knew nothing about it."

"But you wired Lee to come to your home in Los Angeles."

"I never sent him a telegram in my life."

"The telegram is in my desk at Tonto City, and it says: 'Come at once if you can. Wire me if coming and when.' And it is signed by Mary Brant. Rusty Lee left the telegram at his ranch, and it was given to me."

"I never sent it, Mr. Conroy," she told him earnestly. "I want you to believe me when I tell you that I did not know that Rusty Lee was at my home, or had any intention of coming there, until I saw him standing over the body of my father, with a gun in his hand."

"How remarkable!" murmured Henry. "As you have stated, the will gives Mr. Covelle entire charge of the sheep interests— but does that Lee ranch figure in the deal? That is, does Covelle inherit the right to control that ranch? All reports show that your father paid the sum of twenty-five thousand dollars for the deed to this ranch. Would you be willing to sell this back to us at that same price?"

"If I have the right," replied Mary quickly. "Frankly, I am

puzzled over the terms of my father's will, Mr. Conroy. So many things have happened that—"

"I know," assured Henry kindly. "I would be the last to blame you for not knowing just what to do. But will you keep that in mind? We will pay you exactly what your father paid for the ranch. And, Miss Brant, I can assure you that it will never be a benefit to you or to the estate. In all fairness and respect to your father, he made a big mistake when he thought he could put sheep into Wild Horse Valley."

"I know nothing about that, Mr. Conroy," Mary answered, "but I am sure my father would not allow anything that would cause bloodshed."

Henry nodded.

"I am sure he would not, Miss Brant. It has been a pleasure to meet and talk with you."

"Thank you," said Mary. She moved a little closer to him. "Do you—do you know that men are hunting for Johnny Lee?"

"Yes, I believe they are. It seems that Johnny Lee is a much-wanted young man."

"But they haven't found him yet," said Mary, a note of triumph in her voice.

"Johnny Lee," remarked Henry, "seems to be a rather resourceful young man, with a decided penchant for running his nose into trouble."

"That is true," sighed Mary.

After Mary had gone back to her room Henry sat down in the lobby, with Oscar Johnson.

"There is a midnight train, which stops at Scorpion Bend," informed Henry. "We will go home on that train, Oscar."

"Yah, su-ure," agreed Oscar. "Das ha'ar town is not a gude place to stay. Olaf vars de only fighter in de town, and oll he could do vars tear off my short."

"Did anyone else have any remarks to make to you?" asked Henry.

"Yah, su-ure. Von faller says that you are a ha'al of a looking thing. Ay said, 'Hanry may be a ha'al of a looking thing, but—'"

"That is sufficient answer to my question," interrupted Henry dryly. "You have a bad habit of going into details."

RUSTY LEE stayed in the sheriff's root-house until well after dark. The sheriff did not come back home. It was very dark when Rusty opened the outside cellar door, and came outside. There was no moon, and the sky was overcast. At least, Nature was favoring Rusty Lee. He left the sheriff's yard, crossed the street and came up near the main street in the deep shadows of some old buildings.

There was the usual activity on the main street, but Rusty was certain that some of the sheriff's and Covelle's men were watching for him. There were a number of horses tied at the hitch-racks, where it would be possible to select a suitable mount; but he felt very sure that each hitch-rack was under guard.

However, Rusty was not thinking of getting a horse. He knew that Covelle and the sheriff had some sort of a scheme, and he wanted to know what that was. They had mentioned tickets and a midnight train. Rusty knew that there was a midnight passenger train, going West, and he had made up his mind to be at the depot, in spite of possible guards, who might be expecting him to try and board a freight train.

It was eight o'clock when Rusty at last came out of the cellar; so he sprawled in the deep shadow, prepared to wait until midnight. He had no fear of discovery, because he was sure that no one would be hunting him in the darkness.

It was nearly midnight when he got to his feet again. It was a simple matter for him to reach the depot without being seen. The depot platform was badly lighted. As Rusty crouched in the darkness he saw several people together come to the depot. One was a woman, and Rusty felt sure it was Mary Brant. As they came into the lights of the small waiting room he saw that with her were Covelle, Small and the sheriff. They passed through to the train platform.

Rusty heard the train whistle for the station, and he took a chance on being seen, realizing that the guards, if there were any, would be outside to watch the train. He sprinted across an open space and onto the rear platform of the station.

The baggage room door was open on both sides. On a pile of boxes beside the door was a lighted railroad lantern. Rusty hugged the wall beside the wide doorway, as the train came to a stop. He saw the group of people heading for the sleeping cars. He saw Covelle take the girl aside and speak with her, and then she started for the steps of the car, where a porter was standing.

Far down the train a voice called: "Bo-o-o-oard!"

The woman was going up the steps when Rusty acted. Picking up the lantern, he hurried boldly out to the group near the car. The train began moving as he came up to them. The porter swung aboard, and was about to lower the guard and shut the door, when Rusty reached the steps.

Then Nort Covelle recognized him.

"Why, you—" he started to shout. Then Rusty flung the lantern into his face, knocking him backwards. Before anyone else could stop him, he was into the vestibule, knocking the porter backwards over some baggage.

The sheriff, realizing that it was Rusty, ran along the car, yelling to stop the train, which was gaining speed. When he came even with the steps of Rusty's car, Rusty smashed a bullet into the wooden platform just in front of him. The sheriff ducked aside. Before he could recover himself, the train was traveling too fast for him to catch it.

Rusty turned then to the frightened porter.

"Better close her up, pardner," he said.

"Yea-yea-yea-yeassir."

With trembling fingers the frightened Negro closed the entrance. Then he turned to Rusty, his jaw sagging.

"Somethin' mo' fo' you, boss?" he asked.

"A lady came in here," said Rusty grimly. "Where is she?"

"Yessuh, yessuh! She's in Lowah Eight, suh; yessuh! This yeah is huh baggage, suh."

Rusty looked down at the several pieces of expensive luggage. On the top one, in gold letters, were the initials *M.E.B.* Mary Brant's initials.

"Start packin' it in, pardner," ordered Rusty. "I'll foller yuh."

"Yessuh, right now. Yo' just follow me, suh."

"I'll be right on yore heels," promised Rusty.

THEY WENT down the swaying car. Nearly all the berths were made up. In fact, all except Number 8. The girl was sitting there, taking off a veil—and it was not Mary Brant. She glanced up sharply at the porter, and then at Rusty, turning quickly away.

"I reckon yo're Mary Brant," said Rusty.

"Well?" she queried, not looking at him.

"Are yuh?" he asked.

"What's it to you?" she asked.

"Quite a lot—and a devil of a lot to you. Where'd you get Mary Brant's baggage?"

"I didn't know I had Mary Brant's baggage. I don't even know who Mary Brant is, if you ask me."

"I see," said Rusty, tight-lipped. "Covelle didn't tell yuh, eh? He'd run yore neck into a loop, and never give yuh a chance."

"I don't even know Covelle."

"All right, we'll change names, and make it Dud Miles."

The girl jerked around quickly.

"Who the devil are you?" she asked sharply.

"I'm Rusty Lee."

"Oh, I see—the murderer, eh? Well, you've got a lot of gall to be trying to tell me that something is wrong."

"Gall or no gall, sister—I'm tellin' yuh. I've seen you around the Black River honkatonk. Pretty good singer, too. Yuh ought to stick to singin'. Mebbe you don't know what yo're doin' tonight; but yuh ought to know. It might save yore neck."

"If you know so much—tell me what I'm doin'?" she challenged.

"Whereat do yo' want this luggage, Ma'am?" asked the porter.

"Stack it on the seat," ordered Rusty. He waited until the porter went away, before he turned again to the girl.

"Dud Miles hired you to go away on the train tonight, didn't he?"

"Did he? You're doing all the guessing, it seems."

Rusty laughed shortly. "What's yore name, sister?"

"Mazie Brown. My initials are on my bags."

"Must have cost yuh a lot of money."

"That's my business, cowboy."

"All right," said Rusty. "Stick to yore story. But if I was you, I'd drop off this train a long ways this side of Los Angeles, 'cause I'm goin' to send telegrams. When you wake up in the mornin', there is goin' to be a lot of folks lookin' for you, and there might be a lot of stuff in them valises that never belonged to Mazie Brown."

"You won't send any telegrams," she said. "And if you'd use your brains a little you'd realize that a lot of people are *already* looking for you."

"All right, sister," smiled Rusty. "Remember that I told yuh—and you got too bull-headed to listen."

Rusty walked forward to the platform, where he gazed out into the night. He realized that the first station stop was Scorpion Bend, a five-hour run from Black River Flats, and nearly all over heavy grades. He had no ticket and no money, but he knew they could not put him off the train until they made a regular stop.

While he was standing there the train conductor and the Pullman conductor came through the vestibule. Apparently they knew that a woman was the only passenger to board the train at Black River Flats, because they ignored Rusty and went on. No one on the train had paid any attention to the shot he had fired in the vestibule. Apparently, if they had heard it at all, they had thought it some sort of joke.

Rusty went then and sat in a smoking room, listening to several men telling stories, as the train dragged slowly over the heavy grades.

More than two hours had passed since they left Black River Flats, when the train ground slowly to a stop.

Rusty stepped out into the vestibule. The steps were open. The brakeman was down on the ground, with his lantern. Rusty stepped down and looked around.

"Kinda chilly up here," said the brakeman.

"Shore is," agreed Rusty. "What place is this?"

"Apache Siding. We meet Sixty-nine here tonight, and they're late."

There was light enough now for Rusty to see something of the place. There were two long, low buildings, nearly new, like bunk-houses. One was lighted at one end.

"How long will we be here?" asked Rusty.

"Probably fifteen minutes—maybe more."

The brakeman moved away.

Rusty stretched and sauntered over toward the buildings. Through an uncovered window he saw four men seated around a table, playing poker. Rusty grunted softly to himself. The man facing the window was the man who had secured the sheep crew for Covelle in Yuma, and the other three were men who had been recruited at the same time he himself had joined the outfit.

Without a moment's hesitation, Rusty shoved the door open and stepped into the room.

CHAPTER X

COVELLE'S OFFER

AS RUSTY STEPPED into the shack, the men inside turned quickly, staring at the intruder.

"Well, I'll be darned if it ain't the High-Heel Kid!" exclaimed the recruit boss. "Where'd you come from tonight?"

"Covelle sent me," lied Rusty. "Didn't yuh hear my train arrive?"

"Hell, no! A lot of 'em come and go. Covelle sent yuh, eh?"

"Yeah, he said I'd be worth more up here than down there. He said you'd have plenty beddin'; so I didn't bring my roll."

"Shore, we can fix yuh up all right. How about a little drink?"

"Somethin' to eat would suit me a lot better. Got a snack?"

The recruit boss turned to another of the men.

"Heat up the coffee, Mac," he said. "I'd like some, too. Plenty cold beans and a hunk of roast venison. I reckon yuh can keep from starvin'. How's everything down in the city?"

"Little slow," replied Rusty. "Covelle is takin' it easy. He ain't in no hurry. Slow and sure, that's Covelle."

"He's pretty smart. I'll dig out some grub."

Rusty had no idea what these men were doing. He had merely taken a chance that they were still connected with Covelle, and it seemed that he was welcome. There was little chance that they knew anything about him being hunted by Covelle.

As if answering any doubts he might have on that score, one of the men at the table now complained, "We don't never hear a damn thing up here. No way of gettin' any mail, unless somebody comes up here especially to see us—and there ain't been anybody since we came."

"What do yuh hear about things in Wild Horse Valley?" asked the one they called Mac. "We don't know a damned thing."

"We couldn't get much news from over there," replied Rusty, "but Covelle said that things were about to start movin'. Guess he had some trouble with that Brant girl over the will—but that's fixed, I understand."

Rusty was afraid to ask questions, because he was supposed to know what this small crew of men were doing here at Apache Siding. While they were eating a cold supper an idea struck him.

"How many cars can they handle on this sidin'?" he asked.

"Only about fifty," replied Mac.

Fifty carloads of sheep! The scheme was clear enough now. The sheep would be shipped to Apache Siding, unloaded and— Rusty helped himself to more beans.

"How long a drive will it be from here?" he asked casually.

"The biggest part of a day," replied Mac. "It ain't a bad grade."

"Unless Wild Horse Valley gets wise to the scheme," laughed one of the men. "This sidin' ain't been in here over a month, and they think that Scorpion Bend is the only place we could unload."

"They ain't wise—yet," declared Mac. "Covelle worked out the idea. Yuh see, that TL Ranch runs right to the summit of the mountain. We can throw sheep right onto our own ground, and nobody can stop us."

"Won't Wild Horse Valley watch the rim?" asked Rusty.

"Why should they? This is the only route there is where sheep could come over the mountain—and they don't know anything about this spot. Covelle and Butch lived out in these hills for a month, workin' out the scheme. Why, there's a natural pass into the TL."

"Covelle is pretty smart," said Rusty.

"He's smart enough. This looks like an air-tight cinch to me. But if there's any slip—a pile of us will probably get wooden overcoats. Them punchers shoot straight."

"And after all," said one of the men, "I'd hate to lay my life down for a sheep."

"Same here," grinned Mac. "And I don't mind tellin' you that I won't be along with the first sheep that go over the rim."

"Like I said a while ago," remarked Rusty, "Covelle is smart. But it shore looks to me as though he thought the cattlemen are dumb. They won't watch Scorpion Bend—they'll watch the TL. They'll know that the sheep *have to come up over the rim.* And Covelle can't put enough rifles into these hills to force his way over the top. The punchers will set up there in the rocks and pick us off. They can dynamite the sheep. Why, I'll betcha they know about this sidin'—and they're settin' up there, laughin' at us right now."

Mac shrugged shis shoulders.

"Quien sabe, Kid? Covelle says not. Of course, this delay may make a lot of difference. If King Brant hadn't been killed, the scheme was to have sheep over that rim before Wild Horse Valley even knew that Brant owned the TL. Now—I'm not so sure about it."

"It shore looks like suicide to me," declared Rusty.

"Well, let's go to bed," suggested Mac, "and let Covelle do all the worryin'."

"I reckon he's got plenty to worry him," said Rusty dryly.

RUSTY LEE was right when he said that Nort Covelle had plenty of worries. His chin and right cheek had been cut by the flung lantern, and as he paced up and down the sheriff's little office he cursed Rusty Lee in no uncertain language. James

Small, Butch and the sheriff sat there, waiting gloomily for Covelle to make a suggestion.

"Damn him, he fooled all of us with that railroad lantern," complained Covelle. "Everybody thought he was one of the trainmen. Three of us standing right there, and two men guarding each side of the train—and we let him get away."

"There is no use wiring officers at Scorpion Bend," said Small. "Their sheriff and jailer are on the day coach of that same train. But we could wire Yuma."

"What about that girl?" queried the sheriff nervously.

"Forget that!" snapped Covelle. "Lee don't know her. All he wanted was a chance to get out of here. And we won't wire Yuma, because he won't go that far."

"If he drops off in Wild Horse Valley—" began Butch, caressing his swollen head.

"They'll lynch him," finished Covelle. "Well, I'm glad he's out of this country."

"When do we start?" asked Butch.

"Tomorrow morning," replied Covelle. "You ride to two of the camps tonight, so you'll be there by daylight. Start the sheep this way. We'll load as soon as they get here. Damn 'em, I'm going to eat my Sunday supper on the TL Ranch if I have to shoot my way through a hundred cowpunchers."

"A hundred," muttered Butch. "Well, I hope they ain't as tough as Rusty Lee. One of his kind is plenty for one man to handle."

"One man!" snorted the sheriff indignantly. "A dozen, yuh mean."

"Well, we won't have *him* to deal with any more," said Covelle. "He's going a long ways from this country—or I miss my bet."

"I hope yuh win," groaned Butch, and went to get his horse.

Covelle and Small went out to the ranch, but Small did not want to go to bed. It would soon be morning, and he was too nervous for sleep. Small was worried about Rusty Lee, because

Rusty knew too much. Covelle snorted at his fears, but Small paced the living-room floor of the ranch house.

"Lee knows about Quincy Adams," he insisted. "Butch told us he did. Butch said Lee wouldn't tell anybody. Maybe he wouldn't as long as he was with us. And you say that Lee told Mary Brant that you and I killed her father. He told her that Mike Finley forged that deed and the will. And you laugh at me, because I can't sleep."

"Don't let little things worry you," smiled Covelle. "Lee can't prove a word of what he told her. He's guessing at everything."

"What about tonight?" asked Small. "Maybe Mary told him that she was leaving on that midnight train; that's why he was there. I tell you, Covelle, he didn't take all those chances just to escape from here; he wanted to see Mary Brant. And when he found that dance-hall girl—I wonder what he would do?"

"Don't worry about that girl; she knew what to say and do. All we wanted was proof that Mary Brant left Black River Flats. What happens to her after that is no affair of ours. Why, even the depot agent will testify that he saw her leave. The hotel clerk saw her walk out of the hotel with me, and with Butch carrying her bags. No one saw the substitution made, halfway to the depot. Have a drink and forget it; we're as safe as a church, I tell yuh."

"I'll feel a lot safer when I know Rusty Lee is behind bars."

THEY HAD a number of drinks and sat around until daylight. After breakfast Covelle sent all the men to Black River City to assist in loading the sheep. As soon as the men were gone, Covelle went to the door of the room which Butch and Rusty had formerly occupied, and unlocked it.

Mary Brant, fully dressed, was sitting on the edge of the bed. She had not been to bed at all that night.

Covelle smiled at her. "I hope you are feeling well, my dear," he said.

Mary came abruptly to her feet. "What is the meaning of all this?" she demanded. "You force me to come out here, lock me in a room and leave me there all night, without any explanation."

Covelle shrugged. "The explanation is simple, Mary. You were foolishly trying to block a move which will mean many thousands of dollars to your estate; so I was obliged to take drastic steps. When we have succeeded in putting a few thousand sheep on the TL Ranch in Wild Horse Valley, you will be free to do as you please, because it will be too late for you to interfere."

"So you add kidnaping to your other crimes," said Mary.

"That would be difficult to prove, my dear. You are on a ranch belonging to you. This is as much your home as the mansion in Beverly Hills. If you are under a sort of restraint, it is because you are attempting to interfere with work which your father wished me to handle. I'm sorry, but it was the only thing I could do."

Mary's eyes blazed hotly and she stamped a foot. "My father never wished any such a thing, Nort Covelle. That was a forgery!"

"Still believing that murdering cowboy, eh? All right," Covelle's voice hardened, "believe what you want to; but I am in charge of the sheep—and the sheep go to Wild Horse Valley. We are loading today."

"How long are you going to keep me a prisoner?"

Again Covelle shrugged his shoulders.

"At least until you decide to leave the sheep business alone."

"Do you really think you can get away with this, Nort? Suppose there is an investigation started—a search for me. What then?"

Covelle laughed at her.

"My dear, that is all covered," he said. "You went away on the midnight train. The hotel proprietor saw you leave the hotel. At least six people, including the depot agent, saw you get on that train. Oh, I'll admit that the girl was not as beautiful as you are—but she wore a veil. She had your baggage, your ticket and reservation."

"I guess Rusty Lee was right," said Mary quietly. "He said you were crooked. I didn't want to believe you guilty of the things he charged, but I guess he told the truth."

"Possibly," smiled Covelle. "But he couldn't prove one thing, my dear—and the law requires proof, you know. So you may as well resign yourself to a period of inaction."

"You didn't capture Rusty Lee?"

"Instead," replied Coveile, "we chased him out of the country."

"And he left his trademark on your face."

"Who told you?"

"I heard Butch tell the cook that Rusty threw a lantern in your face, and went away on a train."

"You did, eh?" said Covelle.

"Yes."

"Well, I don't suppose that information helps you any."

"I wonder if it does," said Mary calmly.

"What do you mean?" asked Covelle quickly.

Mary had a sudden inspiration. "I told Rusty that I was taking that train," she said.

Covelle's eyes narrowed as he looked intently at the girl.

"And of course," continued Mary, "he would find another girl in my place. If you are as wise as you think you are, you will take me to Black River City and send me away on the first train going west."

COVELLE LAUGHED at her and shook his head. "I don't scare that easily, my dear," he said. "Rusty Lee is too busy trying to save his own neck to bother about you. Listen to me!"

Covelle came closer to the bed, his voice tense, as he spoke quietly.

"For the first time in my life I've got a chance to make money; and nothing can stop me. What you know or don't know isn't going to change the situation. We can produce plenty of evidence that you left Black River City last night. If Mary Brant never shows up again—we are in the clear. In fact, it might entirely solve the problem. These men are all loyal. You haven't got a chance. Jim Small is not only executor of your father's estate, but has a power of attorney to handle all the affairs of the estate. Think that over, too."

"Forged, I suppose," said Mary.

"Too clever to ever be proved a forgery. Mike Finley knew his job."

"His cleverness did not save his life."

"I suppose Rusty Lee told you something about that, too, eh?"

"Perhaps he did. He told me about that lawyer from Scorpion Bend, too. I believe his name was Adams."

"You know quite a lot, it seems," remarked Covelle. "It's a good thing I took you out of circulation. For a young lady of great social standing, and if I might say so, of gentle breeding, you are rather a dangerous person. And you seem to have nerve. Would it make you just a trifle nervous if I were to tell you that—well, that you have a small chance of ever using your knowledge, or beliefs, against me?"

"You wouldn't dare harm me, Nort Covelle." But her face paled a little.

"I should hate to, my dear," he said. "There is still one way out for you."

"What is that?" asked Mary.

"Marry me. A wife may not testify against her husband."

The color came back to Mary's face. "You are ridiculous!" she snapped.

"I am," admitted Covelle, "but the offer still stands. Think it over, Mary; it might take you out of a bad situation."

With that, Covelle left her, went back to the living-room. There he found Small. The lawyer's eyes were red from nervousness and lack of sleep.

"Well?" he queried. "You talked with her, Nort?"

"Yes," replied Covelle grimly. "She knows too much, Jim."

"I was afraid of that. What is the answer?"

Covelle shrugged his shoulders, shoved both hands deep in his pockets and looked at the nervous lawyer.

"Give her time to think about it, Jim. I showed her a way out."

"What was that?"

"Marriage with me."

"Yes, that would be all right. But does she realize—her situation?"

"Oh, I guess she does. She says that Rusty Lee knew she was leaving on that midnight train."

"Good Lord! Nort, I told you last night—"

"I think she's lying, Jim."

"You *think!* Suppose he did know. He is fool enough to run his own neck into a rope to save her, if he knew she was in trouble."

"But he doesn't *know.* Even if he did find that other girl on the train, her orders were not to claim to be Mary Brant. She was Mazie Brown—same initials. Rusty Lee would be the only one who knew that Mary did not leave Black River City last night—and what is the word of a hunted murderer against six or seven of us?"

"But just suppose somebody should come here and see her— talk with her. You and I can't stay here to guard her; and I won't trust anybody. Look what Len did, when we had Lee tied up here."

"I've got that all figured out," smiled Covelle. "After breakfast she gets locked up again. Later, I'll tell you my scheme."

CHAPTER XI

PRISON SHACK

THE NEXT MORNING Rusty Lee had a good chance to study the situation at Apache Siding. Bunk-houses for thirty men had been built, about thirty acres of land had been cheaply fenced, and a large supply of food had been brought there. Mac showed Rusty twenty-five new rifles, a dozen Colt .45s, and plenty of ammunition. In addition to all this, there were two fifty-pound boxes of high-percentage dynamite.

Rusty knew the men only by their first names. Mac was in charge. The others were Lou, Slim and Jules. They knew Rusty as the High-Heel Kid, because that was what Mac had called him. There was little to do now, except to cook and eat—and Mac did most of the cooking.

He and Rusty sat in front of the shacks, and Mac pointed out the course of a trail which would lead down through the mountains to the Black River Flats.

"Covelle tried to figure out a way to herd sheep into here," said Mac. "But there's only that one trail, and it's damned narrow. You can travel it on a horse, but it would take a month to bring a dozen sheep up this far—if yuh ever got any at all."

"But it's a cinch to cross the divide into Wild Horse Valley from here, eh?" remarked Rusty.

"Well, it's pretty easy," admitted Mac, "but sheep go slow. You've got to take 'em easy. By leavin' here early in the mornin', yuh can take a herd into the valley by dark."

"If nothin' happens," amended Rusty.

"That's right," agreed Mac.

"How long would it take to ride a horse from Black River City to this place, over that trail?"

"I've made it in eight hours. Slim and me was almost up to the divide the other day, kinda scoutin' around. Didn't see a soul up there. Covelle says that the land of the TL reaches right to the top of the divide. He says there's a thousand acres—and that'll hold a lot of sheep—for a while. Says the feed is great, too."

Mac led the way and they walked about a mile along the side of the mountain to a spot where Mac could point out the pass in the hills, where they would take the sheep. Rusty smiled to himself. It was all very simple now. At the first opportunity he would go over to the TL Ranch, tell Swan River Grush all about the scheme—and let the old hill-billy cowboy muster forces enough to smash the advance of Covelle and his sheep. Rusty knew the pass. In a few hours the cattlemen could throw a barb-wire fence across it—and with plenty of rifles behind that fence, the sheep could never get further than the line of the TL.

They sat there on the hillside for an hour, talking about Covelle's plans to sheep out Wild Horse Valley, before they wandered back to the camp.

"It's about time to put on the feed-bag," remarked Mac. He opened the door and walked into the shack, where Slim and Jules were arguing.

At what he saw there, Rusty jerked back quickly.

Roped to a chair sat Swan River Grush, the old hill-billy rawhider whom Rusty had left in charge of the TL Rauch. Swan River was tall and as gaunt as a greyhound, with long, stringy mustaches, well stained with tobacco. At sight of Rusty his jaw sagged for a moment, but his teeth snapped together and he glared with malevolent hate at his pardner, whom he believed a traitor to the cattlemen. Rusty tried to flash him a signal, but was not sure the old cowboy got it.

"Mac," said Slim, "we found this old gallinipper wanderin' around here, pokin' into things; so we stuck him up, took his guns and tied him up. He done a fine job of cussin' and then shut up. Me and Jules figured he's from over the hill."

"Wild Horse Valley cowpuncher, eh?" grinned Mac. "How's all the little cows over in yore country, Old-timer?"

SWAN RIVER glared at Mac, refusing to answer. Then he shot a quick glance at Rusty, who seemed to be enjoying the situation.

"Well, why don'tcha talk?" asked Slim.

"I'm damn perticular who I talk to," replied Swan River. "And I don't mind tellin' yuh that you've got the gall of a sidewinder, feller. Puttin' a gun-muzzle on me and ropin' me up thisaway. What fer kind of a shebang you runnin' here, anyway? Can't a feller drift 'cross this here country, without bein' captured? Who the heck do yuh reckon you are?"

"Who do you reckon *you* are?" countered Mac coldly.

"Th' name's Jones," replied Swan River calmly. "Father's name was Jones, and I've got a brother named Jones. Outside of that, what's it to yuh?"

Swan River spat viciously and glared at Mac, who laughed shortly.

"What was yore name before yuh left Wild Horse Valley?" Mac asked.

"Wild Horse Valley?"

"Don't try to be funny. You never came from Black River Flats; so yuh had to come over the hill. And if yo're interested in knowin' somethin' of the future, you ain't goin' nowhere until we get ready to let yuh go. Slim, you and Jules put him in the far end of the other shack, and lock him up. See that he's well tied."

Rusty stood aside as they shoved Swan River out of the place. He could hear the old-timer cursing them roundly, as the two men took him down to the other shack.

"That old coot is a spy," declared Mac, as he stuffed wood into the sheet-iron stove. "Lucky the boys nailed him. We've been expectin' 'em all the time; but he's the first one we've grabbed. I shore hope he came alone."

Jules and Slim reentered the shack. "Whooee-ee, how that old feller can cuss!" exclaimed Slim. "I shore learned me a lot of new words. If yo're fond of good cussin'—that feller's an education. I told Jules to put his horse in the stable."

"What brand is on that horse?" asked Mac.

"Circle C on the right shoulder."

Rusty could have told him that, without looking. Swan River's favorite mount was a tall, raw-boned sorrel, mean as dirt and about as reliable as a rattlesnake.

"I'll betcha his name ain't Jones," said Slim. "He gave it up too quick."

"What'll yuh do about him?" asked Rusty.

"Keep him here, until he can't do us any harm. That's orders from Covelle. I wish t' hell he'd get busy and bring in the sheep. We'll have to unload two, three trainloads, before we start a drive—and every extra minute we're here is givin' Wild Horse

Valley a chance to get wise to the scheme. What do you think, Kid?"

"Well, I'll tell yuh what I think," replied Rusty soberly. "Unless I miss my guess there's goin' to be a hell of a lot of shepherds buried up there on the rim. Mebbe a few punchers will bite the dust, too, of course, but I'll make yuh a little bet that we never put any sheep over that rim."

Mac shrugged his shoulders. "That's up to Covelle, Kid."

"I'll make yuh another bet, Mac—that Covelle won't ever get in range of any shootin'."

"Well, I wouldn't take that bet," laughed Mac. "As long as he's willin' to pay a hundred a month he can get plenty men to do the shootin'."

TIME DRAGGED heavily for Rusty that day. He wanted a chance to exchange a word with Swan River Grush, but one of the boys was always with him. Furthermore, Rusty was sure that something had happened to Mary Brant; and that the dance-hall girl, who said she was Mazie Brown, had been substituted for Mary in order to make it appear that Mary had left Black River City.

Rusty could not make up his mind what to do—whether he should take Swan River's horse, ride up over the rim and warn Wild Horse Valley, or find the trail to Black River City and try to discover what had happened to Mary Brant. If he could help Swan River to escape, the old hill-billy cowboy could get back to the valley and spread the alarm, while Rusty could take the horse and search for Mary.

It was about ten o'clock that night when the first trainload of sheep came clanking over the grades and halted at the siding. Rusty and the four men were over there quickly. Rusty kept away from the swinging lanterns, until he found that the crew consisted of half a dozen sheepherders who had never known him.

The sheep would not be unloaded in the dark. Covelle had sent no instructions to Mac. One of the men said that another train would arrive next day, as soon as word was sent that the siding was clear. After a brief parley at the train, they went over to the bunk-house. The men had not stopped for any supper, and Mac grumbled over having to cook them a meal.

"I'll help yuh," offered Rusty. "I'm a pretty fair cook."

"Kid, you've got a job. Stoke up that stove, will yuh? We'll feed 'em on bacon and eggs, 'cause it's the quickest thing we can cook."

Rusty had made up his mind now. While the men were eating he would take Swan River's horse and head for Wild Horse Valley. He would go to Tonto City and spread the alarm, giving himself up, if necessary. Within twenty-four hours Covelle would be moving his sheep, and any delay now would be disastrous.

The small room was full of smoke from frying bacon. Rusty manipulated a full pan of bacon while Mac was busy with a pan of frying potatoes.

The door opened behind them. Rusty, intent on his job, paid no attention, until he heard Mac say:

"Hello, Mr. Covelle!"

Rusty whirled, smoking pan in hand. Just inside the doorway stood Nort Covelle and Butch, peering through the smoke at him.

Rusty acted in a flash. With a sweep of his arm he flung the smoking-hot pan straight at the one lamp on the table, and at the same instant he dived straight ahead.

His hope was to take them by surprise and crash his way past them in the darkness. But his foot slipped on the hot grease, and he was flung sideways, striking his head against the table as he fell. One of his feet crashed against Butch's right shinbone, and the big man came down on top of Rusty, cursing painfully.

"I've got him," groaned Butch. "Get a light, can'tcha?"

Someone lighted a lantern. Rusty had been knocked cold, but was rapidly recovering. Covelle kicked him sharply in the ribs, but the young cowboy was too dazed at the moment to feel the kick.

"Gimme a rope," panted Butch. "I want to fix this whippoor-will so he can't do any more funny things."

"Here's some rawhide thongs," said Mac. "They'll sure hold him. But what—"

IN A few moments Rusty was tied hand and foot. Butch lifted him up and banged him against the wall. Mac was explaining to Covelle how Rusty happened to be there, and Covelle was telling how badly they had wanted Rusty.

James Small came through the door then, peered closely at Rusty.

"What luck!" he exclaimed. "Nort, do you have any idea who our other prisoner is—the one the boys caught?" And when Covelle shook his head, he announced, "Well, it is Swan River Grush, partner of this unlucky young man."

"The devil it is!" Covelle exclaimed gleefully. "Well, that *is* luck, Jim."

"I tell yuh, I suspected somethin' like that," declared Mac.

"Aw, don't lie about it, Mac," said Rusty painfully.

"Able to argue already, eh?" laughed Covelle. "I guess you *are* tough."

"He won't be so tough when I get through with him," gritted Butch. "I'll pay him back for droppin' that chair on my head."

"I notice I marked yuh with that lantern, Covelle," said Rusty.

"Get all the satisfaction you can out of it, Lee," replied Covelle. "You've come to the end of the blind cañon—and there's no way out."

"Then why go to all the trouble of makin' me a prisoner?" asked Rusty.

Covelle laughed. "The estate of the late King Brant is offering a ten thousand dollar reward for the murderer of King Brant. At that price we don't mind turning you over to the law. You're worth a lot more alive than dead, Mr. High-Heel Kid."

"Yeah," added Butch, "and they've promised to let me have yuh for about five minutes, before they turn yuh over to the law."

"With my hands tied, I suppose," jeered Rusty. "That's about yore style, Butch. But don't look forward to it, 'cause mebbe you'll be dead long before that."

"What do you mean?" growled Butch quickly.

"Try goin' over that rim up there," said Rusty. "What do you think I stayed here for?"

Covelle whirled on Mac. "What has he done since he got here?"

"Why—nothin' that I know anything about," faltered Mac.

"You've watched him—been with him all the time?"

"No, I—damn it, Covelle—he said you sent him."

Nort Covelle scowled thoughtfully, his lips compressed.

"Wh-what could he have done?" asked Small nervously.

"Nothing!" snapped Covelle. "He's bluffing. Butch, you and Mac take him down with the others. Let Slim go on guard, until we figure things out."

Butch and Slim picked Rusty up bodily and carried him down to the room where they had put Swan River Grush. They slammed Rusty down on the floor against the wall.

Rusty paid no attention to their treaty merit of him. He was staring at Mary Brant.

Mary was seated on a rough bench, her hands and feet tied with ropes. She was pale and disheveled, but defiant. Slim sat beside the door, a rifle beside him. Old Swan River Grush sat against the wall, grim-faced.

THE ROOM was rough, unfinished, with wide cracks in both sides and roof. Butch leered at Mary, as he and Mac backed away, but she did not look at him once.

"Keep yore eyes open, Slim," ordered Butch. "This is prob'ly the last of the collection."

They went out and closed the door.

"I been wonderin' if you was as crooked as Wild Horse Valley folks think yuh are, Rusty," spoke up Swan River. "It kinda looks to me like you wasn't liked around this gang. What'd yuh try to do—doublecross them, too?"

"Thanks," replied Rusty dryly. "I thought that at least *you* might figure I was innocent."

"You ain't given me much edge for such thinkin', Rusty."

"We'll pass that part of the pot, Swan River. Mary, are yuh all right?"

Mary nodded grimly, tried to smile, but it was a failure.

"So that's the girl that telegraphed yuh, eh?" remarked Swan River. "Well, I don't blame yuh much. If I was thirty, forty years younger, I'd sell out for one like her."

Rusty ignored the garrulous old hill-billy.

"Mary, they sent another girl on the train in your place," he said. "I talked with her."

Mary nodded quickly. "They told me about it this morning, Johnny."

"What are they aimin' to do with you?"

"I don't know. They were afraid I might stop them from shipping sheep up here. Mr. Conroy, that funny fat man from Tonto City, wanted to buy that TL Ranch. Nort Covelle realized that something might happen to prevent them from using it for sheep; so they—well, it seems that they will go to any length to accomplish their purpose."

"Was Henry Harrison Conroy over to see yuh?" asked Swan River.

"Yes," replied Mary.

"I met him in Black River City and had a talk with him," said Rusty.

"Didn't he arrest yuh?" asked Swan River quickly.

"I had a six-shooter, and all he had was a cane," replied Rusty.

Swan River laughed huskily. A cool breeze was blowing through the cracks of the building. Rusty spoke to Slim.

"How about some blankets, Slim? It's shore goin' to be chilly in here tonight."

"I was just thinkin' the same thing," replied Slim. "Soon's some of the boys show up, I'll have 'em bring some."

"Kinda feels like rain," remarked Swan River. "All signs pointed to it this mornin'. Course, I ain't been lookin' at signs since I came here. I'd shore like to see a heavy rain now."

"Butch said it looked like rain," offered Mary.

"Yuh better not pray for it," grinned Slim. "This here shack would leak like a sieve. Ain't none of 'em got very tight roofs."

The lamp guttered in the breeze through the cracks, and Slim moved the rough table nearer the partition wall. Jules looked in on them, and Slim ordered him to bring some blankets.

"Yuh might bring a bucket of water and a cup, too, Jules."

"At least, our guard is human," said Mary.

"I ain't bein' paid to make women suffer," replied Slim.

"I'll chalk that up in yore favor, Slim," said Rusty.

Slim laughed shortly. "I don't reckon that'll help me much," he said.

"Still," remarked Rusty, "you'll have that much satisfaction, when they tighten the loop under yore left ear."

Slim scratched his lean neck, swallowed heavily, and began rolling a cigarette.

CHAPTER XII

OSCAR COMMANDS A TRAIN

THINGS HAD QUIETED down in Wild Horse Valley. Following the discovery that Rusty Lee had sold out to the sheep interests, there had been several meetings of the cattle-men. They denounced Rusty Lee, and swore that sheep would never come into the Valley. Not one of them had ever thought of the possibility of a siding having been built in the mountains.

They knew how inaccessible that side of the mountains was

from the Black River Flats; so they began to suspect that the purchase of the TL Ranch by the Brant interests was merely the acquisition of a piece of rangeland. No further effort had been made to occupy the ranch, since the time when Swan River had whipped Quincy Adams.

Several cattlemen came to see Henry on his return from Black River City, and Henry told them that he believed he could buy the TL Ranch from Mary Brant for twenty-five thousand dollars. An hour later five of them came from the Tonto City bank with a certified check for that amount.

"Go back and buy it," said Bill Sneed, owner of the Circle C. "We donated five thousand apiece—and we'll split the rights."

Henry thanked them for their confidence in his ability. Danny Regan, Henry's foreman on the J Bar C, rode in and informed Henry that he had been out to see Swan River Grush, but did not find the old hill-billy at home.

"I found a note on his kitchen table," said Danny. "Read it."

It was crudely penciled on grocer's paper, and read:

I've gone down the hill lookin' for sheep. If you only find my remains my right name is Oswald Bertram.

SUAN RIVER GRUSH

"Well," said Henry, "the old man must have been resigned to his fate, when he asks for *that* name on his tombstone."

"Ay had a yackass named Osvald vonce," remarked Oscar. "Yust de two of us vars prospecting in Vyoming. Osvald ate two hurse blankets and died."

"And only one of you came back alive?" queried Judge Van Treece.

"Yust von, Yudge," replied Oscar sadly.

"Well, I don't know," sighed Judge. "After knowing you for more than a year, I have a suspicion that it was Oswald who came back."

"Yah, su-ure," agreed Oscar blandly.

"I don't like the idea of that TL Ranch not being guarded,"

said Danny. "I feel just like Swan River did about it. Of course, the other cattlemen laughed at his idea, but it sounded possible to me. He said it was possible to bring sheep from Black River Flats, across the mountains and through that pass at the rim."

"Utterly impossible," declared Judge. "The distance is too great, the country too broken. Why, I doubt if there is enough flat land in forty miles of broken hills to hold a dozen head of sheep. I am merely quoting the opinions of a dozen cattlemen, who have investigated."

"I hope you are right, Judge," said Danny.

Henry showed Danny the check for twenty-five thousand dollars, and told him what it was to be used for.

"When are you goin' over there?" asked Danny.

"Tomorrow, I believe."

"Are you goin' along, Oscar?" asked Danny, grinning.

"Yah, su-ure."

"Opinions differ," said Henry quickly. "You are staying here with Judge. I refuse to jeopardize my life, limb and liberty by taking you along again."

"Va'al, you need body-guard, Hanry."

"Not the kind you have to offer, my boy. No, I can do very well by myself, thank you. My mission is a peaceful one."

"Damme, I wouldn't take him to a dog-fight," declared Judge. "For no apparent reason at all, he would challenge the whole Army. Like Ajax, he would defy the lightning."

"Yes," sighed Henry, "and very likely win the argument, Judge."

At that moment Al Sneed, a young cowboy who worked at the livery stable, came into the office, stopping just inside the doorway.

"I was over at the Tonto Saloon a while ago," said the young man, "and there was a whisky drummer, who just came in a while ago from Scorpion Bend. He said that when his train came through Black River City, they was gettin' ready to load sheep on a train. I dunno if it means anything, but—"

"Thank you very much, my boy," said Henry. "Your information is interesting, even if they are merely taking their sheep for a ride."

The youth grinned and went back toward the stable.

"Well, what do you think of that information?" queried Danny.

"Of no value whatever," replied Judge. "It merely means that Brant's outfit is loading sheep to send to an Eastern market."

"I hope you're right, Judge."

Henry squinted thoughtfully for several moments.

"There is a passenger train through here about four o'clock in the morning," he said finally. "It will stop on a flag, and will discharge passengers at Black River City. I believe I shall take that train."

"Same ha'are," said Oscar.

"You will *not* take that train," declared Henry. "I do not need you, Oscar. I hope you understand my orders."

"Ve are yust alike, Hanry," said Oscar.

"Just alike? In what way?"

"Hord-headed."

Henry got to his feet and walked to the doorway, his eyes filled with tears.

"There are tut-times," he choked, "when my blood-pressure goes up so high that I see red. I believe I shall go over to the Tonto and converse with the whisky drummer. Oscar, you stay here and see that no criminals occupy our nice, clean cells while I am away."

"Yah, su-ure; Ay vill take snuze."

"That's about all you are good for—taking a snooze," said Judge.

"Yudge, did you ever hear me sink?"

"God forbid!" exclaimed Judge.

"Ay can yodle in Svedish."

"He is breaking my heart!" gasped Henry. "Let us away."

AT FOUR o'clock next morning a red light blinked at the engineer of an incoming passenger train, and he drew the long train to a stop at Scorpion Bend. Henry Harrison Conroy climbed aboard the chair-car. Down near the rear of the train a porter opened a vestibule for a look at a possible passenger, and Oscar Johnson shoved past him into the train.

"You-all got rese'vation?" asked the sleepy porter.

"Hah?" grunted Oscar, as the train eased ahead. "Who de ha'al do you think Ay am—an Inchun?"

The porter grumbled and shuffled away. This man was too big and powerful for him to start an argument. Anyway, that was up to the conductor. Oscar yawned widely, shoved open the door and wended his way clumsily toward the front of the train.

A few miles from Scorpion Bend it began raining. Oscar reached a nearly empty day-coach, where he eased into a seat, pulled his hat over his face and proceeded to go to sleep.

He was only one car removed from the one in which Henry Harrison Conroy sat, dozing slightly, as the rain slashed against the car window. The conductor, half-asleep, took Henry's ticket.

"Only one passenger at Scorpion Bend?" he asked.

"Just one," smiled Henry. "In fact, I believe I was the only person awake in the town at that time."

The train roared on through the mountains, while Henry dozed fitfully. Daylight came, but the rain had not ceased. The train was running slowly now. Henry peered out at the dripping trees, the overcast sky. Finally the train came to a full stop.

With his nose against the pane Henry found himself staring at a string of sheep-cars on a sidetrack, where a crew of men were unloading. Henry gasped, got to his feet and stumbled down the aisle. The vestibule door was open, and the conductor was standing on the steps, trying to shield himself from the rain and look the length of the train. Henry shoved past him and dropped to the muddy ground.

"What place is this?" he asked.

"Apache Siding," replied the conductor. "Must be sheep on the track."

"They seem to be well scattered," said Henry, and started down the track, ignoring the downpour.

The conductor called to him, but Henry paid no heed. A few moments later the train started on. Two men were coming up along the stock cars, shielding themselves from the rain, and Henry went straight to them.

"I beg your pardon," said Henry loudly, "but I should like to—"

Then words failed Henry Harrison Conroy. The two men were Nort Covelle and Butch—and both of them were covering him with their guns.

"I—I seem to have made a mistake," said Henry.

"You have," agreed Covelle. "A decided mistake, Mr. Conroy."

Henry motioned weakly with his right hand.

"I happened to see the sheep—you know."

"And got nosey, eh?" grinned Butch. "What'll we do with him, Covelle—add him to the collection?"

"Right now."

Covelle stepped in behind Henry and quickly felt him over for a possible weapon.

Then he punched Henry in the back with the muzzle of his gun.

"Straight ahead, clown."

"Well," observed Henry, "it is not exactly a nice day for it."

"Nice day for what?" asked Covelle.

"Clowning. Too wet for motley trappings, I am afraid. However, needs must when the devil drives."

OSCAR JOHNSON saw the sheep, too. He awoke as the train pulled out of Apache Siding, blinked in amazement at the sheep, scattered all over the fir-clad side hills, the rapidly emptying cars on the siding.

"Yumpin' Yudas!" he exclaimed aloud and got to his feet.

As swiftly as possible he surged into the next car, looking wildly for Henry. The long train was rolling heavily down the grades now, as Oscar stopped at the far end of the car. Then he banged his way into the next car, but did not find Henry Harrison Conroy.

Back he went, like a halfback carrying the ball, and crashed into the conductor in the vestibule. The conductor was a slight, meek-looking man. His cap went flying as the huge Swede grasped him by both shoulders and his glasses were knocked out on the end of his nose.

"Where in de ha'al did Hanry go?" Oscar yelled in his face. "Did he get off back dere?"

The conductor gasped.

"The—the fat man?" he asked.

"Yah, sure!"

"A fat man got off there."

"Why didn't you say so? Yumpin' Yudas!" Oscar looked wildly around. "How in de ha'al do you stop dis ha're t'ing?"

"I can't stop the train for you."

"Somet'ing you yerk," said Oscar.

"You can't pull that emergency on my train!"

"De ha'al Ay can't! Take look and you see me yerk!"

The conductor tried to prevent it. The next moment they were both driven against the wall, as though held by a giant hand, as the brakes bit into the steel rails.

"Open de door!" yelled Oscar. "Quick before Ay throw you right through de glass!"

The conductor, more than willing to get rid of this wild man, opened the vestibule door. Oscar dropped off against a rocky wall on the upper side of the grade. He was nearly back to the rear of the train, before it started again. With the rain beating down in his face, he started trudging back over the ties.

CHAPTER XIII

WORK FOR OSCAR

"WE HAVE HERE a surprisingly fine group of representative people, Mr, Conroy," stated Nort Covelle to Henry. The sheriff stood in the middle of the dripping room, while his hands and feet were being securely tied with wet ropes.

"If you haven't met them," Covelle went on smilingly, "I suppose introductions are in order. This is a clever young lady by the name of Mary Brant. The tall man with the decorated upper lip is Mr. Grush—known as Swan River. This handsome and talented young man is Johnny Lee, known as Rusty—and wanted for murder. Now that you have met everyone of any importance, suppose you take a seat against the partition wall."

"Thank you very kindly, Mr. Covelle," replied Henry. "You are very considerate. I do not suppose there is any use of my asking for an explanation."

"None at all, Mr. Conroy. Your presence here at this time forces me to extremes. Sorry, but there is no alternative. For the next few days, at least, I hope you can enjoy the situation. After that—who cares?"

"Quite right," replied Henry. "In fact, it is rather ripping to be in such company."

"Get all the fun out of it that you can, Conroy," Covelle answered, no longer smiling. "The finish might not make you laugh."

Covelle walked out and slammed the door. Slim grinned and tilted his chair against the wall.

"Go ahead and talk it over, folks," said Slim. "Don't mind me."

Henry wiggled his nose, his eyes traveling from Mary to Rusty and over to Swan River.

"Well, I will be damned!" he said quietly. "How long have you folks been in here?"

"They got me yesterday mornin'," said Swan River. "I'm Swan River the First."

"They brought Mary from Black River Flats," explained Rusty. "I was trapped in the cook-shack, last night. Where in the world did you come from, Conroy?"

"I was on my way to Black River City to see Miss Brant, when I saw all the sheep. My train had stopped; so I got off to investigate."

"And ran yore big nose slap into trouble," said Swan River.

"Thank you," sighed Henry. "And me, being behind that nose, so to speak, came right along with the proboscis. Tell me something about the sheep situation."

Rusty explained Covelle's scheme to put the sheep into Wild Horse Valley.

"Good Lord!" blurted Henry. "We must get word over there—at once!"

"Have yuh got any mind-readers over there?" asked Slim.

"I guess I was a little hasty," admitted Henry. "We must get word over there as soon as possible."

"Too late now," grinned Slim. "We start the drive in the mornin', if the rain lets up. Pretty heavy travelin' for sharp hoofs now—if that's any satisfaction."

"It ain't goin' to let up," declared Swan River. "This yere storm has been a-buildin' up quite a while."

"This whole thing is a criminal act," declared Henry. "Even if he does keep us prisoners until he has put sheep into Wild Horse Valley, doesn't he realize that as soon as we are free we can prosecute him?"

"Yeah, I reckon he does," replied Slim. "He's got that lawyer with him to do the advisin'."

"Then why does he do these things?" asked Henry.

"Well, jist between me and you—I don't reckon he's goin' to turn any of yuh loose. Nobody knows yo're here."

"Covelle isn't—quite human," said Mary painfully. "I never realized the sort of a person he could be. The man is mad."

"Man!" snorted Swan River. "He's a hy-dro-foby skunk."

WITH SLIM listening to their conversation there was no chance for them to even think of planning anything. But Rusty, remembering his success with Len, decided to go to work on this man.

"Do yuh know where Len went, Slim?" Rusty asked him.

"I jist wondered, Kid."

"He went to Mexico. I explained things to him; so he cut me loose and headed south."

"No guts, eh?" grunted Slim inelegantly.

"Plenty," corrected Rusty. "But Len was bright enough to realize that he only had *one neck*."

"Meanin' what?" asked Slim curiously.

"Meanin' that every man close to Covelle will stretch rope."

"Yea-a-ah?"

"It's true enough, Slim. They've prob'ly caught Dud Miles, the sheriff, by this time. Dud will talk his head off when they catch him. He'll put the deadwood on Covelle and all you fellers, jist to save his own neck. I don't know how much you had to do with the murder of Quincy Adams, who was killed somewhere between town and the ranch, but—"

"Quincy Adams? My gosh, I ain't never heard of him! You can't hang no murder onto me."

"Didn't you murder Mike Finley?"

"Hell, I didn't even know him!"

"Yuh don't have to *know* a man—to kill him, Slim."

Rusty was merely talking for effect, hoping against hope that Slim might, like Len, lose his nerve. But Slim apparently did not have Len's imagination.

"I'll take a chance and play the hand out with Covelle, Kid," he declared.

"All right," replied Rusty calmly. "Don't say I didn't give yuh a chance."

"Thank yuh."

NORT COVELLE was not at all satisfied with the way things were going. He sat on the partly dry side of the cook-shack and cursed the weather, cursed his own oversight in not furnishing tar-paper roofing for the shacks, and then cursed the four prisoners. James Small echoed all of Covelle's complaints, and then added some more of his own. Small was a city man, and this rough life did not appeal to him at all, especially the dangerous end of it.

"There should be another trainload in after dark," remarked Small. "But I don't see the good of them being here. Why, the sheep are knee-deep in mud now."

"Mud or no mud—we drive in the morning," declared Covelle. "There is only one deep swale to cross. One of the boys looked at it today, and it isn't too bad. Doesn't drain a lot of country. But I'll put sheep over that rim tomorrow, even if I have to build bridges."

Night came, but the rain did not cease. The clouds hung low over the tops of the mountains, while fog drifted up from the lower hills. Slim, Jules and Joe fed the prisoners, and brought them dry blankets. There was no way of heating the shack, and none of them had any heavy clothing.

Covelle and Small were toasting their shins at the kitchen stove at about nine o'clock, when Jules came surging into the cook-shack.

"There's hell to pay!" snorted Jules, a huge, bewhiskered sheepherder. "That trainload of sheep is out there and they can't get onto the sidin'."

"Why not?" asked Covelle sharply.

"Damn good reason!" panted Jules. "Somebody's pried a rail

loose jist beyond the switch, and let it slide clown the mountain. They used that pinch-bar we had for movin' a car and—"

"Somebody?" exploded Covelle. "Why, damn it, no one man—"

"Come and look," invited Jules. "One whole rail gone."

Covelle and Small grabbed their hats and went out into the storm, following Jules with the lantern. The rail had been pried up, slid over the sharp edge of the embankment, and they could see one end of it sticking up in the air, thirty feet down the mountain.

Covelle's language would have ignited asbestos. There was no chance to repair the damage until another rail could be secured and spiked into place. The train crew shivered in the rain around the switch.

"Our only move is to either back to Black River City, or pull on to Scorpion Bend," the conductor told Covelle. "We can wire a crew to make the repairs, but it'll take time. It would require a wrecking crane to recover that rail."

"The line will be open for five hours, between here and Black River City," added the engineer. "You better make up your mind."

"Take 'em back to Black River City," said Covelle, "and have a repair crew in here as damn quick as you can."

When the crew went back to the train, Covelle ordered Jules to have all the men report to him at the cook-shack at once.

"There are traitors in our own gang," he declared, "and I am going to smoke them out. No one man ever did that job alone."

Including Covelle and Small, the gang amounted to ten men. Only nine of them came to the cook-shack. Pete Lawson was missing.

Lining the men up along the wall of the shack, Covelle told them what had been done. They looked grimly at him, apparently knowing nothing about it until told.

He questioned them, but there was no sign of guilt.

"Where's Pete Lawson, the big feller?" asked Joe.

No one knew.

"Find Pete," ordered Covelle. "Bring him here to me."

"Could he have done it alone?" queried Small, after the men had gone.

"He's as big and as strong as a horse," replied Covelle coldly.

THEY FOUND Pete Lawson and brought him to the cookshack. They found him in the muck at the bottom of a fill, his right arm broken, his nose flattened, and suffering from concussion. Pete was a huge man, with the physique of a heavyweight wrestler.

For the first time, as he looked at the unconscious man, there was a flicker of fear in Covelle's eyes.

"Do you think one man did that?" asked Small huskily.

"One man?" queried Covelle under his breath. "By the Lord, I wonder. Wait."

Covelle walked swiftly down to the shack where the prisoners were held, flung the door open and walked in. He leaned back against the door and looked at Henry Harrison Conroy. He was breathing heavily.

"Well, Conroy, we just killed your big Swede," he said.

Henry blinked at him, a puzzled frown on his brow.

"You killed my big Swede? You must be mistaken, Mr. Covelle."

"He came here with you."

"I am sorry to contradict you—but he did not, sir."

"You are sure of that, Conroy?"

"Just as sure as I am sitting here, being uncomfortable."

Covelle drew a deep breath, started to say something, then changed his mind. He left the shack, going back to where James Small shivered beside the stove.

"For a moment I thought I had the answer," he told Small. "There is only one man I know who would be capable of manhandling Lawson, and that man is the Swede who works for Conroy. After questioning Conroy, I'm sure the Swede is not here. But who did it?"

"Jules is in there with Lawson," said Small, indicating the partition. "Lawson might wake up and be able to tell us."

Covelle sat down beside the stove, his brow furrowed, as he tried to puzzle out who had done these things. Then he heard queer sounds outside the shack. He went quickly to the door, flinging it wide. Wet, crowding sheep blinked at the lamplight. They seemed everywhere. Joe came kicking his way through them.

"Somebody tore down a lot of fence," he told Covelle, "and the damn sheep are huntin' shelter. They're all over everything. Why, they're even driftin' down the tracks and over the grades. They was huddled up here against the fence—that's why they came this way, I reckon."

"*Somebody* cut the fence!" rasped Covelle. "Who? Why didn't some of you fellows see them cut the fence? Good Lord, do I have to go on guard? Get the men together and shove 'em back where they belong."

"Try it," retorted Joe.

The next moment he was flat on his back from a right-hand punch on the jaw.

"Tell me to try it, will you?" rasped Covelle. "Get up, before I kick your ribs loose. When I give an order—you obey it. Now get started."

Joe limped away, stumbling over sheep in the darkness. Covelle spat viciously and went back to the stove.

"I'd give a thousand dollars for daylight," he declared.

"You might as well offer a million," groaned Small. He got to his feet and began pacing up and down the small shack.

"Sit down, you damn bundle of nerves, before I knock you down," growled Covelle.

But the lawyer paid no heed to the threat.

"Damn the sheep," muttered Small. "As far as being balked with the sheep—that isn't so serious. Oh, I want money as badly as you do, Nort. Don't misunderstand me. But suppose we get caught with those four prisoners. There are things that we can't explain. Especially—that girl. And we've got a sheriff, too. We are not in the clear, as far as he is concerned. The conductor of that train *saw him get off here.* You know that as well as I do. And now, Nort, there is somebody out there in the dark, working against us. You can't laugh at that."

"Probably some crazy sheepherder, who—"

Crash! A ten-pound rock smashed through the one window of the shack, tearing away the gunny-sack covering, struck the side of the sheet-iron stove, knocking it aside. The whole section of stovepipe came clattering down.

Covelle dived out of his chair and into a corner, gun in hand. The small room was full of smoke. From outside came a chuckling laugh, as Covelle moved along the wall and fired his gun wildly into the darkness. Men came running around from the bunk-house and into the smoke-filled room.

One of them, taking a chance, managed to cover the broken window, while others replaced the stove and pipe.

"All under cover, eh?" snarled Covelle. "Not a damn one of you on guard duty!"

"Look what happened to Lawson," said one of the men in answer.

"Yellow, eh?" sneered Covelle. "Get out there and kill that fellow, before he chases you all into the brush, you saffron pups. Take rifles and guard this place. Shoot everything that moves. Damn it, some of you should get him. Or are you too yellow to shoot at a man?"

CHAPTER XIV

RUSTY WAITS

THE MEN FILED out and went back to the bunk-house, but none of them made any move to take a rifle and go outside. The rain beat dismally on the roof, dripping through on the rough floor, making it impossible for the men to keep their blankets dry.

"To hell with Covelle," whispered a sheepherder. "Look at Lawson. Fence tore down. And then he heaves a rock as big as my head through the window and busts up the stove."

"Yeah," added another, "and he unspiked a iron rail and shoved it down the hill; a rail that a dozen of us couldn't handle. If it's one man—he ain't human. Hundred a month! I wish I was back in Yuma."

Down in the prisoner's end of the shacks there was speculation regarding the pistol shot. Slim walked nervously across the room.

"Covelle probably tried to enforce an order," said Rusty. "They say he's noted for that. I was told that he'd shoot a man for disobeyin' an order."

"He would," agreed Slim.

"Pleasant character," mused Henry Harrison Conroy. "Even the despised Simon Legree rarely resorted to worse than a lash."

"Who was he?" asked Slim.

"Have you ever seen *Uncle Tom's Cabin?*" asked Henry.

"I ain't been around here much," replied Slim defensively.

"I guess you haven't," agreed Henry soberly.

Rusty chuckled quietly. Mary was too miserable even to smile. The strain was telling on her nerves.

Jules came in. He looked wet and uncomfortable.

"Everything all right here, Slim?" he asked, looking around the shack at the four bound prisoners.

"Shore. Was Covelle wonderin'?"

"Yeah, I guess he was. Him and Small are keepin' warm against the kitchen stove. Didja know what happened?"

"No, I ain't heard anything. What was the shootin' about?"

"You heard about the railroad track, didn't yuh?"

"Not a word. What's wrong?"

Jules explained about the ruined track which had forced the sheep train back to Black River City, and about finding Pete Lawson, all broken up. He told about the fence being cut, allowing the sheep to scatter all over, looking for shelter.

"And jist a while ago somebody threw a big rock through the winder of the cook-shack, knocked the stove across the room and down came the pipe. Covelle shot through the winder, but the feller jist laughed at him."

"Lovely dove!" snorted Rusty "We must have a friend in camp."

"I see now!" exclaimed Henry. "That is why Covelle came and told me they had killed Oscar Johnson. He thinks it is Oscar."

"Well, there ain't been nobody killed," stated Jules.

"But it can't be Oscar," said Henry. "I left him in Scorpion Bend; and anyway, he wouldn't know about this place."

"This is shore a hell of a situation!" snorted Slim. "Jules, you watch this gang, while I have a talk with Covelle."

Jules nodded and sat down beside the door. Slim hurried out.

"Is Covelle losin' his nerve?" asked Rusty.

"Covelle ain't got no nerves," declared Jules.

"It's a lucky thing for him. Would yuh mind givin' me a drink of water, Jules?"

Growling a little, the big sheepherder got up, dipped up a cupful from the bucket and held it out to Rusty.

"I can't take it, Jules," said Rusty. "My hands are tied."

"That's right."

Jules came in close, leaned over and held the cup to Rusty's lips.

IT WAS then that Rusty acted. His feet were drawn up, his shoulders braced against the wall, and as the guard leaned over him two bound feet shot straight out, catching Jules' legs just at the ankles, knocking them out from under him.

The big sheepherder yelped with surprise, plunged head first against the wall almost directly over Rusty. But Rusty rolled swiftly aside and came up on his knees, as Jules crashed to the floor. His two hands were free. He jerked Jules' six-shooter from his holster. The big fellow sagged back from the wall. Rusty hit him a slashing blow on the head with the barrel of the heavy gun.

"Simple-minded fools!" panted Rusty, as he dug into Jules' pocket, secured a knife and cut his ankles apart. "They tied my wrists with rawhide, and I've been soakin' 'em for two hours. They didn't even *know* that wet rawhide stretches!"

Rusty discovered that his legs had been bound so tightly that he was hardly able to walk. As he staggered a little, Slim suddenly threw the door open. He saw Rusty there, on his feet.

Slim was fast with a gun, but Rusty's move was disconcerting. He kicked over the stool on which they had placed the lamp, and dived sideways away from the rest of the prisoners. Slim's bullet smashed into the wall, but did no harm.

Slim yelled loudly for help—but just then Rusty dived through the doorway, straight into the yelling man. Men were running from the upper bunk-house as Rusty got to his feet. Slim was somewhere there in the mud, but Rusty was not interested in him. He crouched in the darkness, backing slowly. Luckily he still retained the gun.

Covelle was running up, demanding to know what had happened. No one seemed to know, except Slim—and Slim's bellows were not in working order, it seemed. Rusty crouched low in some dripping jack-pines, trying to hear what was being said. In the shack now, someone was lighting matches.

When Covelle discovered that Rusty had escaped, his language would have done credit to any muleskinner.

"Get out and find him!" he bellowed. "Scatter out. Some of you are bound to run into him."

"That's right," replied a sheepherder out in the darkness. "And what chance would one of us have? He's got Jules' gun."

"Then guard these shacks, you damn cowards," rasped Covelle. "At least, you'll protect your own lives—I hope. Where's Butch?"

Nobody seemed to know.

"We ain't seen him for a couple hours," said a sheepherder.

"Send him to me as soon as he shows up," ordered Covelle. "Slim, you guard the prisoners, but keep the door locked inside."

"You better stack Jules along with Pete Lawson," somebody said. "He's in here, tryin' to recite his A B C's."

Covelle went back to the warm stove, where Small was still pacing the floor. The lawyer was panicky. He wanted to run away from something, but he didn't know where to run. Covelle sneered at him.

"Take a grip on your nerves," he said. "These things don't amount to anything."

"Don't they? Lawson and Jules are out of the game—and where is Butch?"

Covelle laughed. "We'll clear up everything in the morning. Give us daylight to work in, and everything will be all right."

"It's a mighty long night," sighed the lawyer.

THE RAIN had ceased, and the clouds were breaking, giving an occasional slant of moonlight. Rusty Lee crouched in a shallow cut near the siding switch, trying to puzzle out just what to do next, when a break in the scudding clouds gave him light enough to see a huge figure, about fifty feet away on the railroad track.

Rusty knew that there were guards around the shacks, but he did not think this was a guard. Taking a chance on getting a bullet in reply, he called:

"Is that you, Oscar?"

"Ha'lo, shiphorder!" replied Oscar's unmistakable voice. "Who in de ha'al are you?"

"This is Rusty Lee."

"Yumpin' Yudas! Ay have been looking for you, feller."

"Lookin' for me? What for?"

"Ay vant to knock ha'al out of you, vit de compliments of Vild Hurse Valley."

Bang! A rifle-flash licked out from the shadow of the upper shack, and a bullet screamed off the steel rail.

"Yu-u-dus!" yelped Oscar, and rolled off the track. There was a commotion at the shacks, as the rest of the men came out, seeking information.

Something struck the shack wall, and a man yelped:

"Look out!"

"You bat you!" snorted Oscar. "Ay can t'row rocks awful gude."

"It *is* that damn Swede!" yelled Covelle. "I know his voice!"

In spite of his own predicament, Rusty crouched in the cut and chuckled. The situation was ridiculous. A big Swede out there, unarmed, throwing rocks at riflemen; and none of the men willing to chance an encounter with him.

"Go and get him, one of you fellows!" cried Covelle. "He hasn't any gun."

"Coom on!" yelled Oscar from behind the embankment.

"Where in the hell is Butch?" asked one of the men. But Butch didn't seem to be anywhere around.

Crash! One of Oscar's rocks wrecked a window, and from inside the shack came a howl of agony. It was James Small, the lawyer. Several rifles blasted bullets into the night, but the only result was a mocking laugh from Oscar, and another rock, which landed on the top of the shack.

"Oscar!" called Rusty.

"Hollo, shiphorder," replied Oscar.

"Go to Tonto City," urged Rusty. "Send out the alarm that sheep are comin' over the hill at the TL Ranch."

Oscar merely laughed and heaved another rock. From over at the shacks Covelle was telling his men to spread out and block any attempt of Oscar or Rusty to get away. Three or four men, properly spaced, could prevent either of them from escaping in the moonlight. Rusty could see several men as they left the shadow of the shacks, crouching low, forming a picket line between the shacks and the sheer bluff beyond the unloading spot on the spur track.

Rusty knew he would have to shift his position before daylight. The moonlight was not bright, but bright enough to prevent anyone from moving about undetected. He was looking up the track, past the spot where Oscar had disappeared, when he saw something crossing the track. It looked like a man, crawling on his hands and knees.

Was Oscar Johnson trying to work his way past the guards, he wondered? The figure passed over the track and into the shadows on the other side. It was about a hundred feet from that point to the temporary barb-wire fence, and there was not even a blade of grass for cover.

Suddenly a rifle shot broke the stillness. Another shot crashed out, echoing back from the cañons. Rusty could see the dim figure of a man, running ahead, crouching as he ran. Then a triumphant cry:

"We got him that time!"

A cloud drifted across the moon. From the shack came the banging of a door, the voice of Nort Covelle asking what had happened. A group of dim figures were going toward the shacks, and Rusty knew it was the rifle guards, bringing in their victim.

Covelle was barking orders for two men to stay on guard.

Rusty hunkered back in his place of concealment and swore at poor Oscar for taking such a dangerous chance. He could tell by the sounds that Covelle and his men must be taking the luckless Swede down to the second shack, where the prisoners were confined. He heard them bang the door open, but there was no light in the place.

CHAPTER XV

SALT-RISIN' TALKS

SINCE RUSTY HAD made his escape the rest of the prisoners had had no information as to the situation. They merely sat there in the dark, listening, wondering, and hoping. They heard the shots.

"Judging from what we can hear," remarked Henry Harrison Conroy, "I was just a trifle mistaken about Oscar Johnson not being here. But how and when that Vitrified Viking discovered this situation, I have no ideas. I sincerely hope that either Oscar or Rusty will do something to alleviate our condition."

"I have been praying for an hour," stated Mary simply.

"So have I," remarked Swan River Grush. "I wasn't askin' for much. All I want is one hand loose and a six-shooter—I can handle the rest of the deal."

"Does the—er—rope feel any looser?" queried Henry.

"Not a danged bit!"

"My prayers work the same way," sighed Henry. "But I suppose we both direct our pleas at such a time that any reply at all would be a miracle."

At that moment the rifle shots rang out, and in about a minute they heard the man's triumphant:

"I got him that time!"

"Who?" queried Henry quietly. "Rusty or Oscar?"

Soon they heard the sound of men walking, arguing breathlessly.

The door was flung open and Covelle's voice said:

"Light the lamp, Slim. Well, Conroy we got your damn Swede."

None of the prisoners spoke. Slim lighted the lamp. The chimney had been broken, but it made sufficient illumination to show Covelle, two of his men, and the huddled, muddy figure on the floor.

"My God!" gasped Covelle. "Who shot—why—it's Butch!"

"His clothes—torn off—" muttered Slim foolishly. "Look at his face! Them bullets never hit him in the face. He—he's had a fight."

"Possibly he met Oscar," said Henry, but added, "if it is Oscar."

Covelle, his face white in the flickering, yellow light, glared at Henry, too angry to speak.

"You really should give it up, Covelle," said Henry. "It is a bad job you are doing."

"Give it up? You mean—to not put sheep in your damn valley? Why, you poor fool! Listen to me..." Covelle's voice had husked to a whisper... "I'm taking what sheep we've got over there in the morning. Possession is nine points in the law. I'll take a thousand sheep in there—and wait for the rest. As for you three—you might as well pray—if you believe in prayer. When the sheep go over the hill—you will never be able to testify against me."

He turned then to the men.

"Drag that out and dump it in the cañon—if you're sure he's dead."

"Shall I blow out that lamp?" asked Slim.

"Yes, blow it out. Maybe they can pray better in the dark."

WHILE THE trouble was going on at Apache Siding, Dud Miles, the sheriff of Black River City, and Salt-risin' Reed, the cook from the Brant ranch, rode over the treacherous trail from Black River Flats to Apache Siding. Salt-risin' Reed's hands were roped to his saddle horn, while the sheriff rode behind, knowing that his prisoner had no choice, save to ride straight ahead.

They had been drenched by the downpour, torn by the brush and scraped by the rocky cliffs along the trail.

"I ain't goin' to kill yuh, Salt-risin'," stated the hill-billy sheriff, "but I ain't makin' no promises of that kind for Covelle."

They rode up out of the cañon depths half an hour after Butch had been killed, and drew up at the upper shack. Rusty, crouched in his place of concealment, saw them, but in the moonlight he could not tell who they were until he heard the sheriff's voice, complaining about everybody shoving guns in his face.

The sheriff herded his prisoner into the cook-shack. There Covelle and Small, red-eyed and weary, met him. At once they asked him for an explanation of his appearance and why the cook was a prisoner.

"Herd everybody else outside and I'll tell yuh, Covelle."

When only Covelle and Small were there to hear his story, the sheriff said swiftly:

"They've done found Adams' body, Covelle. The boys didn't bury him deep enough. That damn hotel-keeper identified him as the man who left the hotel with you that night. Judge Myers and the prosecutor started a investigation, and they got this old fool of a Salt-risin' cornered and he talked too much. They know that Mary Brant never took that train out of Black River City that night, 'cause Salt-risin' said you had her at the ranch all that night.

"I had to work along with 'em, tryin' to figure a way out, but they didn't give me no chance. They made me arrest Salt-risin' and put him in jail, while they're tryin' to find out where you are; so I took him out of jail, after dark—and here we are."

"Didn't I tell you?" wailed Small. "I told you—"

Covelle smashed the lawyer full in the face, sent him sprawling beneath the table. He grasped the bound cook, whirled him around, drove a fist into his face, knocking him against the wall. Salt-risin' slid heavily to the floor.

"That's all right," said the sheriff calmly, "but it ain't goin' to figure out what to do about things, Nort."

"Why in hell didn't you stay down there?" roared Covelle. "They couldn't have proved anything. Now you've raised hell—coming up here, and bringing that old fool along with you. You're finished—as sheriff."

"I know it—that's why I pulled out. But what went wrong up here?"

"How do you know anything went wrong?"

"That sheep train went back to Black River City."

In a few words Covelle informed the sheriff of the conditions at Apache Siding, and why the train had gone back with the sheep.

"So Rusty Lee and the big Swede are both loose, eh?" grunted the sheriff. "Why ain't somebody killed 'em by this time? There ain't but three ways out for 'em, Nort. They could foller the railroad, go over the trail we jist came in on, or up over the hill to Wild Horse Valley. You say you've got 'em blocked from Wild Horse? All right. None of 'em know the trail to Black River Flats. Hell, you ain't bad off."

Covelle eyed him angrily. "Is that a fact?" he said. "Butch is dead, Jules and Lawson are busted up, and the sheep are all over hell's-half-acre. We can't ship any more until the railroad is repaired. Rusty Lee is out there somewhere, armed with Jules' gun, and don't forget that big Swede. Not bad off!"

THE SHERIFF shrugged his shoulders and helped himself to a chew of tobacco.

"All right," he said, nodding slowly, "then there's only one move left for me and you, Covelle. Them two horses are pretty fagged, but you've got others."

"What do you mean?" asked Covelle.

"Mexico. We can pull out ahead of daylight, stay in the cañons until dark tomorrow evenin', and then cut across the border."

"And give up everything I've fought and planned for?" Covelle snarled. "Don't be a fool! I'm not whipped. I'll eat supper tomorrow night at the TL ranch; and to hell with the law. They can't prove anything. Salt-rising Reed is the only one who can testify against me—and they'll never have him on any witness stand. You stick with me, Dud, and you'll wear diamonds."

"What about Small?" queried the sheriff, pointing at the lawyer. Small was sitting on the floor, holding a hand over his bruised nose and mouth. "You've got to *save* him, Covelle."

"I wonder if I have?" said Covelle grimly. "Is he worth saving?"

"You'd better," whined the lawyer. "I hid that will—just to be safe."

"You lie!" snapped Covelle. "It's in your brief-case."

"You try to find it in there," retorted Small.

The leather case was on a box in the corner of the cook-shack, but Covelle, looking, found that it did not contain the will of King Brant. He swore and threw the case aside.

"Get up and wash your face, Jim," he said.

Small got to his feet, a hideous grin on his bloody features. "That will," he said, "is hidden at the ranch—and a lot of good it will do us, if we don't dare go back there."

"All right," gritted Covelle, "if you're so damn smart—what's to be done?"

"I believe Miles is right, Nort. Turn the prisoners loose—and head for Mexico."

"Not I," declared Covelle. "I'm putting sheep into Wild Horse

Valley tomorrow. After that I'll be in shape to fight all charges. They can't prove a damn thing. Let's have a drink."

"What about the men?" queried Small painfully. "You've got Mac, Lou, Slim and Jules, who might be loyal; but you've got six sheepherders out there that probably wouldn't be. Oh, they'll fight for you, if it comes to a battle against the cattlemen—but will they fight for you in court? They all know you've got prisoners. They know that one of them is a girl. Personally, I think you were crazy to bring her here."

Covelle yanked the cork from a bottle of whiskey and began pouring it into tin cups. At that point someone knocked gently on the door, and he turned quickly.

"It's Slim," called the man outside.

"All right, Slim," replied Covelle.

"Wasn't there supposed to be three horses in the stable?" Slim asked.

"No—four," replied Covelle.

"Well, they're gone," declared Slim. "I took Miles' two horses out there, and the other four are gone. I thought maybe you had 'em moved."

"All right, Slim," replied Covelle calmly. He handed cups to Small and Dud Miles.

"You didn't have them moved, did you?" asked Small huskily.

"I did not!"

"Some—somebody stole them?"

"He-e-ey!" exploded the sheriff, banging his cup on the table. "If they stole your horses, what's to keep 'em from takin' mine?"

Covelle's face twisted grimly, but he ignored the question.

"That stable," he said slowly, "is back of this building. If they took those horses there's only one way they could go."

"To Wild Horse Valley," finished Small.

"That's right—to Wild Horse Valley."

"Rusty Lee's work," whispered Small. "Why *didn't* you kill him, when you had the chance?"

"To hell with all that stuff!" snapped the sheriff. "Stay here and get salivated, if yuh want to, but I'm headin' south right now. If—"

HE DIDN'T finish. From outside came the reports of a rifle, the echoes rattling back against the wall of the shack. Three times the rifle blared into the night, and in a few moments running steps thudded on the muddy earth in front of the shack. Covelle sprang over and unlocked the door.

It was Slim, panting heavily. "Them other two horses—gone!" he managed to say.

"My horses?" yelped the sheriff.

"The fence was cut—beside the stable," panted Slim. "I went to one of the boys to guard the place, but we got back too late. The—the moon went under a cloud."

"And the horses headed for Wild Horse Valley, eh?" said Covelle.

"Up the hill—yes."

"Who is watching the prisoners?" asked Covelle.

"Lou. He's outside the door—with a shotgun."

"All right. Get out there and try to locate Rusty Lee or the Swede."

Slim nodded. Still panting, he hurried out.

"This is a hell of a note," wailed the sheriff. "Not even a horse left."

"All right," said Covelle grimly. "We're here—and here we stay."

"That," remarked Small, "is little satisfaction to me. I might flag a passenger train at the siding and get out of the country. Yes, I could do that, I suppose."

He stared thoughtfully at the floor.

"But you won't," declared Covelle. "You'll stay here until this deal is completed, and then you'll go back to the ranch and dig up that will. You try to renege—and I'll blow your head off, Small."

"I think we better have another drink," said the sheriff. "That's about all there is left to do—until daylight. But I wouldn't be a bit surprised to see somebody from Black River City drop off the next passenger train through here from there. Salt-risin' told Judge Myers all about this place and about yore scheme to put sheep in Wild Horse Valley."

"How wonderful that would be!" exclaimed Small. "And they would find all of Covelle's prisoners."

Covelle whirled on him like a wolf. "Don't forget that you are in this as much as I am, Small."

"I haven't actually killed anybody yet," reminded Small huskily.

"You haven't got guts enough to pull a trigger, Small. But you know the law well enough to realize that we are equally guilty; so don't crow about your hands being so damn clean."

"We might move the prisoners," suggested the sheriff mildly, as he helped himself to another drink. "It might be the thing to do. What they don't find, yuh know...."

"You've got more brains than I thought you had, Dud," said Covelle. "I believe your idea is all right."

CHAPTER XVI

ONE-MAN ARMY

WHEN RUSTY LEE crawled far up the spur track he had no idea of what he was going to do. In the heavy shadow of the sheer cliffs, he slid across the tracks. There were guards between him and the upper shack, where the cook-house was located, although he could not see any of them.

Still crawling, he reached the corner of the barb-wire fence, he crawled under. There were plenty of sheep scattered around. Rusty was soggy with mud, but he did not mind discomfort.

Slowly he crawled down among the sheep—slowly, so as not to disturb them any more than was absolutely necessary.

He was behind the line of guards, who were watching the other way. Finally he reached the shed-like stable and discovered that someone had already cut the fence at that point. There was no door on the stable, no guard in sight. Speaking softly to the three horses—Swan River's horse was not there—Rusty quietly moved them outside, tied up their ropes and eased them away from the stable. In a few moments they had disappeared.

Rusty was at the corner of the stable when he heard Slim coming with the two horses which the sheriff and the cook had ridden.

Slim left the two saddled horses outside the door and went inside. He came out very suddenly, stepped to the corner, not over twenty feet from Rusty, and discovered the cut fence. Then he whirled and ran back toward the shack.

Rusty got up and went to the corner. He heard sounds in the cook-shack, as Slim informed Covelle about the missing horses. Rusty ran over to the stable doorway, mounted one horse, grasped the reins of the other, and spurred quickly around the corner.

He was only a short distance from the stable when Slim, back again, cut loose at him with the rifle. The first bullet buzzed close to Rusty, but the others went wild as he raced away in the darkness. But Rusty did not go far. He reined up, swung to the left, and rode a short distance up the slope, where he tied the horses in a little fir thicket. It was too late for him now to ride to Tonto City to spread an alarm.

"This looks like a one-man job," he told himself. "I can't expect any help from Oscar Johnson, 'cause it looks like that blamed Swede is against me as much as the sheepmen are."

TIME DRAGGED heavily for the prisoners. Sitting there in total darkness, listening for every sound, remembering that Covelle had advised them to pray, there was little conversation for a while. Finally Swan River said:

"Shucks, I don't reckon I'd ever be a success at prayin'."

"In my case," said Henry, "I find a lack of practice. I find myself groping for words. After seeing the expression in Covelle's eyes, I wonder if prayers would be of any use. The man is mad."

"I can't understand him," said Mary Brant weakly.

"You have known him a long time, Miss Brant?"

"Nearly five years. Dad believed in him. He wanted me to marry Nort Covelle. I trusted him, but I never trusted James Small. It was Small who persuaded dad to give Michael Finley a chance, after Michael came from the penitentiary; and I'm sure now that the plot was in Small's brain all the time. Michael was a clever forger. I've seen the signature on my father's will—and it is perfect."

"You kinda like Rusty Lee, don'tcha, ma'am?" asked Swan River.

"Why, I—I suppose I like him," replied Mary.

"He's pretty much of a danged fool—but he's honest."

"I don't believe this is any time to discuss likes and dislikes," said Henry quietly, "and we are all more or less fools, much against them.... Miss Brant, no matter what happens to us, I would like to have you know that you are, by long odds, the bravest of the three of us. We have both voiced fears and sorrow over our situation, but you have not complained at all. Thinking on that, I feel more cheerful."

"Well, I don't," said Swan River quickly. "Somebody's comin'."

The door opened. After the lamp was lighted they discovered that the "somebody" was Covelle, Small and the sheriff. Covelle carried some strips of flour sacks, with which they proceeded to gag all three prisoners.

There was no explanation. The ropes were removed from their ankles and they were forced to their feet.

"Keep in single file," growled Covelle, "and watch where you step."

MOMENT'S LATER, as Rusty came back from hiding the

horses, he saw the headlight of an engine coming up the grades. It was the wrecking crew, coming in to replace the missing rail on the siding. Rusty knew that all the guards would be watching the train; so he took advantage of this fact and got back to the stable in safety.

Quickly he went around the end of the lower shack, where the prisoners were kept, and came up to the front corner, which was only a step from the door. Rusty expected to find a guard at the door, but was surprised not to find one, and to find the door open.

The wrecker was at the switch now, and as he stepped into the empty room, Rusty saw two of the guards near the engine. The absence of the prisoners caused his heart to miss a beat. Had Covelle done away with them? He went back to the doorway and looked around, but no one had seen him. Then he ducked back into the room.

About a dozen men were coming toward the shack, talking as they came. Rusty was cornered, but trusted to the darkness to break his way through the crowd, if they came in, They stopped short of the doorway. Rusty heard the door of the next compartment open, and the men filed in. He could hear Slim's voice saying:

"Each one of you fellers take a rifle and a six-gun. There's plenty shells in that big box; so load up enough. We start drivin' just as soon as it gits daylight, and we don't quit until we're into the valley. Covelle will be back here by daylight. I don't think we're goin' to have any trouble, but we better be all set, if it does happen."

They all filed out again and went up toward the cook-shack, disappeared inside. Rusty waited a few minutes before making his way up to the next door, which was unlocked, the padlock hanging open.

He went in, helped himself to a new Winchester, filled his pockets with ammunition, and went back around the corner.

It was evident that Covelle's belated forces had arrived on

the wrecker, and now they were all armed and ready to start the drive. Even with Butch, Lawson and Jules out of the lineup, the odds would be at least twenty to one against Rusty being able to stop the drive.

Skirting the stable, Rusty took advantage of a strip of jack-pines to get further up the hill, where he had to crawl across a wide space. The first rays of dawn were painting the eastern sky when he reached the brushy foot of the sheer cliffs west of the shacks.

By using all his skill as a climber, he managed to work his way up over the broken rocks and brush to a point where he could crawl up through a narrow crevice to the top of the cliffs. From there he was about two hundred yards from the nearest shack, and about a hundred feet above them. Sprawling flat on the rock, he ripped open boxes of cartridges and stuffed the magazine of his thirty-thirty.

Sheep were straggling about now, as the light grew stronger. The crew at the switch were working swiftly to repair the track, and in a few more minutes they had pull onto the siding to let a passenger train pass them. One of the horses that Rusty had let loose from the stable was feeding down toward the shacks, its rope dragging.

Sunlight painted the east slopes of the hills now, as the wrecking outfit pulled out, their job done. The herders began gathering in the loose bunches of sheep, driving them in past the shacks. Rusty could see Slim down there, giving the men their orders, sunlight glinting on their rifles.

Off to Rusty's left were several hundred sheep, feeding on the slope, and the smaller bunches began drifting toward the main body. Some of the men were making up packs of food and blankets. But there was no sign of Covelle nor Small, whom Rusty believed had taken away the prisoners.

FINALLY THE men were ready to start the drive. But as they left the corner of the cook-shack, Rusty lifted his rifle and drove a bullet into the ground directly in front of them. For a moment they hesitated, and then raced back toward the shack. Several of the men dropped their packs in their haste.

At the front of the cook-shack they halted, looking in every direction, trying to locate the source of that bullet. Rusty chuckled and added the extra cartridge to his magazine. Slim came to the corner of the shack, looking cautiously around as he argued with the men.

Rusty saw three of them leave the group and disappear down the fronts of the shacks. They circled the last shack, suddenly racing over to the stable. A hundred feet from the back of the stable was a growth of jack-pines.

Rusty shifted his rifle, watching carefully. In a few moments he saw a man crawling into the open, heading toward the jack-pine cover. The man was lying flat, drawing himself along by elbow power alone.

Rusty lifted his rifle, aimed carefully, and drove a bullet into the soft dirt about a foot ahead of the crawling man. Forward motion immediately ceased, and the man went scrambling back for protection.

Zee-e-e! A bullet struck a rock and went whining over Rusty's head. Slim had discovered him now, and was shooting from the corner of the cook-shack. As Rusty ducked below the rocky rim, two more bullets whined over his head.

"All right," he said grimly. "No more foolin'; so take what yuh get."

Now that Rusty's position had been discovered the men realized his strategy. His position commanded the situation, and they were loath to take chances. There was no place they could get to drive him out. Three of the men were still behind the stable, while the rest were just close to or inside the cook-shack, holding a council of war.

Rusty lined up his sights and smashed a bullet into the ground just short of them. The bullet splattered them with mud. A moment later they were all inside the cook-shack. Then, realizing that the flimsy walls of that shack were not at all bullet-proof, they all piled out and went down to the rear of the shack, out of Rusty's sight.

The loose horse was working closer to the stable now. Rusty did not want any of them to have transportation; so he splattered a bullet in front of the feeding horse, intending to drive the animal back up the hill. But the bullet had the opposite effect. The animal trotted through the break in the fence and entered the stable.

DOWN BELOW Slim and Lou, with thirteen men, were grouped at the end of the shack, talking it over. Over at the side of the stable were Mac and two others. Eighteen in all, heavily armed, but afraid to start the drive because of one lone cowboy on the cliff. Slim cursed bitterly, but was no more ready to start than the others.

"Is this here High-Heel Kid a good shot?" asked a man.

"Yuh can't prove it by me," replied Slim gloomily. "But I do know he's in a spot where he can sure stop us from goin' any plane. Hell, I wish Covelle would come back."

"I wonder what became of the Big Swede," said Lou. "He was shore prominent enough around here last night."

"How about tryin' to circle that cliff and come at the kid from behind?" queried one of the men. "Mebbe we can git above him."

"That's easy—unless the preachers are wrong," remarked one of the men. "All you'll have to do is make a break out there toward them sheep—and you'll be plenty high up—*pronto.*"

"We could make a break—all in a bunch," said Lou. "He couldn't stop all of us."

"You go ahead, mister," grinned one of the men. "I'll stay here and keep a tally. And if anybody wants to know about me—I'm stayin' here just as long as that High-Heel Kid is up in them rocks."

"We could starve him out," said another.

"Nothin' to stop him from movin', though," Lou assured him. "At dark he could make a sneak further back on us. You won't never starve that red-headed devil; he's too smart. Mebbe Covelle will know what to do."

A few minutes later Covelle, Dud Miles and Small came out of the cañon just beyond the end of the lower shack. Rusty saw them for a moment, but not long enough to afford a shot. If there had been time, that shot would not have been a warning. Rusty was all through warning the sheepmen.

Covelle, Dud Miles and Small joined the fifteen men at the end of the other shack, and Slim quickly explained their predicament.

"So you're a bunch of brave gunmen, are you?" sneered Covelle. "You'd let one man drive all of you to cover. Those sheep should be a quarter of the way to the divide right now. Well, what are you going to do—quit on me?"

"It looks like suicide to me," said one of the men.

"He's got to raise up to shoot," Covelle retorted. "About six men shoot at him every time he raises up, while the others start the drive. We can place a man at every corner of the cook-shack and the stable. We can keep him from doing any damage. When the rest of you get higher on the hill, you can cut loose at him."

"Yeah, I reckon we can do it that way," agreed Slim. "Anyway, it's worth tryin'."

CHAPTER XVII

FLIGHT

THE THREE PRISONERS had no idea of their destination, when Covelle, Small and the sheriff took them from the shack in the darkness. Stumbling along, with Covelle in the lead, they went down the trail into the cañon. Mary knew it was the trail to Black River Flats, over which Covelle had brought her.

Because of the dangerous nature of the trail they were obliged to proceed at a snail's pace. With their hands tied behind them it was very difficult to keep their balance. There was no conversation, except an occasional curse from Covelle, as he stumbled over sharp rocks, or gave a low-toned warning of the narrow turns.

After about two miles of the nightmare trail Covelle stopped them. He lighted several matches before he found the exact spot he was looking for. It was a little trail, hardly visible, leading up over a jumble of broken sandstone. Here the moonlight gave them some illumination. Covelle led them up this trail.

"I hope he knows where he's goin'," grunted the sheriff. "I don't."

About a hundred feet off the main trail they came to a ledge, where the moonlight showed the sheer walls of the cañon. Here was sort of a cave, under the overhang of a huge slab of sandstone. There was apparently no way of going further.

The prisoners were forced to sit down against the wall, while Covelle and the sheriff tied their feet again. None of their gags was removed. Covelle lighted a cigarette, laughing quietly. Then he said:

"With no chance of any argument, I feel I am safe in saying that you are here to stay. You were in my way; so I removed you. That is, I left you safe and sound, merely forgetting where I left you. You see the idea, I hope. In case my conquest of Wild Horse Valley is a success, I may look in on you as I go back to Black River City. But do not count on that, because I shall be a busy man. Good luck to you, and my very best to the buzzards; they are plentiful around here."

Quietly the three men slithered back over the rocks, leaving the three prisoners, incapable of speech or action. There was no chance of loosening their bonds, no way of traveling. If their suffering became too great, they could always roll off the ledge....

RUSTY HAD been enjoying his advantage, and did not realize that a concerted attempt was being planned until a regular barrage of bullets began humming over his head and screaming against the rocks behind him. Rolling over quickly he slid to a fissure in the cliff, where he could not see the shacks, but could cover the slope behind them.

Several men were running swiftly up the slope toward the sheep, when Rusty opened fire. On the second shot a man dropped his rifle, went to his knees and sprawled flat. Another man, further to the right, stumbled and went to his knees, sat up and lifted both hands.

But there were more men, running from beyond the stable, ducking, dodging, weaving toward the jack-pine cover. Rusty emptied his rifle at them, but scored no more hits. Two more raced across the opening as he reloaded his rifle. Then he squirmed back to his original spot, where he peered down at the shacks. He saw a man, whom he thought was James Small, the lawyer, run from the corner of a shack and disappear into the stable.

Far down the grade a locomotive whistled, and Rusty wondered if it could be another trainload of sheep. There was no more shooting at Rusty. He lifted his hat above the rim, and two bullets hummed off the rocks.

"Well," he mused, "I thought I could keep 'em away from the sheep, and now they think they can keep me up here. Mebbe we're both wrong."

Scooping up his scattered cartridges he slid back on the ledge, and dropped a few feet to the rocks below. From there he come whirling to the front of the shacks, quickly angled down the narrow fissure, skinning his elbows and knees in his haste. Over rocks and through the brush he went along the hillside, heading for the thicket where he had left the two saddled horses. Once in the saddle, he would have an advantage over the men on foot, who were working feverishly to bunch the sheep and get them started.

As he reached the horses, he heard the sharp blast of a locomotive whistle. From further up the mountain sounded the clatter of rifle shots, but no bullets came his way. He selected the best horse, swung into the saddle, and held quiet for a moment, trying to plan out his first move.

NORT COVELLE was jubilant. He did not care because two of his men had gone down and were still out there, wounded and afraid to move. The bulk of his men were out of reach of fire from the cliff top now, and were herding sheep toward Wild Horse Valley. He looked around for Small, but the lawyer had disappeared.

"Crawled into a hole, I suppose," he told Dud Miles.

"Don't blame him much," mumbled the sheriff. "There'll be hell raised over this, Covelle. I git to thinkin' about what we've done, and it scares me. Too many men shot and missin', I tell yuh. It's got me plumb worried."

"Don't turn yellow, Dud," laughed Covelle. "I told you I'd give you a cold ten thousand dollars for your end of the deal, didn't I?"

"Yeah, I know all that, Nort. I ain't no damn dude. But mebbe I can't think far enough ahead to see myself enjoyin' that money. I'd shore trade my chances for that ten thousand to be in Mexico, and still headin' south. You didn't exactly mean that you was goin' to leave them three people down there for the buzzards to eat, didja?"

Covelle looked at the sheriff. His eyes narrowed and his lips twisted in a grin.

"I meant just what I said, Dud—they'll never come back."

"Aw, I know, but that girl ain't hurt nobody. I wouldn't let her—"

Covelle was only three feet away from Dud Miles; so he shot from his hip—once… twice. Miles' tall frame jerked from the impact of the forty-fives; his eyes shut tightly. Then his knees buckled and he collapsed heavily on the cook-shack floor.

Covelle whirled and walked to the doorway. He heard the whistle of the approaching train, and he remembered what Dud Miles had said about Judge Myers and the prosecuting attorney investigating things at Black River City. He listened for a moment and then walked swiftly down to the door of the room where the guns and ammunition had been stored.

From a box he took out a dynamite bomb, made up of six sticks of dynamite, all capped and fused. The fuse was rather long, the end split for a quick spit. He shoved the bundle inside his shirt and walked outside, his mind working swiftly.

He heard guns barking up on the slope of the mountain, and wondered if his men were still fighting against Rusty Lee. The engine sounded a sharp blast as it came laboring up the grade. It was a passenger train, coming from down in the Flats, and it was grinding to a stop at the siding.

Covelle stepped to the corner, watching closely. Four men got off the train and stood there, looking intently toward the shacks. Covelle recognized Judge Myers.

There was plenty of shooting up on the mountain now, and the four men moved out to see what was going on. Covelle walked to the rear corner, nearest the stable, and looked toward the hill. A man came running down from the jack-pines, his shirt torn, a bloody smear across his face. He dropped flat and rolled under the barb-wire fence, almost into Covelle.

"Get out of here!" he yelped. "The cowboys! They drove us back!"

COVELLE HALTED for a moment. He had not expected the cowboys of Wild Horse Valley to bring the battle down to him. The four men from Black River City were coming down toward the shacks now. The sound of shots seemed closer.

Covelle dashed for the stable door, just as a horse surged out. In the saddle was James Small.

Covelle grasped the headstall and whirled the horse around, almost throwing Small out of the saddle. Small went desperately for his gun. Apparently the little attorney was too frightened to shoot straight, because he missed Covelle at four feet.

Covelle did not miss. He shot across his left arm, and Small pitched off the saddle, almost on top of him. Covelle jerked the frightened horse around and went into the saddle.

There were riders thundering down the slope as Covelle spurred past the rear of the lower shack. He swung the plunging horse into the old Indian trail, and went lurching down into the cañon. The four men from the passenger train saw him go over the edge, but were unable to prevent it, and the next moment saw five riders come whirling to the front of the shacks, smoking guns in their hands.

They were Rusty Lee, Danny Regan, foreman of Henry's J Bar C, Tom O'Rourke, Oscar Johnson, the Vitrified Viking, and Judge Van Treece, Henry Conroy's deputy.

"Where's Covelle?" yelled Rusty.

"Down in that cañon!" shouted Judge Myers. "He went over the edge—a suicide!"

"Like hell, he did!" snorted Rusty, and spurred straight for the old trail.

Rusty knew what that trail was like. He had looked at it before, and it certainly was not built for running horses. But Covelle was traveling that trail, and Covelle knew where the prisoners had been taken; so Rusty threw caution to the winds.

Luckily he had selected a mountain horse, sure-footed as a goat. At certain spots Rusty rode with his left knee on the saddle, in order to give his horse room. He knew that he must watch for Covelle, who might block him at any turn in the trail.

Down along the cañon wall twisted that trail, across slide-rock, through manzanita and jack-pines, where a slip or a misstep would send the rider down a sheer wall or dangerous slope. But Covelle was still ahead, or down in the cañon.

Rusty galloped around a right-hand turn and was on a slight upgrade, where the wall broke sharp into the cañon, when he saw it across the trail: a streamer of smoke ahead; the unmistakable spouting plume of a dynamite fuse.

With a jerk of his body, Rusty flung himself backwards out of the saddle. He landed safely, although painfully—and a second later the side of the hill seemed to explode. It drove

Rusty back against the rocks, while the debris of the explosion rained around him.

Bruised and shaken, he got to his feet. His face was bleeding from a cut, his hands were cut and bleeding, but there were no broken bones, nothing to stop him; and he still had his six-shooter. If Covelle had intended wrecking the trail behind him he had miscalculated. He had dropped the bomb too far to the left, and the force of the explosion had only widened the trail.

Of the horse there was no sign. Rusty judged that the poor beast had just about reached the bomb when it exploded, and had been blown off into the depths. Limping a little, he went ahead, and in a few minutes he saw Covelle's horse, standing on the trail, tied to a projecting rock.

CHAPTER XVIII

OVER THE CLIFF

THE THREE HELPLESS, voiceless prisoners saw Nort Covelle come crawling over the rocks. He was panting, cursing in whispers, as he reached them—a murderous animal, defeated, but coming back to render and tear weaker creatures. He halted near them, laughing mirthlessly, the glare of near insanity flaming in his eyes.

"I blew away the trail," he told them huskily. "They can't follow me. There is no trail between here and Apache Siding."

Henry Harrison Conroy nodded helplessly. They had heard the explosion.

Covelle turned on Mary, his thin lips drawn back in a sneering smile.

"We're going away, my dear—you and I. The rest of you can stay here and rot; but Mary goes with me. Not because I want you," he told Mary, "but to keep Lee from ever getting you. You'll go with me—to Mexico—or to hell. We're going over the old trail, and we'll be there long before they can block us. Small is dead, Butch is dead—the rest are dead by this time—but Nort Covelle is alive."

He laughed insanely, picked Mary up bodily. Covelle was powerful, in spite of his slender body, and handled Mary with no effort. Bound as she was, she could make no resistance.

He turned to the others. "The buzzards will soon be here," he told them. "It would be better for you if I dropped you over the edge, but I'd rather have you sit here and realize that it doesn't pay to fight Nort Covelle."

He started away then—and at that moment, Rusty Lee came over the raise in the rocky trail.

Covelle stopped short, staring at him as though he were a ghost. Rusty's face was bloody, and there was blood on his arms and hands, but the gun in his right hand was as steady as a rock.

Covelle's gun was in his holster, but because he had Mary in his arms Rusty could not shoot. Covelle, realizing his advantage, backed quickly to the edge of the precipice.

"All right, Lee," he said harshly. "I don't know how you got here, but it doesn't matter. Stop where you are, or I'll throw her over the edge."

Rusty stopped, his shoulders hunched.

"You can't win, Lee," said Covelle. "My life doesn't matter. I'll be as well off down in the bottom of the cañon as on the end of a rope. You alone are responsible for my failure. You want this girl. Well, you don't get her. She goes with me—or into the cañon. Toss your gun away."

Rusty stared at Covelle, and realized that in the madness caused by his defeat, the man was fully capable of doing just what he threatened to do. He looked at Mary, and her eyes seemed to tell him to do as Covelle ordered. It was her only chance.

Rusty tossed away the gun. It clattered on a rocky ledge above Covelle. He laughed gloatingly.

"Covelle still gives orders and has obedience," he said. "Back up to the trail."

Rusty began backing carefully, wondering why Covelle did not put Mary down and shoot him. Perhaps he had something more spectacular to do than merely to shoot Rusty down. Covelle did not hurry, did not try to get close to Rusty, but his eyes were never off the young cowboy, as he packed his burden, feeling carefully with his feet as they crossed the rocky ledges.

"Back down the trail," he ordered Rusty. "That's far enough. Would you like to say a few words of farewell to the young lady? You'll never see her again. No? Well, suit yourself, High-Heel Kid; don't say that Covelle wasn't considerate."

They had reached the spot where Covelle's horse stood. Edging in against the cliff, he lifted Mary behind the saddle. With a slash of his knife he severed the bonds of her ankles.

"Ride straddle," he ordered sharply.

Mary tried to obey, but her cramped limbs refused to function. Covelle laughed brutally.

"Suit yourself," he said. "You always were a little prude."

Then he flung the tie-rope across the horse's neck, grasped the bridle reins and saddle horn. He looked back at Rusty, a laugh on his lips.

"*Adios,* High-Heel Kid," he said. "Covelle wins the consolation pot."

The nervous horse started, as Covelle threw his weight into the stirrup—but the sheep boss did not mount.

As quick as a flash the saddle turned, dropping Covelle flat on the back of his neck against the cliff. The sudden lurch of the horse unseated Mary, and the horse went plunging ahead, snorting with fright. Rusty had already started on a run toward them, as Covelle started to mount. It was not over twenty feet, and he got there just in time to prevent Mary from going off the trail.

Covelle, badly dazed, was struggling to get back on his feet, pawing at his holster. Rusty dived past Mary as Covelle came up, and struck the sheepman's arm with his fist. It knocked the gun back against the wall—and as Covelle turned around, Rusty drove a stunning blow to his jaw.

That blow did more than he had intended. Covelle spun around on one heel, threw up his hands and went backwards off the narrow trail. He struck the sharp slope fifty feet below the trail, bounced outward and went hurtling downward into the depths.

Nort Covelle was through with scheming and with murder.

FOR A moment Rusty stood there, speechless and unmoving, startled by the suddenness of Covelle's death. Then, from behind him, came a shrill yell. He whirled to see three riders and several men on foot coming down the trail. They were Judge Van Treece, Danny Regan, Oscar Johnson, Tom O'Rourke, Judge Myers and the men who had come with him on the train.

Rusty, panting heavily, turned then to Mary and quickly removed the bandage from her mouth. For a moment she was unable to talk, so tight had the gag been. He then cut the ropes off her wrists. By now the others had come crowding up and were questioning Rusty. He merely pointed over the rocks toward the little cave.

"Henry and Swan River—over there a little ways," he said.

"Yumpin' Yudas!" snorted Oscar. "Das ha'ar Rosty is a fighting fule!"

But Rusty was only interested in Mary. He chafed her wrists clumsily, grimacing with her as the pains of returning circulation became almost unbearable. He heard, though, the yelp of triumph from the throat of Oscar Johnson as he found Henry and Swan River.

"Everything is all right now," he told Mary. "There ain't a thing to worry about. You can go back home again and forget all this trouble."

Mary shook her head slowly. It was still difficult for her to speak, but she managed to whisper:

"I'd rather stay in Arizona, Rusty."

"After all this—trouble you've had?"

"But the trouble is all over. You just told me it was."

"Yeah, that's right—but, gosh! I dunno—"

"We'll sell the sheep," she said. "Dad would want me to do that. And we could buy cattle."

"We?" queried Rusty. "You mean—the Brant estate?"

Mary looked at him, and in spite of her pain she smiled.

"Was Nort Covelle wrong?" she whispered.

"Wrong about what, Mary?"

"He—he said you—wanted me," she answered.

"Well, my—gosh!" Rusty was finding it hard to talk. "No! That's the one time in his life that he was right. But I didn't—I didn't—"

"I did," said Mary.

"Lovely dove!" breathed Rusty foolishly.

The men were coming back over the rocky trail. Henry and Swan River were hardly able to walk or talk, but they were doing the best they could to make the others understand what had happened to them.

Rusty picked Mary up and put her on her feet.

"Red-headed son-of-a-gun!" whispered Swan River. "I knowed you'd find a way out."

"Liar," replied Rusty calmly. "You gave yourself up for dead hours ago."

"*I* did," wheezed Henry. "I admitted defeat. I hope I may never go through anything like that again. Even when you came after Covelle, it was only a fading ray of sunshine, my boy."

"I don't understand Covelle," complained Swan River. "After he made you throw away yore gun—why didn't he kill yuh, Rusty?"

Rusty turned and walked over to Covelle's gun, which was lying on the trail. He picked it up and examined it quickly.

"The reason he didn't shoot me is because the gun is empty," he said. "I guess he forgot to load it, bein' in so much of a hurry; so he ran his bluff."

"Did he also forget to cinch up his saddle?" asked Danny Regan.

"No," replied Rusty, "he didn't. But before I went up over that trail, after him, I cut the latigo off the saddle and threw it into the cañon. I wasn't goin' to give him any chance to get away."

"Yu-udas!" snorted Oscar. "And to t'ink Ay vanted to kill Rosty."

"Well," said Judge Van Treece, "the whole thing sounds like a nightmare to me. Luckily some of us were already coming to investigate, when Oscar came to warn us of the sheep. I still don't know what it is all about, but it doesn't matter as long as right wins."

"Ay tank it vars Rosty who von, Yudge," said Oscar admiringly.

Judge Myers stepped up to Mary. "Miss Brant, I want to congratulate you on your escape," he said. "It happens that Covelle's aim was not exactly deadly, when he shot James Small. Oh yes, Small died; but he lived long enough to confess to his and Nort Covelle's crimes. It seems that he had hidden that forged will, and had refused to divulge its hiding-place. I believe you can now claim your father's entire estate, with no provisions."

Before Mary could answer him, Sheriff Henry spoke up.

"I think," he said, looking keenly at Mary, "that this is a terrible place to transact business. I am still jerky from thinking of buzzards, and I can not get any place until someone moves the horses off the trail, or leads them back ahead of me."

MARY RODE one of the horses, and Rusty led the animal, as the cavalcade went back to Apache Siding. They kept Mary away from the shacks, where the casualties and prisoners were held. Judge Myers and his two special deputies took care of everything.

They had been at the siding but a few minutes when they

heard the whistle of a passenger train. It was coming up the grades, heading toward Scorpion Bend.

The job here was done; there was no reason to remain. Oscar had found a red flag—and he used it.

There were sheep on the hillside. Henry, seeing them, smiled and rubbed his over-red nose.

"Not intending to be facetious," he said, "but I remember a little rhyme. Something about 'Mary had a little lamb, it's fleece was—'"

"Red as ha'al," blurted Oscar soberly. "Ay am not so dumb."

There were tears in Mary's eyes as she looked up at Rusty.

"Lamb?" she said. "You—Rusty."

But just at that time the flagged train ground to a stop. The conductor peevishly threw open an entrance, leaning out to see who would have the temerity to stop a passenger train at such a spot. He saw Oscar Johnson, and drew back sharply.

"You?" gasped the conductor.

"Oh, ha'alo dere!" exclaimed Oscar. "You are de faller who said Ay couldn't stop it. What do you t'ink now?"

"You stopped it," replied the conductor quietly. "But never do that again."

"Ay hope not," replied Oscar. "It yerked pretty hord. Did you see de pretty girl and de red-headed faller who yust vent inside?"

"Yes, I did," replied the conductor gruffly, "and they look as though they had been fighting."

"Yah, su-ure. He yust proposed to her."

Oscar swaggered into the car, leaving the conductor trying to puzzle it out for himself, and sat down opposite Mary and Rusty. Henry had turned around in his seat, looking back at the young folks.

"I would love it," said Henry soberly. "I doubt if he would understand what it meant, but I am sure he would consider it a great honor, after he found out."

Rusty turned and looked at Oscar, huge and placid.

"Oscar," he said quietly, "Mary and I are going to be married in Scorpion Bend tonight. Would you like to be the best man at the wedding?"

"Vould Ay like to be de *best* man?" he queried. "De best man at a vedding? Yumpin' Yudas, Ay have always been de best man at a vedding or a funeral or a fight. Yah, su-ure, Ay will be dere."

"Well, that is settled peaceably," sighed Henry. "Isn't it wonderful—peace and love—and perfect relaxation. Why, only a short hour ago we—"

"Please," interrupted Mary. "I don't want even to remember it."

"From now on is all I want to remember, Mary," said Rusty soberly.

"Same ha'are," agreed Oscar Johnson.

"You won't have any trouble in doing that, Oscar," said Judge, "until about tomorrow. What are you doing tonight?"

"Sleep," replied Oscar. "Dem ships kept me avake oll night."

Rusty looked fondly at Mary and said:

"It's shore wonderful to be goin' home, Mary. The law don't want me now—and to Wild Horse Valley, I'm still a cowpuncher in good standin'. It was tough travelin' for a long time, but I've been well paid."

"You allus was a feller that could fall in a hawg-pen and come up smellin' like a rose," declared Swan River Grush.

"Why Oswald Bertram Grush!" exclaimed Henry.

Swan River raised halfway out of his seat, his jaw sagging, and sank slowly back.

Then there was only the *clickety-click* of the car wheels, as the belated passenger train roared toward Wild Horse Valley, where the cattlemen could sleep nights once again, forgetting that there had ever been a menace from Black River Flats.

GALLOPING GOLD

*On the trail of vanished treasure
with the Sheriff of Tonto Town*

CHAPTER I

OUTLAWS ALL

"ROARIN' BILL" ROSE sprawled in a home-made rocker, his booted feet elevated to the top of a crude table, on which was an oil lamp, numerous and sundry ancient magazines, old newspapers, scattered playing cards, and a half-filled bottle of whisky.

Roarin' Bill's shirt-collar was hiked up around his ears, his chin sunk down inside the collar. One hand, dangling over the arm of the chair, held a letter, the envelope of which rested on Bill's lap. Bill was tall and gaunt, as hard as the Arizona hills which surrounded his Lazy R ranch house. His face was deeply lined, his hair grizzled. Taken as a whole, Roarin' Bill was a typical old Arizona rawhider. Because of the fact that he seldom raised his voice they called him "Roarin'."

The main room of the Lazy R was furnished with home-made stuff, very serviceable, but not beautiful. Midway of the room, seated at a card table, were "Thunder" and "Lightnin'" Mendoza, Roarin' Bill's hired hands. More Yaqui Indian than Mexican, they suited Roarin' Bill.

"I like 'em," Bill had said; "'cause they ain't got brains enough to tell what they shoudn't tell—even if they was smart enough to know anything."

Just now Thunder and Lightnin' were absorbed in a game of their own. With the stakes at two-bits a corner, they eagerly watched a pair of Mexican jumping-beans in the center of a penciled circle on a piece of paper. A larger circle indicated the finish line. When the winner's bean managed to edge over

the outer circle, another stake was put up, and the two beans replaced in the starting circle.

"How yuh comin', Lightnin'?" asked Roarin' Bill.

Lightnin' turned his head for a moment—and in that time, in some unaccountable way, Thunder's bean was balancing precariously on the finish line. After a jerk or two it went rolling back to the center, where it collided gently with Lightnin's entry.

"Sometheeng ees wrong," declared Lightnin'. "Every time I'm turn your head away, theese damn bean from Thunder ees go like strick. I'm lose feety centavos, biccause I'm not keep your eye open."

"W'at ees a strick?" queried Thunder.

"W'at you theenk?" asked Lightnin'. "You theenk I'm pay you feefty centavos and also learn you w'at ees a strick? *Por Dios,* I'm theenk my bean got rheumateesm."

"Did yuh see Ab Morgan in Tonto City?" asked Roarin' Bill.

"Sure," nodded Liglitnin', keeping his eyes on the two beans. "He ees there weeth hees *hija.*"

"She ain't his daughter—she's his step-daughter."

"Huh?"

MR. H. HARRISON CONROY

"Step-daughter. She's the daughter of his wife. I mean—the wife he had, before she died."

Lightnin' scratched his head violently for several moments.

"You mean, hees step on her, when she was leetle?"

"I don't reckon we'll go into that," said Roarin' Bill. "Jist go ahead and play with them worm-infested beans. Watchin' a jumpin'-bean roll six inches won't tax yore brains—much."

"Lightnin' ees ver' dumb," declared Thunder, fondling the six hairs which comprised his mustache. "W'en a man ees married, biffore hees wife died—*cuidado!* Ha, ha, you pay men twenty-five centavos!"

"*Madre de Dios!*" snorted Lightnin'. "I light one cigareet— lose twenty-five centavos! I queet. Seex-beets, eh? I'm geeve you payday."

"You geeve me now," demanded Thunder. "I'm play for cash— only."

"Eef *you* lose—how the hell you pay me? You got notheeng."

Thunder shrugged his shoulders.

"Ver' true—I'm got notheeng. But I'm—well, I'm not ask for *oro Americano.* Ver' likely I'm be satisfy weeth necktie, mebbe some pair socks."

"Madre de Dios! So? You look een my war-sack, eh? You see those rad necktie and those green sock, eh? Leesten to me, you pock-picket—"

"Sh-h-h-h!" warned Roarin' Bill. At the sound he heard, his right hand slipped down beside him, gripping a heavy Colt .45. Quietly, he cocked it.

"Somebody outside," he said.

A MOMENT later, two quick knocks sounded on the door. They were followed after a short interval by two more. Bill relaxed in his chair again.

"C'mon in, boys," he said.

The door swung open. Four rough-looking men filed in, closing and fastening it behind them. They were "Pecos Charley" Peters, "Sody" Slade, Ed Clovis and Zibe Tucker—as tough a quartette as ever came out of New Mexico with a posse on their heels.

They strode over without a word and helped themselves from Roarin' Bill's bottle. Tonto Valley did not know this bearded quartette, dressed in worn and faded clothes, although they had been holed-up at the Lazy R for more than two months.

Pecos Charley was a skinny little person, bow-legged, large-nosed, with a nervous Adam's-apple. Sody Slade was huge, clumsy, big-fisted. Clovis was of medium height, dark, narrow-eyed, always alert. Zibe Tucker was short and fat, good-natured until riled, and inclined to be a peacemaker.

"Well, Bill, we got it all moved," announced Pecos Charley after a stiff drink. "We shot a small blast fifty feet back in the second tunnel, and shook down enough stuff to keep anybody from gettin' inside. We can clean it out in a week."

"Did yuh dig it all out?" asked Roarin' Bill.

"Every ounce," declared Pecos Charley. "It was a pocket—like I said it was. But—" Pecos shoved his thumbs inside his belt and expanded his chest—"it'll run close to seventy-five thousand dollars."

"I wish I had my split of it right now," put in Clovis. "I dunno how we've kept out of sight this long."

"It ain't seemed long," mused Sody Slade. "That's 'cause we've all been busy, I reckon."

Roarin' Bill went to the kitchen and brought back tin cups and another bottle of whisky. Filling the cups and passing them around, he said:

"Well, here's hopin' our luck don't ravel out, gents."

They drank deeply, thoughtfully.

"Luck is shore a funny thing," said Roarin' Bill. "I drifted in here eight years ago, with a bundle of money and with a past that was full of black spots as a leopard's hide. This cattle outfit was spindlin' when I bought it. Shucks, the law must have knowed I was here. I never changed my name. I was right here—if they wanted me.

"But I was aimin' to go straight. I never slick-eared one damn calf in Tonto Valley; I paid my debts and acted like a white man. Mebbe that's why they let me alone—I dunno. But I never had any luck—outside of not goin' to the pen. Blizzards, drought, lobo wolves—they all took a whack at the Lazy R. And worst of all—Ab Morgan and his damn Quarter-Circle M outfit moved in right beside me. For six years he's handed me the hot end of the runnin'-iron. It's hell, I'll tell yuh."

"And then we had to come along," added Sody Slade. "We didn't help yuh none, Bill."

"You jist forget that, Sody," said Roarin' Bill quickly. "I ain't forgettin' that the law was hot on my trail—oncet. But it's shore funny the way it worked out. Hidin' you fellers in that old Comanche mine on Morgan's property, and you accident'ly stumblin' onto that vein of gold that everybody had overlooked."

"It's all in yore old abandoned Two-Gun tunnel now, Bill,"

said Pecos Charley. "It was a back-breakin' job, but we moved it over there."

Roarin' Bill nodded and poured more liquor.

"I been figurin' that as soon as possible, I'll reopen my old mine," he said. "I can say then that you four fellers are miners that I hired in Scorpion Bend. Then we can clean out that tunnel, sack up that ore and ship it out. We'll git the money, split it five ways, work a few more days and say it was only a pocket."

"That's fine," agreed Pecos Charley. "All I want is my split of the money, and then I'm goin' to California and start all over again—on the square."

"I like to hear yuh say that, Peeos," said Roarin' Bill. "I've been square for eight years. It's the only life, I'll tell yuh that. Well, you fellers have had a taste of it for two months. The feller who said that honesty is the best policy shore said somethin'."

"I'm jist wonderin' what Ab Morgan would say about it," mused Zibe Tucker. "You forgot about that ore, didn't yuh, Bill?"

"Well, I—huh! Yeah, I did—kinda, Zibe. But I don't figure it's stealin' to take somethin' from a feller that he never knowed he had. Anyway, I've been gettin' the worst of it from Morgan for six years; so that gold ore sorta evens us up—a little. Listen to this:"

Roarin' Bill opened out the letter he had been holding and held it nearer the light.

"This was in the postoffice at Tonto City today," he said. "It says: *'I fenced the water at Outlaw Springs, and you tore down the fence. I claim that water and I aim to keep it. I'm fencin' it again, and if you tear down that fence again I'll fill you so full of holes that the woodpeckers will use yore carcass to store their winter supply of acorns. Yours truly, Ab Morgan.'*"

"WELL, SHUCKS," drawled Sudy Slade. "Let's all ride down there and give the woodpeckers first chance at Ab Morgan."

Roarin' Bill shook his head. "You keep away from Ab Morgan," he ordered. "Everybody in the Valley knows how things are between me and Morgan. If you killed Morgan, they'd hang me—unless they caught you at it. If Morgan kills me, they'll say it's jist too bad—and do nothin' to Ab Morgan."

"Is that the kinda law you got around here, Roarin'?"

"No, it ain't. But Morgan is supposed to be a law-abidin' citizen. I'm Roarin' Bill Rose, ex-outlaw. That's why nothin' will be done to Ab Morgan, in case he guns me down. We've got the dum-dingedest sheriff you ever seen, boys. He's short and fat, with a face like a moon, and a nose—well, it's the biggest one I've ever seen. Kinda like a potato, and red as hell. He's funny, I tell yuh. Before he came here, he was an actor. Never seen a cow until he inherited the JHC Ranch, over near Tonto City. But he ain't no fool, even if he does look and act like one.

"He's got Judge Van Treece for a deputy. He's taller than Sody, and looks like a bloodhound that lost the scent. And the jailer is Oscar Johnson, the dumbest Swede in North America—and the strongest. Takes a horseshoe, twists it in two, without even makin' up a face. But don't never make the mistake of thinkin' any of them three are dumb—except Oscar Johnson. He'll qualify.

"No, I don't reckon there's a crooked thought in all three of 'em—but naturally they'd favor Ab Morgan."

"How soon do yuh reckon you can start yore mine to workin'?" asked Pecos Charley. "I'd shore like to cash in on that ore."

"Well, I'll tell yuh," replied Roarin' Bill. "Next time I go to Scorpion Bend, I'll take a sample along for an assay. Ira Hallam, the assayer, is a danged old woman, with a hinged tongue. He'll tell the world that I've struck it rich. That'll alibi us for havin' a lot of shippin' ore real soon.

"In the meantime you fellers keep under cover. You can load up on stuff to take back to the tunnel now; it's there in the kitchen. And there's a quarter of fresh beef in the shed. I brought plenty tobacco, too! so yuh won't have to worry about that. Reckon I've got enough to keep yuh eatin' for a week or ten days. By that time, I'll have the assay made, and be fixin' to stock up on drill steel and picks."

"That shore sounds good to me," grinned Sody Slade. "Take

care of yourself, Bill; we need yuh." He moved toward the door. "C'mon, fellers, let's pack the grub back to the rustler's tomb. See yuh later, Bill."

"Why not take that assay to Scorpion Bend in the mornin'?" suggested Pecos Charley.

"I've got a job to do in the mornin'," replied Roarin' Bill.

"What's that, Bill?"

"Why—tearin' down a fence. Good night."

The four men filed out of the house. When they were gone, Roarin' Bill turned to the two Mexicans, who had been listening to the conversation.

"Jist remember," he said, "that you ain't seen nobody nor heard anything."

"Sure," agreed Lightnin' quickly. "I am jus' like clem."

"Two clem," added Thunder. "W'at ees a clem?"

"Por Dios!" exclaimed Lightnin'. "The more I'm know from you, the crazier I theenk I am. And," he added with finality, "that ees all I hope."

"Sure," agreed Thunder. *"Buenas noches,* Onkle Beel."

"Yeah! Good night. We're ridin' to Outlaw Springs before breakfast. Better take rifles. Not that you could hit a flock of hay barns—but it looks better. I uhh…" Roarin' Bill rubbed his chin thoughtfully. "Better not take any ca'tridges; yuh might shoot yourselves—or me."

CHAPTER II

PRUNE JUICE AND HENRY

TOM RICKEY, PROPRIETOR of the Tonto Hotel in Tonto City, jerked up from behind his desk, listening in alarm. From the dining-room came the sudden sounds of crashing crockery, thudding blows and mingled battle cries. Rickey raced to the swinging doors which led into the dining-room.

Just at that moment Judge Van Treece, on the other side of the same doors, was leaving the scene of conflict at about the same speed.

Tom Rickey was short and fat, while the deputy sheriff was tall and thin; so Rickey went down on his face just inside the doors, while Judge Van Treece pin-wheeled halfway across the lobby, ending up in a sitting position, holding his head in both hands.

The dining-room was more or less a wreck. Oscar Johnson, the jailer, whom Judge Van Treece had nicknamed the Vitrified Viking, was struggling with another huge man, both of them sprawled across a table from which all the dishes had been swept.

About midway of the room stood Josephine Swensen, maid of all work and waitress extraordinary. Josephine, Oscar's lady love, was over six feet tall and would weigh about a hundred and eighty. She was a stringy-blonde, with little blue eyes and a huge nose. In her powerful right hand swung a pitcher of water.

Tom Rickey tried to order a cessation of hostilities, but his recent collision had done something to his vocal chords. Oscar finally turned his opponent over, and proceeded to hammer him on the head with the side of his huge fist, like a carpenter driving spikes.

Swish! That heavy water pitcher arced across the intervening space, and landed *clunk!* against the top of Oscar's blond head. Oscar said, "Oof!" and sat down beside the table, drawing the crumpling tablecloth off over his head, concealing himself entirely.

The big fellow who had been the victim of Oscar's hammer-like right looked around vaguely, took one step, tripped over Oscar's extended feet, and crashed against another table. The table went over, dumping the remains of Judge Van Treece's meal on the floor.

"Who in de ha'al do you t'ink you are?" queried Oscar through the folds of the tablecloth.

The man didn't say. He got to his feet and headed for the swinging doors, a blank expression in his eyes. That is in one eye; the other was tightly closed and was rapidly assuming a pure mauve tint.

Oscar tore the concealing cloth away, felt of his head. Slowly he got to his feet, glowering at Tom Rickey. His eyes beheld the water pitcher, and he turned accusing eyes upon Josephine.

"We're de ha'al is Olaf?" he asked.

"Get out of here!" croaked Tom Rickey, "You—you damn bull in a china store."

"Damn fool in a restaurant," corrected Josephine.

"Ya-a-ah, su-ure," sneered Oscar. "Va'al, Ay can ta'all you dis much—Olaf is no yentleman."

"Olaf," defended Josephine, "has olvays acted like a yentleman."

"He may be a yentleman on de outside," conceded Oscar, "but inside, he's yust a bum."

"Wait a minute!" wheezed Tom Rickey. "I don't care who is a gentleman and who isn't a gentleman. The fact remains that you two halfwits have wrecked my dining-room, chased out customers and raised the devil in general. Get out of here, you—you damn Swede!"

"Which von?" asked Oscar.

Josephine advanced with clenched hands, and Oscar headed for the swinging doors.

"You'll sure get a bill for this," declared Tom Rickey.

BUT OSCAR was already out in the lobby, heading for the street. On the sidewalk he came face to face with Henry Harrison Conroy, the sheriff, and Judge Van Treece. The sheriff was there by chance; Judge, by choice.

In appearance, Henry was all that Roarin' Bill Rose had told the four men. Just now he was wearing a pearl colored fedora, which was a trifle too small, and carrying a cane.

Henry squinted closely at Oscar, whose face showed plainly that he had been to war.

"Ay am yust looking for Olaf," said Oscar blandly.

"Oh, is he still alive?" asked Henry. "Judge said you might murder him."

Tom Rickey came to the doorway and saw the three men. He strode out to them, a scowl on his face.

"Conroy, can't you control that damn Swede?" he asked. "Him and another big Swede just—"

"Norvegian!" corrected Oscar.

"Well, what's the difference?" asked Rickey warmly.

"De difference is dat I can vip any damn Norvegian on—"

"A certain racial difference, I believe," sighed Henry. "Please continue, Mr. Rickey."

"Well, them two big Swedes—"

"Vait! Von Norvegian and two Swedes."

"Two?"

"Yah, su-ure. Me and Yosephine. Olaf is a Norvegian."

"Josephine wasn't in this!" snapped Rickey.

"Ya-a-ah? Who t'rew de vater pitcher?"

"Well—"

"Yah! Va'all, go ahead."

"I give up," sighed Tom Rickey.

"Send the bill down to the office," said Henry as if this sort of thing were customary. "I'll take it out of Oscar's pay."

The three officers turned then and walked down the wooden sidewalk to the sheriff's office. They entered and sat down. Oscar blew on his sore knuckles, rubbed his swollen head and began making a cigarette.

"Oscar," said Judge, "there are times when I'm ashamed of you."

"Ay done my best, Yudge," sighed Oscar. "Ay had him olmost vipped, when Yosephine t'rew de pitcher."

"I suppose," remarked Henry, "that it will go down on the records as a draw. I saw Olaf crossing the street to the Tonto Saloon. He swam halfway, and treaded water the rest of the distance. Why did you run away from the battle, Judge?"

Uneasily, Judge got up and walked to the doorway. "Well, I—I was between Josephine and the battle," he explained. "I saw the look in her eye and the pitcher in her hand. Unfortunately, Mr. Rickey and I met amid swinging doors. I am still a trifle dizzy—but it will pass. I—"

His gaze straying up and down the dusty main street of Tonto City, he broke off suddenly, added as if anxious to change the subject:

"Here comes Ab Morgan, walking very much as though a scorpion had stung him while sitting down."

"While the scorpion was sitting down, Judge?"

JUDGE GAVE Henry a malevolent glance and came back into the office. Judge Van Treece had, in his earlier days, been a well-known lawyer, with a profound knowledge of the law; but his appetite for hard liquor and high-stake poker games had made a derelict of him, until Henry Harrison Conroy, seeing in Judge a kindred spirit, had made him deputy sheriff.

A moment later Ab Morgan came in, his spurs rattling, a scowl on his bony face. Morgan, owner of the Quarter-Circle M spread, was a huge man, quick of temper, arrogant and avaricious. He sat down, flung his hat on the floor and leaned toward Henry.

"I came in to get a warrant for the arrest of Roarin' Bill Rose," stated Morgan. "Soon's I get it, I want you to serve it."

"As soon?" queried Judge.

"As soon!" snapped Morgan.

"What has our friend Roarin' Bill done?" asked Henry curiously.

"He tore down my fence! Damn him, he's torn it down three times."

"It must be," murmured Henry, "that he doesn't like the fence."

"Yea-a-ah!" snorted Morgan. "What right has he got to tear down my fences?"

"It seems to me," said Henry, "that we could discuss this much better if you would tell us what fence—and why it has been torn down three times."

"Do yuh know where Outlaw Springs is?"

"Yes," nodded Henry.

"All right. I claim that water: so I fenced it. Every time I fence that water, Roarin' Bill Rose tears the fence down. I'm through sendin' him a warnin'. If the law won't stop him—I will."

"Mr. Morgan, have you a legal title to that water?" Van Treece asked.

"Legal be damned! It's on my property."

"Possibly on your range," admitted Judge, "but has never been legally acquired."

"I didn't buy it—no! But I've claimed it for six years. I've got a moral claim."

"I—really, I have never seen a moral fence," said Henry quietly.

"As a matter of fact," put in Judge hastily, trying to dim the glare which Morgan gave Henry, "you have fenced Outlaw Springs for your own use."

"I have."

"Those springs have never been fenced before?"

"Not till I fenced 'em."

"I see. That is about the only water on that side of the range, except for a spring further over on your range."

"That's right."

"What will Roarin' Bill Rose do for water?"

"Move his damn cows over on the other side of Broken

Wheel Canyon, I reckon. What the hell do I care what he does with 'em. That's his funeral."

"If he did that," remarked Henry, "it would also give you all the feed on this side of the canyon."

"Wait a minute!" snapped Morgan. "Are you intimatin' that I'm tryin' to run the Lazy R off that range?"

"If there's no water for them—" suggested Judge quietly.

"All right, all right! But no damn man can intimate—"

"Period!" interrupted Henry sharply. "We are merely trying to determine whether my office has any right to interfere. I never intimate. In fact, I don't like the word at all. It is very obvious that if the water is taken from the Lazy R—they must leave that range. Ergo—your cows get the benefit. But does Roarin' Bill confiscate the fence?"

"What's that got to do with it?"

"Merely a point of law, sir. You might have him arrested for stealing your fence. As I see it, the matter is between you and Mr. Rose."

"It's a shootin' matter," declared Morgan grimly.

"Oh, I hope not. Life is too short to kill over water. Now, if it was whisky—"

"Yo're a hell of a sheriff!" roared Morgan hotly. He jumped to his feet and grabbed up his hat.

Henry did not move from his chair.

"Better judges than you, sir, have told me that," he answered. "In fact, long ago, I discovered it for myself."

"All right—I'll protect myself!"

"That, sir, is the very first law of nature," smiled Henry.

MORGAN STALKED out of the office then, grumbling to himself. When he was well out of earshot Judge sighed. "I'm afraid there will be trouble over that water," he said. "Roarin' Bill Rose has only those two dumb Mexican cowboys while Morgan has six or eight pretty tough riders. The odds are against Bill."

"And still," murmured Henry, "I believe Roarin' Bill Rose can take care of himself. Do you know much of his past life, Judge?"

"A little. I believe he was a fugitive from justice when he came here. Perhaps the money he used to purchase his ranch was part of his ill-gotten gains. However, he has gone straight so no one has molested him. His dealings in Wild Horse Valley have all been on the square. I do not believe that Morgan and his Quarter-Circle M outfit have made life any too pleasant for old Roarin' Bill. Personally, I feel that in this case Bill is within his rights."

"I feel the same," Henry said. "I believe I shall speak to Bill. He could get an injunction against Morgan to prevent him from fencing the water."

"Bill Rose will never go to law to settle his troubles," declared Judge. "His only injunction will be a gun."

"Ay vonder vere Olaf vent," said Oscar, feeling of his sore scalp.

"Do you want to apologize to him?" asked Judge.

"Ay vant to poke him in the snu-ute. Yudge."

"You stop poking people in the snoot. Why can't we have some dignity in this office? No wonder they call this 'The Shame of Arizona'."

"True," sighed Henry. "It irks me sore. Oscar, were you ever irked?"

"Ya-ah, su-ure," nodded Oscar. "Von time Ay bought a diamond ring from a drommer for fifty dollar, and Ay found out—"

"Oh, hell!" snorted Judge. "I wish Frijole would bring in some of his abominable prune whisky. Anything to break the monotony. By the way, Oscar, has Frijole quit distilling?"

Frijole Bill Cullison was the cook at Henry's JHC Ranch, and a distiller of prune juice. The finished product was liquid dynamite to the interior of man.

"Ay yust brought gallon yesterday," replied Oscar. "Yumpin' Yudas, das last prune yuice is gude. Ay took t'ree drink at de ranch and Ay saw t'ree hurses. Ay got on de middle von, and de odder two coom along."

"Hm-m!" murmured Henry. "There must be virtue in it, Judge. At least Oscar knew which horse to pick."

"Yust prunes," declared Oscar. "Free-holey says he put in squirt of hurse-leeniment to make it taste gude."

Oscar lumbered into the back room and came back with the jug and some tin cups. Henry sniffed at the liquor.

"Whew! Squirt, eh? Well, gentlemen, my very best to you both."

They drank. Judge and Henry choked, wiped away the tears and looked at each other.

"Not bad," whispered Henry. "It warms the cockles of my heart. I must remember to compliment Frijole."

"Sulphuric acid on a kerosene base," whispered Judge huskily. "My gullet is still smoking. That cook can distill the most damnable concoctions I have ever swallowed. Henry, I wonder what a man would do, if he were to get drunk on that stuff."

"I think," replied Henry, a queer expression on his face, "that if you will watch real close for about ten minutes you'll find out."

"Whooee-e-e!" snorted Oscar, without changing expression. "Ay am about to sink."

"Go ahead," urged Judge expansively. "We will join you in the chorus."

CHAPTER III

WANTED FOR MURDER

AB MORGAN WAS still smarting over his failure to impress the sheriff. Somehow he had expected Henry to be willing to take up the case. He knew the courts would not interfere, because he had no legal ownership of the water. He wanted the water and he also wanted to force the Lazy R cows off that side

of the canyon. Having suffered for the time being a set-back
to his plans, he stalked over to the Tonto Saloon, where he
proceeded to drink too much liquor. It was not often that Ab
Morgan drank to excess, especially when as today, Sally Morgan,
his step-daughter, had come to town with him.

Sally had driven the buckboard team to Tonto City, and when
she finished her shopping she discovered that Ab Morgan was in
no mood to go home. She left him to return to his drinking and
walked worriedly down the street. Sally was twenty, a tall, lithe
young lady—the hope and despair of every cowboy who saw her.

Henry Harrison Conroy, fortified with two drinks of Frijole's prune whisky, met Sally on the street. He doffed his fedora
and bowed.

"It must be," he declared, "that there is a holiday in Heaven.
Otherwise, how could an angel have the time to come to Tonto
City?"

Sally smiled. "Are you ever serious, Mr. Conroy?" she asked.

"My dear Miss Morgan, if I were—er—forty years younger,
I would really be serious. How in the name of all Arizona suns
do you manage to keep so fresh and beautiful?"

"I am neither fresh nor beautiful, Mr. Conroy—I'm just plain
worried. It seems that Dad is—well, he is over at the Tonto
Saloon, and—"

Henry pursed his lips. "I see-e-e. Hm-m-m. Dallying unduly
with the juniper juice."

"I believe so," sighed Sally. "I don't know what to do about it.
I sent word to him that I was ready to go home, and he—sent
word back to me, saying to drive carefully, so as not to break
the eggs."

"Mr. Morgan is a trifle upset over Roarin' Bill Rose, I believe."

"Breathing fire and brimstone," said Sally. "Oh, I hope they
don't get together. They each have a hair-trigger temper."

"I hope not," agreed Henry. "But if you want my advice, Miss
Morgan, I would tell you to go back home alone. You might have

some of the boys come in later, bringing an extra horse. Perhaps, by that time, he will have drunk himself into a state of docility."

"That's true," she agreed. "Maybe your advice is good."

"My advice is always good," smiled Henry, "if you understand what I mean. Judge says that my advice comes from the heart, rather than from the brain; kindly, but rarely consistent."

"You're very honest. Mr. Conroy."

"When Diogenes met me he threw away his lantern," said Henry soberly. "I still have the scar on my head."

Henry walked with her to the buckboard, untied the team for her. She handled the half-wild sorrel team well, waving back at him as they swept out of town.

Pursuing his prune-juice inspired saunter, in front of the post-office Henry met Danny Regan, foreman of his JHC Ranch. Danny was young and impulsive, but competent.

"I've been listenin' to Ab Morgan," Danny announced. "He's shore got a big war-talk, Henry. Says he's goin' to run Roarin' Bill Rose out of the Valley, and then he's goin' to get the Commissioners to force you to resign. He's gettin' pretty drunk. Course, he'll forget it all when he gets sober, but if I was you I wouldn't go over there. Just as well keep away from him while he's in that mood. I reckoned he was kinda workin' around to include me in the talk; so I stepped out."

Henry nodded contemptuously. "I believe he will be all right, unless Roarin' Bill Rose comes to town," he said. "Morgan is inclined to talk big."

EVENING CAME and still Ab Morgan talked. In spite of heavy drinking his intoxication never got beyond the swaggering, boasting point. Cal Essex, Morgan's foreman, and several of the boys rode in, bringing an extra horse.

Later came Roarin' Bill Rose, all alone, and with no information that Ab Morgan wanted his scalp. He went blithely into the Tonto Saloon, where he met Morgan face to face. One glance at Morgan, and Roarin' Bill Rose knew he was facing trouble. Both Rose and Morgan wore holstered guns. Several men, who were directly behind Morgan, moved aside quickly, so as to be out of line of the two men.

"I've been waitin' for you to show up, Rose," said Morgan.

"Sorry to keep yuh waitin'," replied Roarin' Bill grimly. "Hope I ain't too late."

"Yo're just in time."

Roarin' Bill's keen eyes watched Morgan's hands, and there was a thin smile on his face.

"Fingers nervous, Morgan?" he said. "It ain't possible that yo're lookin' for trouble, is it? I never did think yuh had nerve enough to reach for a gun. Still don't think so. What's eatin' yuh, anyway?"

"I sent you a warnin' about that fence, didn't I?" asked Morgan.

"Yeah, that's right."

"And you went out next mornin' and tore it down again."

"That's right. I ain't much of a hand to believe what I read."

"Yuh ain't, eh? Well, I'm goin' to tell yuh somethin'—and you better believe it."

"Go ahead. Mebbe I still won't believe it, Morgan."

"Yo're through in Wild Horse Valley, Rose. I've put up with yuh as long as I'm goin' to. Yore damn outfit ain't worth two whoops in hell, anyway. I'm givin' yuh twenty-four hours to get out of this valley. I hope you understand what I mean."

"Well, yuh didn't leave much for my imagination," said Roarin' Bill. "Twenty-four hours? That's awful funny, Morgan. Or are you so drunk that you don't realize what yo're sayin'?"

"I said—twenty-four hours!" snarled Morgan. "After that— look out for yourself."

"I've been lookin' out myself for years, Morgan. I think yo're a big-mouthed, lantern-jawed, bat-eared bluffer. How about finishin' this deal right here—now? You've got a gun. It'll be an even break. Why wait twenty-four hours? Hell, I'm not movin'; so yuh don't need extra time."

Morgan moistened his lips with his tongue. In spite of the

fact that he was intoxicated he realized the danger of starting a draw. Roarin' Bill, sober, possibly a faster man with a gun at any time, had all the advantage. It would be suicide to move now.

"That twenty-four hours still stands," he said stubbornly. "When that time limit is up—watch out."

Roarin' Bill turned on his heel then and left the saloon. The crowd sighed with relief. The games resumed, and the men proceeded to forget what had been said. Ab Morgan stood moodily at the bar for quite a while, and no one paid any attention when he walked out.

Henry Harrison Conroy heard about the quarrel. He was told that Roarin' Bill had left the saloon and had likely gone home, but a little later Henry saw Roarin' Bill's horse tied in front of the general store. Thinking that trouble was twenty-four hours away, Henry went back to the office, where Judge was reading by the office lamp, and told Judge about Morgan's ultimatum to Roarin' Bill.

"Mr. Morgan must think he is dictator of the valley," said Judge, marking his page by folding it. "Twenty-four hours is rather a short time for a man to dispose of his holdings. I am afraid that Roarin' Bill Rose will still be here when the twenty-four hours have—What was that?"

From somewhere nearby came the muffled thuds which sounded very much like revolver shots. Henry and Judge ran to the doorway. A group of men had left the Tonto Saloon, apparently for the location of the shots. From over in front of the general store a man was calling to them, and they came running. Henry and Judge joined them. The man was Tom Rickey, proprietor of the hotel.

"In the store!" he yelled. "I just went past, when the shooting started!"

They crowded inside the building. Lying on the floor about midway of the room, his head and shoulders against the counter, was Ab Morgan. His six-shooter was lying a foot away from his right hand.

Henry bent down quickly and examined him. When he looked up again his face was very sober.

"He's dead," he said. "But who—how—you!" he blurted at the storekeeper, who stood there, a kerosene can in his hand. "Where were you?"

"Good Lord!" gasped the man. "Why, Roarin' Bill Rose came in here a few minutes ago. He wanted some kerosene. I had to tap a new can; so I—why, he was in here alone, when I left."

Someone yelled outside, and the yell was echoed by the thudding of hoofs. It was then that Henry remembered seeing Roarin' Bill's horse outside the store. Among them, Morgan's men.

"Get your horses and go after him—all of you!" ordered Henry. "I deputize you. We'll be with you as soon as we can get horses. He's gone to his ranch."

"That horse of his couldn't outrun a goat!" exclaimed Cal Essex, Morgan's foreman. "C'mon, boys!"

Henry and Judge hurried to their stable. They saddled clumsily, with Judge complaining about his rheumatism. Judge abhorred horseback riding and he did not care who knew it.

"Roarin' Bill went out the back door, after the shooting," deducted Henry. "He circled the building, while we were inside, and made his escape."

"It dovetails," groaned Judge, as he mounted.

"Dovetails with what?"

"With other asinine deductions you have made. The thing is obvious. Any nine-year-old child could have figured that our."

"I don't suppose I ever will."

"Does that make sense? You don't suppose you ever will. Ever will what?"

"Be a first-class detective, Judge. Now, if you can possibly browbeat that oat-destroyer to a gallop, we might get there before the cowboys get back."

THE EIGHT riders, headed by Cal Essex meanwhile were

thundering in at Roarin' Bill's ranch house. In hopes of overtaking Bill they had run the hearts out of their mounts.

There was a dim light in the main room. A door at the rear closed softly. Two cowboys ran around the house, glimpsecl a dim figure heading for an old shed.

"Stop, before I shoot yuh!" yelled one of the cowboys. As he called he stumbled over an unseen rock. That error saved his life—for on the instant a bullet answered him from the darkness, neatly parting his hair and practically ruining a nearly-new sombrero.

The other cowboy fell over him and went sprawling on the ground. Strangely enough three other figures were running away from the house now, in an entirely different direction. When Cal Essex yelled to them to halt, a volley of bullets whined so close to the six other men of the posse that they dived for safety.

The two cowboys came stumbling around the house and nearly got shot by the six. They finally became normal enough to ask if anybody had shot Roarin' Bill Rose.

"I seen him all right," declared the cowboy whose scalp was still tingling. "I'd have got him, too, except that I stumbled."

"Me, too," added his companion. "Only I fell over you, Gus."

"That's fine," said Essex sarcastically. "Well, we seen three of him—and not a damn one of us fired a shot."

"Three of him, eh?" said the cowboy foolishly. "Well, two of 'em might be Thunder and Lightnin' Mendoza."

"Aw, hell!" snorted Essex. "Them two Mexicans don't even pack guns. You fellers seen one man and we seen three. That's four."

"Eddication is wonderful," sighed a cowboy.

"Yea-a-ah! Yuh ort to get some for yourself. But what four men would be here at the ranch—ready to shoot at us?"

"It's a cinch it ain't Henry and Judge," chuckled one of the men.

They opened the door and crowded into the ranch house.

There were empty cups on the table, and an empty bottle, all smelling strongly of liquor.

Further investigation showed that there were no horses in the stable.

"Well," observed Essex, "it's a cinch that Roarin' Bill didn't come home."

THEY WERE back in the ranch house when Henry and Judge arrived. Essex explained about the shooting in the dark. The one cowboy exhibited a bullet burn across his head, and the damaged sombrero.

"Rather mysterious," agreed Henry. "Four empty cups and an empty whisky bottle."

"And four men, who opened fire upon a command to halt," added Judge soberly. "Who are they, why were they here, and why were they so anxious not to be stopped?"

Henry looked around at the sober faces.

"If any of you pupils can answer any of the teacher's questions—do not hesitate," he said, beaming upon them.

"Hell, he can't answer his own questions!" snorted Cal Essex. "It seems that we can't do a thing here; so I better get back. Are yuh sure Ab Morgan's dead, Henry?"

Henry nodded. "I'm very sorry," he said. "It will be a blow to Miss Sally."

"I hope to tell yuh," agreed Essex.

"You better find Roarin' Bill Rose before we do," said one of the Quarter-Circle M cowboys meaningly.

"Yes, I believe it would be better," replied Henry soberly. "But if you take my advice, you will make it 'we' and not 'I'. Roarin' Bill shoots very straight, they tell me."

They filed out quietly and mounted their horses, leaving Henry and Judge to make their own pace on the return journey.

"There is something complicated about this, Judge," declared Henry, as they rode away from the ranch house. "What four men would be in that house tonight? Roarin' Bill never seemed to have any cronies who knew him so well that they would enter his home, while he was away, and help themselves to his liquor. It smacks of mystery."

"And my old legs smack of rheumatism," groaned Judge. "Mystery! The only real mystery is how I can ever get my two feet close enough together to take a few steps, after riding a horse five miles."

"You are getting old, Judge."

"I am not, sir! Old, indeed! My mind is more alert than when I was twenty."

"Then you should ride standing on your head, Judge. Your underpinning is getting worn. The other day I was reading an article about termites—"

"Are you suggesting that I have termites, sir?"

"Possibly only dry-rot. The article said—"

"Rot! I was just thinking about Sally Morgan. This will hit her very hard, Henry."

"Very. While I am not inclined to wear sackcloth and ashes because of Ab Morgan, I really feel sorry for Sally."

The two rode on in silence then.

CHAPTER IV

MISSING MEN

DAYLIGHT DISCLOSED THE fact that there was blood on the floor of the Tonto general store near the back door, and several splashes on the wooden pavement, where Roarin' Bill Rose had apparently crossed to his horse at the hitch-rack. One cartridge in Ab Morgan's gun had been fired.

"It is evident that Ab Morgan shot Bill Rose," said Henry.

"If it was a fair fight, why did Roarin' Bill run away?" asked Cal Essex.

"My dear boy, that is a question," replied Henry. "Panic, perhaps. Roarin' Bill's reputation is not the best in the world, and perhaps he was afraid it might react against him, in the event that he was arrested. With no witnesses to the shooting, Bill might have felt that the law might not listen kindly to his explanation."

"If Roarin' Bill is wounded, we better look for him," said Judge. "He might be dying out there along the road."

There were plenty of volunteer searchers. They started out promptly. Where the old road winds along the rim of Broken Wheel Canyon there is a pot-hole in the solid rock, known as the Devil's Chimney. It is about twenty feet wide across the top, sloping inward to a ledge, two hundred feet down. This ledge blocks off about two-thirds of the hole and is a mass of broken rock and stunted brush. Here the Chimney narrows to what seems a bottomless hole.

About fifty feet from the edge of the Devil's Chimney one of the searchers discovered Roarin' Bill's old sombrero, recognized by all of them. Near the edge of the hole were sharp marks on the rocks, where shod hoofs had scraped. Sprawling along the rim and peering into the depths, the searchers were able then to see the broken remains of Roarin' Bill's horse and saddle, where the horse had crashed onto the ledge.

There was no sign of Roarin' Bill's body, but there was no doubt in the minds of the searchers that Bill's body lay some-where down there in that tangle of rocks and brush or on the bottom, smashed beyond recognition.

"It was dark as heck last night," said a cowboy. "He was foggin' around this turn, probly runnin' kinda blind, and went right over the edge. You can see them marks, where the horse tried to stop. I figure that Roarin' Bill sunk his spurs pretty deep, when the bronc shifted his stride—and they went over."

"That seems to be the picture," sighed Henry. "But I suppose we may as well ride out to the Lazy R, anyway."

They found Thunder and Lightning Mendoza at the ranch.

They had been down near the Mexican Border, visiting friends, and had just returned. They gazed with apprehension on this group of riders.

"Have yuh seen Roarin' Bill Rose today?" Cal Essex asked them.

"We no see since yes'erday," declared Lightning.

"Where were you fellers last night?"

"We go veesit yes'erday," informed Thunder. "Las' night we stay weeth hees onkle."

Thunder pointed at Lightning.

"Ain't he yore uncle, too?" asked one of the riders.

"I'm theenk so—but I'm get damn tired from argue. Lightning hee's always mak' claim. W'at you want, eh?"

"Perhaps I'd better do the talking," suggested Henry. He turned to the two Mexicans. "Last night Roarin' Bill Rose shot and killed Ab Morgan, in Tonto City."

"*Bway-noo!*" exploded Lightning. It was merely his pronunciation of "*Bueno!*"

"That ees damn good," agreed Thunder.

"Wait a moment, boys," warned Henry.

At that, some of the Quarter-Circle M cowboys started to dismount.

"It is merely a matter of opinion."

He turned to the two Mexicans. "After Roarin' Bill shot and killed Ab Morgan, Roarin' Bill rode out of Tonto City. We suppose he was coming out here, as fast as his horse could run. However, he made a mistake in the dark, and rode his horse over the edge of the Devil's Chimney."

"*Madre de Dios!*" gasped Lightning. "Onkle Beel ees died?"

"It seems that such is the case," replied Henry soberly.

"Well," remarked Thunder, "that ees the firs' time Onkle Beel ever do those."

"He prob'ly won't do it ag'in, either," said a cowboy dryly.

Henry and Judge searched the house, accompanied by Thunder and Lightning. Henry was curious to know if Roarin' Bill had any relatives whom they might notify. Thunder and Lightning did not know. In a table drawer they found a letter from Sam Hartridge, a lawyer in Scorpion Bend.

It was several months old, and was in regard to a will. The lawyer advised Roarin' Bill to rent a safety deposit box in the bank, and keep the will there, instead of in the lawyer's safe. Whether Roarin' Bill had done this remained to be seen.

"That will, wherever it is, might disclose some living relative," said Judge. "We will get in touch with Mr. Hartridge, Henry. I happen to know him, and I can assure you that he is not a credit to the profession. In fact, I feel sure that he is not a bit reliable, when it suits Mr. Hartridge to be otherwise."

"That," remarked Henry soberly, "seems to be part of the curriculum."

"I resent that, sir!"

"I always have," sighed Henry. "But what can be done about it?"

They rode away, leaving Thunder and Lightning wondering what was going to happen to them, with no one left to pay wages.

FROM THE nearby brush, Pecos Charley Peters, Sody Slade, Ed Clovis and Zibe Tucker watched until the riders disappeared.

"It's shore got me fightin' my hat," declared Pecos. "What the hell was the idea of that bunch of riders last night, yellin' at us to stop? And here they are again, along with the sheriff and deputy. I'd shore like to know what's happened to Roarin' Bill."

"Somethin' damn wrong," declared Ed Clovis nervously. "Do yuh suppose they've picked up our trail? Mebbe Roarin' Bill got drunk and talked about us."

"I don't believe that," said Sody. "I'm goin' in and see if them two lazy Mexicans know what's wrong."

"Let's all go," suggested Clovis. "I'm gettin' jumpy."

They found Thunder and Lightning on the little porch.

"Where's Bill Rose?" asked Sody.

"Onkle Beel ees dead," replied Lightning.

"Dead? Good Gawd! Who—how'd he get killed?"

"Leesten," said Lightning. "Onkle Beel hees go to Tonto Ceety and keel Meester Morgan. Then hees ride like hell and fall in to Devil's Cheemney."

The four outlaws looked at each other queerly. With Roarin' Bill Rose dead, they would never be able to realize on their stolen gold ore. After all their hard work and planning—everything was lost.

"Good gosh!" wailed Pecos Charley. "Why—he—he just took that assay sample to Scorpion Bend. He said that assayer was a talkin' fool. A gold strike on the Lazy R—and us livin' in a tunnel!"

"I'm not quittin'," declared Sody Slade. "Not after makin' a pack horse out of myself all that time. A fifth of that gold belongs to me, and I'm goin' to collect."

"I feel the same about it," agreed Clovis. "We'll wait an' see what happens. There's at least seventy-five thousand dollars' worth in there."

They started back to the hide-out. Thunder and Lightning looked at their departing forms and at each other. It was the first time they had heard about the gold in the tunnel. Seventy-five thousand dollars' worth!

"How much ees that?" queried Thunder.

"How much? Hm-m-m. You know how much ees one hunnerd dollars?"

"Sure."

"Thees ees more."

"How much more?"

"*Cuidado!* How the hell you s'pose I'm going to theenk, huh? I'm got to use your brain. Thees job ees gone now. You 'member those lawyer from Scorpion Bend? He come here to see Onkle Beel."

"Sure. W'at he look like?"

"That ees the one. I theenk I go see heem."

"See heem for w'at?"

"Mucho dinero."

"You ask heem for money?"

"Sh-h-h! Keep mouth shut. Say notheeng. You wan' be *vaquero* all my life? Hm-m-m! I'm wan' be reech man. You stay here and cook the frijole, w'ile I'm go to Scorpion Bend."

THAT NIGHT in Scorpion Bend the depot agent, working at his telegraph key, glanced up and saw a man looking through the window. His impression was that the man's bare head was swollen, his hair matted, his eyes blank and staring. Then the man turned slowly away.

A freight train had just arrived, and the agent was too busy to investigate right then. So he did not know that the man had stumbled out along the cars. As he passed one, a door was slid carefully open.

"Lookin' for a place to ride?" a voice called out to him.

The man hesitated, stumbled back toward the open door. Several hands helped him into the box car.

After the train was rolling out of Scorpion Bend, one of the men in the car lighted a match and took a look at their latest passenger. The match burned down to his fingers, and with a choice explosion of profanity he tossed it aside.

"We've got to git this feller off our hands quick as we can," he told the others. "He's in bad shape."

"What's the next stop?" asked one of them.

"Black River City's the next town. This feller may die before we can get him there. If he does, I'm travelin' mighty fast, 'cause it'll sure look like murder."

Back at Scorpion Bend the agent looked all over for the strange-looking man, but could not find him.

CHAPTER V

IMPOSTOR

IRA HALLAM, THE assayer of Scorpion Bend, was short, fat and wheezy. He always needed a shave, his fingers were acid-stained, and he invariably needed a clean shirt. Ira was a particular friend of Sam Hartridge, the lawyer, who was six feet, one inch tall, very skinny, and had a great capacity for whisky. Hartridge always dressed in rusty black, affecting white collars and flowing bow ties.

Just now they were in Hartridge's office on the main street of Scorpion Bend, and Hallam was wheezing with excitement. Hartridge sucked on an empty pipe and waited for Hallam to tell him what all the excitement was about.

"It's a million-dollar strike!" whispered Hallam.

"Who made it?" queried Hartridge.

"Roarin' Bill Rose—but he don't know it yet. I just finished an assay from a sample he brought me—and it's so damn rich that I'm almost afraid I made a mistake. Why, the darned thing was shot full of gold! Jewelry ore—or I've never seen any."

Hartridge carefully filled his pipe, but his lean fingers shook.

"Roarin' Bill Rose, eh?" he muttered. "That old Two-Gun mine. It never produced a dollar. Neither did the old Comanche property, on Morgan's ranch. How do you know this sample came from Roarin' Bill's mine?"

"He told me it did, Sam. He doesn't know a thing about ore. Why, you could see the gold in that sample."

"What are you excited about?" asked Hartridge curiously. "Suppose he has made a strike—what of it, Ira? It doesn't mean that we can find that same ledge and locate it for ourselves."

"I don't know," admitted Hallam. "It—it's so damn rich."

He turned and looked through the window at the street,

where the Scorpion Bend-Tonto City stage was pulling in from Tonto City. On the seat with the driver was Henry Harrison Conroy.

"Old Funny-Face coming to town," laughed Hartridge.

Hallam turned back to him.

"It's so damn rich, Sam," he said again, plaintively.

"Maybe there should be a law against it," laughed Hartridge.

"If we only had the money to buy out the Lazy R," sighed Hallam.

"We could pool about a dollar and six-bits," said Hartridge.

At that moment Henry Harrison Conroy opened the door and walked in.

"I give you good afternoon, Mr. Conroy," said Hartridge pleasantly.

"Thank you—I'll take it."

Hartridge introduced Henry to Ira Hallam, offered the sheriff a chair.

"I understand," stated Henry when he was comfortably seated, "that you have acted as attorney for William Rose of Tonto City. Perhaps he is better known as Roarin' Bill Rose."

"Well, I helped him make out his will," smiled Hartridge. "That is all I have done in that capacity."

"I see. Night before last Roarin' Bill Rose shot and killed Ab Morgan. In making his escape from Tonto City, it appears that Roarin' Bill, accidentally, I suppose, rode his horse over the edge of the Devil's Chimney. We have been unable to locate the body, because of the nature of the place, but can see the horse. It would require about two hundred feet of rope—"

"You say that Roarin' Bill is dead?" interrupted Hartridge.

"Unfortunately—yes. A letter from you, in which you advised him to place his will in a safety deposit box at the bank, came to my attention. Naturally, we are anxious to contact some relative—if he had any."

"Yes," nodded Hartridge, "I wrote him to that effect some

time ago, but he did nothing about it. I still have the will in my safe."

"Does it mention a relative?"

"Yes, it does. I believe he left everything to a nephew, named Frank Neilan, who lives in Detroit—or did live there. I don't believe that Roarin' Bill has heard from him in a long time. Of course, I shall try to get in touch with the man at once, Mr. Conroy."

"Yes. I believe that would be the thing to do."

Henry explained about the shooting, and that the evidence showed that Roarin' Bill had been wounded in the gunfight. Then he rose to go.

"Well, I'll get in touch with this heir of William Rose at once, if possible," said Hartridge. "The will is sealed, but I have the name and address. As soon as he reaches here, we will have a reading of the will and present it for probate."

For several moments after Henry left the office, Hartridge and Hallam looked at each other. Hartridge finally looked away and lighted his pipe.

"I've got the man, Sam," whispered Hallam. "He's a drifter—named Slim. Interested in mining. Hasn't got a dime, and I've been feeding him. Damn it, don't you understand what I'm driving at, Sam?"

"How the hell do you suppose I got admitted to the State bar?" asked Hartridge coldly.

"What about identifications?"

"Leave that to me. I'll write him a letter. He'll bring that letter back with him—from Detroit. Find out how far he'll go on a deal like this—and what he'll want. I'm alone in my house. Bring him out there tonight—late—and we'll talk it over."

"I'll do it," replied Hallam nervously. "Good Lord, Sam—it's a million dollar gamble."

Hartridge shrugged. "With my brains behind it, there's no gamble, Ira. Keep your nerve; you're shaking like a leaf already."

"Wait until you see the button of gold I got out of that

small sample. You'll be shaky, too. I'll see you tonight—about midnight."

THE INQUEST brought no new developments, but because of the strong circumstantial evidence the jury decided that Ab Morgan had come to his death from gunshot wounds inflicted by Roarin' Bill Rose. Ever since the night of the shooting the riders from Quarter-Circle M had ranged the hills, still seeking Roarin' Bill. They did not find him. They knew he had been wounded badly, and the only logical answer was that his body was far down there in the Devil's Chimney; but they wanted to be sure.

"Bill couldn't have gotten out of the valley, wounded as he was, without attracting attention," remarked Henry, as he and Judge and Oscar got together in the office after the inquest. "We will take it for granted that he is at the bottom of that damnable hole in the earth. But who were the four men who shot at the posse that night at the Lazy R? That is the real puzzle, Judge."

Judge shook his head. "It couldn't have been that Bill Rose beat them to the ranch. No, that is out of the question. Hm-m-m. As you remarked before, Roarin' Bill has no friends—no one who would feel free to enter his home during his absence and help themselves to his liquor. What did you think of Mr. Hartridge, the lawyer?"

"Very pleasant, Judge—very. My first impression was that he is an estimable disciple of renowned Blackstone."

"Blackstone! He learned his law from mail-order catalogues."

"Well, that may be. And still, if he knows everything contained in a mail-order catalogue, he has a certain knowledge. Their contents cover many things. You couldn't say that they are narrow or bigoted, Judge."

"Ay bought suit from von," remarked Oscar. "It vars narrow."

"But not bigoted," said Henry.

"Yust in de pants."

"I see—the pants were bigoted. Well, that might happen.

By the way, how are you and Josephine hitting it off these days, Oscar?"

"Hitting? Yumpin' Yudas! Ay haven't been to see Yosephine since she t'rew de pitcher. Last night Ay saw her t'rough de vindow and she made a snu-ute at me. Ay made snu-ute right back at her, by Yiminy."

"That is love," choked Judge. "Two adult Swedes making snoots at each other through a window. Who won, Oscar?"

"Ve vere not snu-uting for a prize, Ay'll say dat."

"Go and get Frijole's jug," ordered Henry huskily. "I feel a nervous breakdown coming on. Hurry, Oscar."

THE BLINDS were drawn tight in Sam Hartridge's little home at Scorpion Bend. Sam was a bachelor, living alone, and taking most of his meals at a restaurant. Ira Hallam, the assayer, sprawled in an easy chair, while the third man sat near him, his hat on his lap.

He was the man they called Slim. His clothes were not of the best, but were fairly neat and clean. He was tall and lithe, his features clean-cut. He was perhaps twenty-five years of age.

"Did Hallam tell you anything about this deal?" asked Hartridge.

"Nothing, except that you wanted to talk with me," replied the young man.

"What is your right name?"

"We don't need to go into that, do we?" queried the young man.

Hartridge smiled knowingly. "Not at all, Slim. One name is as good as another. Hallam told me you were from the East."

"This is my first trip west."

"Good. No one knows you in this country?"

"Not a soul."

"Hallam says you are interested in mining."

"I studied it at college. They threw me out, before I had a

chance to graduate. Yes, I know something about it. That was how I happened to meet Mr. Hallam. I saw his office sign."

"That makes it work out fine," smiled Hartridge. "Here is the deal...."

Slim listened in amazement as the lawyer outlined their scheme to get control of the Lazy R and, incidentally, the newly discovered gold vein. He told Slim all about Roarin' Bill Rose, about his troubles with the Morgan outfit, and the subsequent tragedy in Tonto City.

"I believe I understand the deal," said Slim when he had finished. "You want me to impersonate this heir, take over the property, and at the proper time sell out to you—at your price."

"That," nodded Hartridge, "is exactly what we want."

"Isn't it a dangerous undertaking?"

"Where is the danger? Roarin' Bill told me himself that he never saw this nephew in his life. He said he wasn't sure he was still alive—but that the man was his only living relative. I don't need to investigate. What the nephew doesn't know won't hurt him. News of that kind would never get to him. There will be no trouble in probating that will. Why, the deal is air-tight. You sell out to us, leave the country—and that's all there is to the deal."

"And what do I get?"

Hartridge frowned thoughtfully for several moments.

"That is something that Ira and I did not decide."

"Oh, we'll take care of that," assured the assayer quickly.

"Not with me," replied Slim. "A deal is a deal. As long as I'm the main character in the deal, I'll take a third of the profits."

"Oh well, now wait a minute!" exclaimed Hartridge. "You couldn't ask that much, Slim."

The young man grinned slowly. "One-third, gentlemen."

"It might be arranged," said Hallam. "You see, Sam, if he was a partner—well, he couldn't hold us up—blackmail, I mean."

"Well, all right. It might be better, at that. Is it a deal, Slim?"

"Sure," nodded Slim.

The blow landed square on the button.
The foreman went down.

"What about a written agreement?" queried Hallam.

"Not for me," said Slim quickly. "Nothing on paper."

"That's right," agreed Hartridge. "It's too dangerous. We've got to take each other's word for this deal."

"When do we start?" asked Hallam anxiously, now that the deal was assured.

"As soon as the heir gets here," laughed Hartridge. "My letter should get there about day after tomorrow and—"

"Good Lord, you didn't write him, did you, Sam?" interrupted Hallam.

"Certainly not! It will take him about four days to get here. That will be about next Tuesday. Yes, that would time it about right. I'll give Slim enough money for expenses and some better clothes, and he can go to Black River City. He can kind of keep under cover, until Tuesday morning, when he can take a train back here. Is that satisfactory to you, Slim?"

"Sure. I'll take that midnight train tonight."

"Right."

"Just one more detail, Mr. Hartridge," smiled Slim. "You haven't told me who I'm to impersonate."

"The name," replied the lawyer, "is Frank Neilan, and you are from Detroit."

"Frank Neilan from Detroit," muttered Slim. "Why—uh—that's fine. Frank Neilan. Will I have to answer any questions about my relatives, or anything?"

"I don't know why you should. Anyway, you'll know as much about them as the man who asks the questions."

"Yes, I suppose that is true," grinned Slim. "Give me that money—and I'll see you Tuesday. From now on I'm Frank Neilan."

"And don't forget it," added Hallam.

"Don't worry; I won't forget."

CHAPTER VI

CAL ESSEX'S ULTIMATUM

AB MORGAN HAD been proud of his Quarter-Circle M Ranch. He had spent a lot of money to make it liveable. Originally it had been only a huddle of adobe shacks in a sycamore grove; he rebuilt and remodeled until it was to his liking. The ranch house was a two-story adobe and frame, nearly surrounded with a thick patio wall, with arched gates and heavy wrought iron. The patio was flagged, its walls covered with climbing roses.

Sally's mother had died when Sally was twelve, but Ab Morgan had never married again. Sally had been four when her mother and Ab Morgan married, and she had never known another father.

Morgan had always surrounded himself with hard-riding, hard-bitted cowboys, and Cal Essex and the rest of his present crew were no exception. Cal Essex wanted Sally Morgan; he had wanted her ever since he had first seen her, two years ago, but had been careful to hide it from Morgan, who had told him that he was going to select a mate for Sally. Ab Morgan was under six feet of dirt now; so there was nothing to prevent Cal Essex from asking Sally to marry him. Cal was not a man to waste time; so already today he had come to the ranch house and spoken his piece.

Judging from the expression on his face now, though, as he stood at the bottom of the front steps and looked up at Sally, his invitation had not been accepted.

"All right," he said huskily, his face a trifle white under its coat of bronze. "You know how I feel, Sally. But that's all right. I—I reckon you'll want me to take charge of everything—about the ranch—now."

"You'll still be the foreman," Sally told him evenly. "I will run the ranch."

Cal Essex laughed shortly and looked away for a moment.

"Pretty big job for a girl," he said. "The boys won't like it very well—havin' a woman runnin' things, yuh know."

"Well, that's just too bad."

"You know what I mean. They're used to havin' a man boss."

"They've got a woman boss now."

Essex shrugged his shoulders.

"Go ahead. But I'm tellin' yuh that you've got eight tough boys to boss, Sally."

Sally's eyes flashed.

"If I can't boss them—I'll fire them," she declared.

He came up the steps till he was close to her again, and spoke with lowered voice.

"I wouldn't do that," he said. "I don't like to tell yuh this, but before you make any mistakes, I reckon you better know all about it. Those boys stole cattle from the Lazy R—actin' on yore father's orders. If you fire any of 'em—they might talk."

Involuntarily, Sally took a step backward. She stared at him in horrified amazement.

"My father stole cattle?" she whispered.

"Plenty. He wanted to break Bill Rose."

"Oh, that isn't possible! Cal, you're lying to me!"

"You can say that—'cause yo're a woman."

"Woman or no woman, I still say it, Cal Essex. Dad isn't here to defend himself. Oh, it isn't true; my dad wasn't a thief."

Cal smiled thinly.

"Wasn't he? Well, my advice to you would be to set tight. I'd hate to have Wild Horse Valley know what he was. And don't forget that *they stole cattle an his orders.*"

With that Cal Essxex turned away and sauntered down toward the stables. Sally stood there, staring after him, heartsick and helpless.

"I reckon I've got you hogtied, young lady," Cal chuckled to himself, "and I'll be runnin' this ranch, if anybody stops to ask yuh. She don't dare ask anybody if it's true."

SALLY MORGAN tried to think things over calmly. Cal Essex wanted to boss the Quarter-Circle M. It was the first time that she had ever detected meanness in Cal Essex, and she realized that it amounted to blackmail. Unless he had his way he would denounce Ab Morgan as a rustler. She knew Ab Morgan had tried in just about every possible way to run Roarin' Bill Rose out of the valley, but she had never dreamed that he was stealing Rose's cattle. Yet she could not prove that he did not steal them—and Cal Essex probably could prove that he did, because he would have the able assistance of his cowboys.

Sally finally came to a decision. In this extremity there was only one man in the valley whom she felt she could trust—and that man was Henry Harrison Conroy. Sally felt sure that she could tell him the story, and that it would never be repeated.

She hitched up her own buckboard team and started for Tonto City. Her sudden decision to go to town piqued the curiosity of Cal Essex. He promptly sent one of the cowboys after

her on the trail to Tonto City, in order to find out where Sally
went and whom she talked with.

By the time the cowboy arrived, the team was tied at a little-
used hitch-rack, with Sally and the Sheriff Henry sitting in the
buckboard, talking earnestly.

If Henry felt any amazement over the story Sally told him,
he did not show it. He merely rubbed his red nose with two
fingers and a thumb, his small eyes squinting thoughtfully, until
she finished.

"My dear, I am not surprised at Mr. Essex," he said dryly.
"My own idea is that, given the opportunity, Mr. Essex would
be what the Mexicans call a *mucho malo hombre.* As far as your
stepfather being a cattle rustler—I go into my Spanish again
and say, *'Quien sabe?'* "

"You believe he really did steal Lazy R cattle, Mr. Conroy?"
Sally asked.

"Merely an old custom—revived at times, I believe, Miss
Sally. But it is bad form on the part of Mr. Essex to taunt you
with it. I can see his reasons. Your refusal to consider his prop-
osition of matrimony—and I really could not blame him for
that—caused him to show his real colors. My advice would be
to continue to run the ranch as you see fit. After all, a denunci-
ation from him would also implicate him as a rustler."

"But I don't want it to be said that Dad was a thief," sighed
Sally.

Henry nodded.

"Cal Essex realizes that. That is his strength." Then he told
her: "By the way, I got a letter from Samuel Hartridge, attorney
at law at Scorpion Bend, saying that a young man named Frank
Neilan, nephew and heir to the Lazy R, is on his way here from
Detroit, and will arrive very soon."

"I heard that he had left everything to his nephew," Sally
answered. Then she added, impulsively, "Mr. Conroy, in spite of
everything that has been done, I liked Roarin' Bill Rose. Before
there was real trouble between our ranches he used to come over

and visit. He seemed to be a kindly man, but lonesome. All he had to talk to were Thunder and Lightning."

"He was all right," nodded Henry soberly. "His past was rather checkered, I believe, but he played a square game in this valley. I feel that the gunfight was an even break. Roarin' Bill was shot. Perhaps in his panic and injury, and with no witnesses, he felt that the law would not give him an even break. No doubt they would dig up his past—which might not look good to a jury."

"That was why I came to see you," said Sally. "You seem to always make allowances for failings in human nature. I'm sure our conversation won't be repeated."

"You may rest assured of that, my dear lady."

He climbed down from the buckboard then, bowed and left her. Sally went on to the post-office for the mail, and Cal Essex's spy rode back to the ranch ahead of her.

"She went to see the sheriff," he reported. "They set in the buckboard for quite a while, talkin' together."

"Now what the heck is she framin' up with that potato-nosed hunk of lard?" wondered Cal Essex. "If he gets smart with me, he'll wish he'd stayed in a theater, I'll tell yuh that."

"I heard a feller sayin' in the Tonto Saloon that Roarin' Bill's nephew will be here pretty quick to take over the Lazy R," the puncher said. "He's a city man, and prob'ly don't know beef from bull's-foot."

Cal Essex grinned thoughtfully. "We'll make life tough for that tenderfoot, Art. I'll figure out sometin', after I get a look at him."

"Sure."

"Are you and Steve still watchin' the Lazy R Ranch?"

"We was out there the last two nights until midnight, but all we seen was them two Mexicans."

"Uh-huh. I'd sure like to know who them four men were that shot at us that night."

"So would the sheriff's office," laughed Art. "I heard Judge

Van Treece talkin' about it. They don't know any more than we do."

HENRY WAS back in his office when Lawyer Sam Hartridge appeared. The man he brought with him seemed far more presentable than Slim, the drifter, had been in Scorpion Bend. His suit was fairly new, shoes shined, a new hat and he was well barbered.

"Sheriff Conroy," Hartridge said, "I want you to meet Frank Neilan, heir to the Lazy R. Frank, this is our sheriff, Mr. Conroy."

Henry showed no surprise. "Frank Neilan, I am glad to meet you, sir," he said. "Welcome to Tonto City. I want you to meet Judge Van Treece, my deputy—and Oscar Johnson, the jailer. Gentlemen, this is Mr. Neilan, new owner of the Lazy R."

Judge and Oscar shook hands solemnly with the newcomer, welcoming him to Wild Horse Valley.

"Mr. Neilan knows all about the trouble here," said the lawyer. "I have told him all the history of the feud."

"My uncle," said Frank Neilan, "must have been rather an interesting character."

"He vars a fighting yigger," declared Oscar blandly.

"Yes, I believe he was," smiled Neilan.

"Is this your first trip west?" asked Henry.

"Yes, sir."

"Do you know anything about cattle or horses?"

"Very little," admitted the young man. "I have studied mining, but have had no practical experience."

"You will probably get very little around here," said Judge.

"Mr. Neilan will learn," Hartridge assured them.

"They usually do—in Arizona," said Henry dryly. "You are going out to the ranch today?"

"We are on our way out there," replied Hartridge. "I believe Mr. Neilan will live out there, waiting for the will to be probated. He can learn ranching only by practical experience."

"With Thunder and Lightning to teach him, he should know it all in less than a week," said Henry.

Frank Neilan laughed. "Mr. Hartridge told me about those two. I hope you gentlemen will ride out to see me once in a while."

"Why, certainly," nodded Henry. "You see—"

He broke off, for at that moment Sally Morgan stepped into the doorway.

Henry got to his feet. "My dear lady, come in!" he exclaimed.

Just inside the door, Sally hesitated. "I beg your pardon," she said hastily. "I didn't know I was interrupting—"

"You are not," Henry assured her. "Miss Morgan, you have to meet Mr. Hartridge. May I present Mr. Frank Neilan. Mr. Neilan, this is Miss Morgan."

"Miss Morgan, I am very glad—er—" Then Frank Neilan hesitated.

"Very true," interrupted Henry quickly. "Miss Morgan's stepfather and your uncle—"

The young man stepped toward Sally then, smiling. "But what of it?" he interrupted. "After all, that feud was between Miss Morgan's stepfather and my uncle. I don't see why it's necessary for the two remaining members of the family to carry it any further."

"God forbid!" grunted Judge hollowly. Frank Neilan turned to Sally.

"Miss Morgan," Frank Neilan added. "I did not even know my uncle. In fact, I barely remembered that such a person existed. I hope we can be friends."

She held out her hand.

"I see no reason why not," she answered.

He took the hand. "You're very kind," he said.

Sam Hartridge's face showed the suspicion of a frown.

"I think we will be going on," he announced very quickly. "I have to drive back to Scorpion Bend, you know."

They left then, the young man not without a backward glance at Sally.

Minutes later, as they were driving over the rough road to the Lazy R, he said:

"She's beautiful, Hartridge."

"Sally Morgan? Of course she is. But what of it?" Hartridge growled. "You're in here to help us make some big money; so keep away from women. You can't afford to get mixed up in anything—except our deal."

"I know. Well, the officers accepted me at face value."

"Did they? How do you know?"

"Well, they seemed too, anyway. They didn't ask any questions."

"You were not on trial."

Neilan looked at the lawyer closely. "What's wrong with you, Hartridge?" he asked.

"Not a damn thing. I merely want you to understand that you've got a serious job ahead of you. Don't be too friendly at the Morgan place. We can't afford to have anything go wrong. Remember, Hallam and I are respectable citizens."

"And I'm not, eh?"

"Damn it, *you've got to be.*"

The young man shrugged.

"Oh, all right. I'll take care of my end, but I still think that Sally Morgan's a beautiful girl."

"I won't argue with you."

PECOS CHARLEY PETERS was in the Lazy R ranch house when the horse and buggy came into the yard. He had been trying to get some information from Thunder and Lightning about conditions. There was no chance now for him to leave the ranch house unseen; so he went down into the little root-house under the kitchen, after which Lightning moved the table over the small trapdoor. He had just gotten it in place when

Hartridge, without ceremony, stepped into the kitchen, with the stranger at his side.

"This is your new boss, boys," informed Hartridge, indicating the young man with him. "You will take orders from him, just as you took orders from Roarin' Bill Rose."

"Sure," agreed Lightning heartily. "He tells us go to hell—we not go. Jus' like Onkle Beel."

"That's right," agreed Neilan with a grin.

The two then investigated the little ranch house thoroughly.

"My uncle was not exactly a good housekeeper," smiled Neilan when the inspection was finished.

"You can stand a little dirt," said Hartridge.

The two Mexicans went outside then, and Hartridge and Neilan sat down in the kitchen.

"So far, so good," declared Hartridge. "No one has questioned the fact that you are Bill Rose's nephew; and they won't. Stick around here and boss the place, until after everything is settled. Keep sober and keep away from the Quarter-Circle M. As soon as it is possible, we will discover that rich mine. Hallam and I will buy you out, and you'll head for parts unknown, but before that we'll have an agreement drawn up, which will give you one-third of the profits. Don't you worry—you'll get your share."

"Yes, I believe I will," replied Neilan.

When Neilan went back to the buggy with Hartridge to see him off, a little later, Pecos Charley sneaked out of the kitchen and made his way down to the brush past the stable. Through the cracks in the kitchen flooring he had heard enough of the conversation to know that there was a deep dyed and pretty devious plot against the Lazy R.

Down at the stable Thunder and Lightning, unaware of Pecos' discovery, talked things over.

"So that ees new boss, eh?" remarked Lightning. "I'm bet he don' know one cow from two calf."

"Sure," agreed Thunder expansively. "But jus' like Onkle Beel say, theese rolling stone ees wort' two in the hand."

"Sure. You never can tell, that's all I hope."

"I'm bet you get your weesh," added Thunder. "W'en are you goin' make deal weeth those lawyer?"

"I'm theenk eet over. Pecos Charley hes say to me, 'You damn Mexican, you say one word 'bout us and I keel you too dead to skeen yourself all over.' How you like that, eh?"

"You are my brodder—I'm cry like hell."

"He skeen you, too."

"Por Dios, thees Pecos ees toff jeeger. I'm theenk we better not talk too much, eh?"

"We better not talk any; I'm only got one skeen."

CHAPTER VII

LEAD WITH THE RIGHT

FRANK NEILAN WAS not a horseman. In fact, he had only been in a saddle twice in his lifetime. This, on the second day of his stay at the Lazy R, was to be the third. Lightning saddled a horse for him, and pointed out the trail he had said he was taking, the trail to the Quarter-Circle M.

"I hope this horse is gentle," said Neilan apprehensively as he climbed aboard.

"Those horse ees so gentle that hees eat off your hand," assured Lightning. "Those horse never do notheeng wrong in my life."

It was about five miles to the Morgan ranch house, but the trail was wide, and Neilan had no difficulty in finding the place. He dismounted stiffly at the patio gate. Sally was cutting roses, as he came into the patio. There was no one else in sight.

He walked up to her, doffing his hat, suddenly a little embarrassed.

"I—I just wanted to be neighborly," he told her lamely.

Sally smiled at him. "I'm glad you do," she said. "And how do you like your ranch, Mr. Neilan?"

"It isn't much like this one, Miss Morgan," he laughed. "I'm afraid my late uncle wasn't an adept housekeeper. And those two Mexicans!"

"Funny, aren't they?"

"The way they crucify the English language. Half the time I don't know what they're talking about."

"Neither do they," laughed Sally. "Your uncle liked them, though."

"Well, maybe I will—in time."

They sat down on a shaded bench and Sally told him about the folks of Wild Horse Valley. Neilan was a willing listener. He wanted to know something of the cattle business, admitted that he knew nothing. For an hour or more they talked, while Neilan's old mount dozed beside the patio gate.

Then Cal Essex and two of his riders came home. They recognized the old horse.

"Four bits against a duck egg it's that new owner of the Lazy R," said one of the boys. "Got plenty crust—comin' over here."

A few minutes later Sally came to the patio gate with Neilan, and then went back. Neilan mounted and rode out. Essex, a scowl on his face, accosted him at the main gate.

"Yo're the new owner of the Lazy R, ain't yuh?" he asked.

"Why, yes. My name is Neilan." He was a little surprised at the foreman's angry scowl.

"Names don't mean much to us folks," Essex told him, "as long as yo're from the Lazy R. The less we see of yuh, the better it'll be for all of us."

"Oh, are you the owner of this ranch?" Neilan asked with seeming politeness.

"I'm the boss," replied Essex coldly. "Bill Rose wasn't welcome here; so I don't know of any reason why his relatives should be."

"Yes, that's true," agreed Neilan. "But on the other hand, you'll always be welcome at the Lazy R."

"Don't worry—we won't come there—unless it's on business."

"Business?"

"Sure. If somebody does somethin' we don't like—we come visitin'."

"I see," smiled Neilan. "I hope I don't do anything to incur your displeasure."

"I'm overlookin' yore visit today, 'cause you didn't know better. Stay on yore own range, Neilan. We don't care for visitors."

"Isn't that laying it on a little thick?" queried Neilan, still politely. "After all, I believe this ranch belongs to Miss Morgan, and she didn't order me to stay away."

"Listen, feller," growled Essex, "I'm runnin' this ranch—and if you give me any more of yore lip, I'll yank yuh off that saddle and rub yore nose in the dirt."

"Really?" gulped Neilan.

"Yuh don't think I can?"

"I don't want any trouble. I'm not a fighter. Anyway, you've got a gun—and I don't like guns. I don't exactly want to get shot."

Grinning wolfishly, Essex drew the gun and balanced it on a fencepost. Then he turned back to Neilan.

"Keep talkin', feller," he said. "Yo're safe from that gun now." Neilan backed up a step.

"Really, there isn't anything for us to fight over," said Neilan. "I'm not—"

"Get off that horse, before I yank yuh off," interrupted Essex savagely. "When I get through with you—you won't want to come back."

Neilan seemed to sigh. "Well, if I must," he said.

HE DISMOUNTED clumsily, Cal Essex swung at his jaw before he had both feet on the ground—but Neilan's head twisted just enough for the blow to smash against the saddle. The force of the blow sent Essex staggering against Neilan. The latter merely shouldered him quickly aside, and stepped a few feet away.

Essex stepped back, breathing heavily. At the corner of the patio the two cowboys grinned widely. They could easily visualize what Cal Essex would do to this fool tenderfoot.

"Rather dirty tactics," remarked Neilan. "Good thing I was looking for that blow, or my nose might be in the dirt."

His hands hung loosely at his sides.

"Are yuh goin' to fight, or stand there?" snarled Essex. His knuckles ached from that smash against hard leather.

"I'm afraid you'll have to do the fighting," smiled Neilan. "It was solely your idea."

"Scared to fight, eh?"

"A little."

"All right, feller, you've got it comin'."

Essex rushed in, swinging a right-hand blow at Neilan's chin—but the blow only met open air. The next moment, the foreman was flat on his back—dropped by a left-hook which had caught him square on the button!

The two cowboys, gasping with amazement, came running. Essex was out for a rather long count, it seemed.

"He led with his right," said Neilan quietly.

"Led with his—huh? Well, I'll be danged! First time I ever seen Cal knocked down. Stranger, you better not be here, when he wakes up."

"I was here before he went to sleep," reminded Neilan.

"Yeah, that's right. He's comin' out of it, I reckon."

Essex recovered sufficiently to stand on wobbly legs, but there was no more fight in him. He looked blankly at Neilan, as though trying to understand what had happened. The cowboys took him by the arms and gently led him up to the bunk-house; then Neilan mounted his old horse and headed back toward the Lazy R.

He didn't know that Sally Morgan had seen the fight from

a front window of the ranch house, that there was a smile of extreme satisfaction on her face as she lowered the curtain and turned away.

Meanwhile, a drink of whisky and a few cold towels drove the fog from Essex's brain, and the two cowboys told him what had happened. When one of the cowboys said he was sure that Sally had seen the fight from a front window, a cold rage showed in Cal Essex's face. The cowboy had seen her drop the curtain.

"I thought you'd whip him easy, Cal," said one of the boys. "He don't look like a fighter to me."

"I guess he was just lucky," said Essex painfully.

"If he is, I'd like that kinda luck," said the other cowboy.

"All right," growled Essex. "I'll get him—don't worry."

"Sure yuh will, Cal. But don't lead with yore right hand again."

"Don't tell me what to do! I can whip a dozen like him."

"Oh, sure. You was prob'ly off balance."

"That's right. Guess I slipped."

But down in his heart Cal Essex knew that he had not slipped, nor had he been off balance. All he remembered was that he had lashed out with his right fist—and everything had gone black.

"We'll make it so tough for him that he won't stay," said one of the cowboys.

"You leave him to me," ordered Essex. "He's my special meat."

"You shore can have my helpin'," said the cowboy dryly.

THE HEIR to the Lazy R spent next day helping Thunder and Lightning clean house. With many gallons of hot water, plenty of soap, and a quantity of elbow grease, they made the ranch house presentable.

"Isn't that better?" he asked Lightning that evening, as they surveyed the scrubbed interior of the house.

"Eet ees ver' good," admitted the Mexican. "But w'at ees the use? *Mañana* eet gets dirty again."

"Well, if it does, we'll clean it again."

Lightning looked a little horrified, then shrugged his shoulders. Apparently the man was crazy, he decided.

That night, while Neilan was reading an old magazine by the lamplight, and the two Mexicans were deep in their jumping-bean game at a table, the outside door was suddenly shoved open. With no other warning, in filed Pecos Charley, Sody Slade, Ed Clovis and Zibe Tucker.

Lightning jerked to his feet.

"Madre de Dios!" he blurted.

"That's all right, Mex," assured Pecos Charley. "Set down and play yore game. Don't worry about us."

Frank Neilan got quickly to his feet.

"Good evening, gentlemen," he said pleasantly. "You startled me for a moment."

Pecos Charley laughed shortly. "Prob'ly startle yuh longer than that, before we git through. Set down—don't mind us."

"I—I don't believe I've met you," stammered Neilan. "Are you from the Morgan ranch?"

"That's shore funny as hell," remarked Sody Slade. "From the Morgan ranch, eh?"

"I didn't know," said Neilan. He could see that there was something sinister about these four rough, bearded men, well armed.

"Well, I can tell yuh—we're not from the Morgan ranch," informed Pecos Charley. "We was pardners with Roarin' Bill Rose."

"With my uncle?"

"Uncle—hell! Listen, feller: I was in this house when you and that crooked lawyer talked things over. I know yore game. Yo're just as crooked as a dog's hind laig—and so is he. Yo're makin' out to be Roarin' Bill's nephew. Well, we know yuh ain't—*sabe?*"

"Is that right!" gasped Neilan.

"Ain't much right to it, as far as we can see," stated Clovis.

"We could go down to Touto City and tell what we know,

and they'd tar and feather you, Mr. Tenderfoot," declared Pecos Charley.

Neilan looked very worried. "I—I suppose they would," he agreed.

"All right," said Pecos Charley. "We'll tell yuh *our* story. After you've heard it, *you better set in the game with us.*"

"Well, I—you seem to have the better of me, gentlemen."

"Yo're doggone right we have," laughed Clovis. "Tell him, Pecos."

Beginning with the day they had ridden in and discovered their old partner Roarin' Bill Rose, Pecos Charley told Neilan of how they had hidden in the old mine on Morgan's ranch, until they accidentally discovered the vein of jewelry ore. He told of the nights of back-breaking work in digging out this vein and carrying it over to Roarin' Bill's old Two-Gun mine, where, after the vein was worked out, they had dropped a chunk of the tunnel in, blocking it entirely.

"You can see what Bill's death meant to us," said Pecos. "It sure ruined a stake for us, when he willed this place to his nephew. Well, we stuck around, waitin' to see what happened—and it happened. You and that crooked lawyer talked too much—and I heard yuh. Mebbe you don't know it, but yo're goin' to pick up where Roarin' Bill left off. You'll reopen the mine, ship the ore we gathered, split it five ways—and we get out. How do you feel about it."

"But it's stolen ore," protested Neilan.

"You half-witted road-runner, you!" snorted Pecos. "Course it's stolen. Ain't you stealin' this whole danged ranch? We're not kickin' about yore crooked work, are we?"

"That's true," agreed Neilan.

"All right—that's settled," said Pecos. "Shake hands with yore new pardners, *Mister Neilan.*"

The four men filed past and shook hands with him.

"How soon can we dig that gold out?" asked Clovis.

"Why—er—the will has to be probated first," Neilan

answered hesitantly. "I—I don't know how soon we can dig it out."

"Well," said Zibe Tucker, "we've talked it over among us. We figure that the law has kinda passed us by, by now. Anyway, we was only wanted for stealin' horses—and things; so we'll take a chance. We're danged good and tired of livin' underground; so we decided to hire on with the Lazy R."

Frank Neilan gasped, swallowed thickly, but seemed unable to speak.

"Oh, we're damn good cowpunchers, pardner," Zibe assured him.

"Por Dios!" gasped Lightning. "Seex *vaqueros* for seexty cow."

"Ten cows apieces, eh?" grinned Pecos Charley. "Well, that's about my size."

"But—but they will ask questions," protested Neilan.

"That's all right," assured Pecos. "We heard about you needin' men, while we was over in Black River City; so we rode over the hill—and got the jobs."

"All right," choked Neilan. "I—I guess you're hired, boys."

"THAT'S THE right spirit!" exclaimed Sody. "We'll add a lot of class to this here rancho. Another thing, if them Morgan chickadees come pokin' around here, we'll plumb ventilate 'em for yuh."

"Wait a minute!" gasped Neilan. "I told them they'd be welcome."

"Lovely dove! You ain't buried the hatchet, have yuh?"

"Well—not exactly. I was obliged to knock out their fore-man today."

"You—wait a minute! You knocked out Cal Essex?"

"I think that's his name. He led with his right, and I countered with my left. It was all very simple."

The four outlaws looked at each other for several moments in silence. Roarin' Bill had told them that Cal Essex had whipped every fighter in Wild Horse Valley. They had seen the Quarter-Circle M foreman, and they knew he had a great physical advantage over this young man.

"I reckon we'll go out and pack in our warbags," said Pecos Charley finally; "If I didn't know positively that yo're a danged liar, I'd almost believe yuh *are* Roarin' Bill's nephew."

"What about these Mexicans?" queried Clovis. "Can we trust 'em?"

"Them two?" sneered Pecos Charley. "One peep out of them, and I'll slit their throats. They won't talk. C'mon."

"W'at ees a peep?" queried Thunder fearfully, after the four had gone.

"A peep?" parroted Lightning. "A peep ees—well, you make one."

"You like see me get your neck sleet?"

"Eef you do, I know damn well what ees a peep."

"Good lord!" groaned Frank Neilan. And he quoted, " 'What a tangled web we weave, when first we practice to deceive.'"

"Sure," agreed Lightning soberly. "Theese crooked business get you een trouble clear up around my neck."

"Yes, I think you're right, Lightning," Neilan said. "Well, I've always longed for excitement—and I guess I'm going to get plenty of it. Good night."

"*Buenas noches,*" replied Lightning.

"I suppose I'm going to have to learn Spanish," Neilan said.

"W'at ees the use? Me and Thonder spik damn good from English. I'm learn first, and then I'm learn heem. He's pretty damn good, too."

"Do you and Thunder talk Spanish to each other?"

"No-o-o. You onnerstand theese Spanish ees not so damn good for saying theengs. Eef I am spiking Englis' I can onnerstand myself better than you can eef you are leestening to Thonder spiking Englis' to me. That ees the deeference—I hope."

"I hope so, too," agreed Neilan. He was choking again, but not from fear....

CHAPTER VIII

BULLETS AT THE SPRING

"**MR. HARTRIDGE, I** have no personal interest in the case," stated Judge Van Treece. "I am merely telling you that Judge Myers will not accept that will for probate, because of *corpus delicti*. If you had really studied law, you should know that."

Sam Hartridge flushed quickly. Henry, seated behind his desk in the sheriff's office, emitted a faint chuckle.

"I am aware of that point, sir," stated Hartridge. "But the circumstances are peculiar. We all feel satisfied that William Rose is at the bottom of Devil's Chimney."

"But you can't prove it."

"The law can't prove he isn't," flared the lawyer.

"My dear young man," propounded Judge, "the law doesn't need to prove anything. It will say, 'Produce the body as evidence of death!'"

"An impossible thing, under the circumstances."

Judge nodded with seeming sadness.

"The limit is seven years, I believe. After seven years, the law may declare him legally dead, you know."

Hartridge snorted indignantly. "Why, it would be ridiculous for Frank Neilan to have to wait seven years to get title to the Lazy R." He could see his well-planned scheme falling to pieces.

"You might find a rope long enough to let you investigate the Chimney," suggested Henry.

"Impossible," replied the lawyer. "I've been out there. It's at least two hundred feet to where the horse smashed up on that ledge. Why, if you toss a big rock over there, you never hear it strike bottom."

"Yes, that's true," nodded Judge. "I am very much afraid that poor old Roarin' Bill's remains are not available."

While Hartridge sat silent in glum meditation, Oscar Johnson came riding up the street. He tied his horse in front of the office. In his high-heel boots and big sombrero Oscar Johnson was a giant. He came clumping into the office, brushing his hat off on the top of the doorway. He picked it up, sent it sailing into a corner and looked seriously at Henry.

"Ay vent up dere," he announced. "Yumpin' Yudas, he's got four of de toughest cowponchers Ay ever seen."

"Wait a minute," said Henry. "You went up to the Lazy R?"

"Ay vent to de Lazy R," nodded Oscar. "Yust like you ordered, Ay vent to see how dis tanderfoot vars getting along. Yah, su-ure."

"All right, Oscar. You went to see how this tenderfoot was getting along. And what happened?"

"Ay met four of de toughest cowponchers Ay ever seen. Van of dem says to me, 'What de ha'al do you vant ha'ar?'"

"Ay told him Ay came to see how dis tanderfoot vars getting along. Yust den de tanderfoot coom out, and he introduce me to de four cowponchers. He says he hired 'em."

"Hired four cowpunchers?" gasped Hartridge. "Why—why, there aren't a hundred head of cattle on the Lazy R! What on earth is he thinking about? Who are they and where did they come from? They aren't local men, are they, Oscar?"

"Loco?"

"Not loco!" snapped Judge. "Local! Men who live in the valley."

"Yah, su-ure," nodded Oscar. "Living at de Lazy R."

"Vitrified, even unto the cerebellum," sighed Judge.

"Where are they from?" queried Henry.

"Black River City. Dey are hord-looking fallers, Hanry."

"I'll have to investigate that," declared Hartridge. "Neilan hasn't any money to pay to cowboys. Why, he hasn't enough to pay those two Mexicans. I can't understand what he's thinking about."

He got up abruptly and left the office.

"There is something queer about that Lazy R deal," declared Judge after he had gone.

"Just what?" queried Henry.

"Hartridge is too blamed interested in that ranch, Henry."

"You don't think that Neilan—"

"Is an impostor?" finished Judge. "Henry, I told you I wouldn't trust Hartridge as far as I could throw a bull by the tail."

Henry smiled thoughtfully, but finally shook his head.

"It doesn't exactly make sense, Judge. That Lazy R isn't worth the risk of putting an impostor in there."

"I realize that. Perhaps I am wrong. The young man looked honest."

"Anyway, it isn't our business, Judge."

"That's true. Henry, have you heard that Sally Morgan has made Cal Essex manager of the Quarte-Circle M?"

"No, I did not hear such a statement. Who told you?"

"I suppose that Mr. Essex circulated the report himself."

Henry polished his nose thoughtfully.

"It is possible," he admitted. "I—er—Judge, just how far is it possible to throw a bull by the tail?"

"Not a damn inch, sir. Meaning, of course, that you do not believe Mr. Essex."

"No, no, not at all. I was merely wondering if there were any records in throwing a bull by the tail. Rather impossible, it seems, because of lack of leverage, and the natural animosity of the critter. Still, it might be done. Nothing is impossible."

"One thing is," declared Judge.

"What is that, Judge?"

"Making you look at things seriously."

"You wrong me, my friend. Behind this mask of mirth lies a serious and determined spirit. I might say, a granite interior."

"Hardening of the arteries, Henry. I'll buy a drink."

OUTLAW SPRING was a waterhole about ten feet across and perhaps eighteen inches deep, in the bottom of a brushy swale. On two sides the brushy, cactus-covered hills stretched away for several miles. For possibly an acre the brush had been cleared away. There were several of Ab Morgan's posts still standing, but the barbwire had disappeared.

Dan Leary and Steve McClung, two of the Morgan riders, came down through the swale. McClung carried a shovel across one shoulder, while Leary carried a hammer. Cal Essex had sent them to re-fence Outlaw Spring. With Roarin' Bill Rose entirely out of the picture, there was no danger.

They dismounted near the water and began assembling scattered posts.

"This makes three times we've built this damn fence," growled Leary. "She'll stay this time, y'betcha. That tenderfoot don't even know there's water over here."

"Course he don't," agreed McClung, straightening up a post. "But he shore knows how to hit with his left hand."

"Ain't that true?" agreed Leary. "Wait'll I straighten up a couple more posts, and we'll see how they line up. I like things accurate."

Leary fussed with two more posts, until they satisfied him.

"Take a squint, Steve; she's as straight as a rifle bar'l."

Steve humped over, one eye shut, close to the post.

Sock! The post jerked out of line, and a rifle shot echoed hack from somewhere up on the brushy hill. Both cowboys jumped back. There was a neat, round hole in the fencepost. Possibly fifteen feet away was Steve's hat on the ground, where he had left it.

Pluck! Squee-e-e-e! A bullet ruined the crown of the hat, struck a rock and went whining away down the swale.

Such shooting was too much for Steve and Dan. Risking the chance of more shots, they raced to their horses. They mounted on the run, and headed for the high brush down the swale, then toward home.

"Tenderfoot—hell!" gasped Dan, after they were safe from further shooting. "That rifle was at least two, three hundred yards away, and he hit my hat. Hit that fencepost, too."

"Mebbe he was shootin' *at us*," suggested Steve.

"You can believe that if yuh want to—I don't. That feller's a ringer, Steve. Played tenderfoot with Cal Essex, didn't he? And now he shore made life pre-car-ious for me and you."

"That's a nice soundin' word, even if I don't know what it means. Let's go home and tell Cal Essex he can build his own fences. I'll be blamed if I'm goin' to turn carpenter and git dry-gulched."

THERE HAD been a warm argument between Sally Morgan and Cal Essex that morning. After breakfast Cal had come to Sally.

"It's about my pay," he told her. "As foreman of this spread I've been gettin' sixty a month. As general manager I reckon I'll have to get about a hundred and fifty."

"When and if I ever make you general manager," replied Sally coldly.

"I've taken over the job," he assured her.

"And I still sign the checks for the Quarter-Circle M," reminded Sally. "You'll get sixty—or nothing."

"You're not tryin' to make me mad, are yuh?" he asked.

"You may get mad, if it suits you, Mr. Essex; but you aren't going to blackmail me."

Essex laughed at her. "Blackmail is a hard word, Sally."

"Miss Morgan to you," she said quickly.

"And another thing," remarked Essex calmly. "Tell that tenderfoot from the Lazy R that he ain't wanted here. I don't reckon he'll ever come here again—but if he does—"

"After what I saw," said Sally with the trace of a smile, "I shouldn't think he would be afraid to come here again."

Essex flushed hotly. "It won't be with fists next time."

"From behind a tree?" asked Sally.

"Wait a minute!" snarled Essex. "I'm not that kind."

"Any man," declared Sally coldly, "who will steal cattle on orders will shoot a man from behind a tree."

Essex turned on his heel then and walked swiftly away to the stable. He saddled a horse and started for Tonto City. Sally had more nerve than he had thought she had. He had thought she would knuckle down under the threat of exposing Ab Morgan as a thief—but she was not knuckling down very fast.

Cal Essex realized that Sally Morgan would never marry him. With that hope gone, all he could expect was a chance to run the ranch and try to make some easy money for himself. But he was not going to let Neilan see Sally—not if he could prevent it. That knockout blow still rankled in Essex's heart, especially since he was sure Sally had seen it delivered.

"I'll get that tenderfoot," he swore to himself. "I'll make him wish he'd never seen Wild Horse Valley."

AND WHILE Essex rode to Tonto City, and Steve and Dan rode back to the ranch from Outlaw Spring, Frank Neilan rode up to the patio gate at the Morgan ranch. He dismounted and tied his horse. Sally saw him from a window and came into the patio.

"It was so awful lonesome at my place," he told her.

"You aren't afraid to come here?" she queried.

"My dear lady, what is there to fear?"

"After what happened the last time?"

Neilan laughed and shook his head. "Nothing happened to me."

Sally's eyes were serious as she said, "But don't you understand that some men don't always fight fair?"

"Why, yes, I've heard that said—but Miss Morgan, surely you aren't warning me against your own men."

"I have no control over the personal likes and dislikes of my men, Mr. Neilan."

"No, that's true," he agreed. "Maybe I should have stayed at home. From your angle, it would have been the wise thing to do—but I never have been noted for my wisdom. It—it makes me feel like a trespasser. I—er—really rode over here to ask you a very personal question, but now—"

"What is it?" asked Sally curiously.

"I hope you won't be angry with me, Miss Morgan. Mr. Hartridge told me that you're engaged to Mr. Essex. Of course, if you are, possibly that would account for his actions."

"I see," mused Sally soberly. "Is your object—matrimony, Mr. Neilan?"

"Why, no—that is—well, I didn't want Mr. Essex to think—"

"Just what did you mean, Mr. Neilan?"

"I don't... know," admitted Neilan helplessly. "Golly, I guess I mixed that one all up, didn't I?"

"Then let's drop that subject," suggested Sally with a smile. "How are you getting along at the ranch?"

"Fine. I mean I'm getting along very well. I can almost understand Thunder and Lightning now."

Sally laughed. "Have they explained the difference between a horse and a cow?"

"No, I haven't had that pleasure. I'll ask them. Or do you mean that I don't know the difference?"

"The last time you were here you told me you didn't."

"That's right. But I have learned a lot since then."

They were laughing, as Dan Leary and Steve McClung stalked into the patio. At sight of Neilan the two punchers stopped short, looking keenly at him.

"Is Cal Essex around?" queried Steve.

"He left about an hour ago," replied Sally. "Is there something?"

"I'll tell yuh there's somethin'. Cal sent me and Dan down to fence Outlaw Spring, and some dry-gulcher drove us out with a rifle. If yuh ask me, it's the Lazy R. They'd be the ones to do it."

Sally looked quickly at Frank Neilan.

"What is the meaning of 'dry-gulcher'?" asked Neilan.

"A feller who hides in the brush and shoots yuh in the back," replied Steve, and added, "if yuh don't happen to know."

"If I knew, I wouldn't ask," replied Neilan.

"Yea-a-ah! Well, I don't mind tellin' yuh that you could have been that dry-gulcher. You could have cut across the canyon and beat us here, so yuh could prove an alibi. You cached yore rifle, before yuh showed up, eh? Well, that's fine. If yuh ask me, yo're a smart *tenderfoot*, Neilan."

"Neither of you were hit?" queried Sally.

"Na-a-aw," growled Steve.

"Sounds like my marksmanship," smiled Neilan. "Except for the fact that I don't know where Outlaw Spring is located, and that I haven't fired a rifle in over a year, it might have been me."

"We didn't expect yuh to admit it," growled Dan.

"It couldn't have been Mr. Neilan," declared Sally.

Steve scowled darkly, by no means convinced.

"We'll see what Cal Essex has to say about it."

The two cowboys stalked out and went to the bunk-house.

"If I were you, I wouldn't be here when Cal Essex comes back," said Sally. "No, I'm not asking you to run away, Mr. Neilan; but there's no use for you to be inviting trouble."

He turned and looked for a moment at the retreating cowboys; then he nodded.

"You're right, Miss Morgan," he said. "And thank you for the advice. There really is enough accidental trouble, without looking for it purposely. Thank you for a pleasant hour."

He walked to the patio gate. Then he turned and looked back at Sally, who had stopped at the door.

"You really haven't answered my question, you know, Miss Morgan."

"You might tell Mr. Hartridge that he was misinformed," she replied.

"Golly! Say! Isn't this a wonderful day?"

But the door had closed. Neilan smiled foolishly and went to his horse.

Down at the stable, Dan and Steve watched him ride away on the old horse.

"Wait'll we tell Cal about that dry-gulchin'," said Steve.

"Yeah! And when he knows Neilan has been courtin' Sally in the patio. Whooee-e-e-e!"

When Cal Essex came back from Tonto City and was told what had happened at Outlaw Spring, his wrath blazed profanely. But when he was told that Frank Neilan had come to see Sally, he went, in the vernacular of the range, straight up. Cal was already about half drunk, and now he was completely mad.

"All right," he said ominously. "Don't say anything where that woman can hear it, but just as soon as it's dark, we're goin' to the Lazy R. Either me or that tenderfoot are leavin' this valley— and I like it here pretty well. We'll wear masks, in case them two Mexicans are there. No use advertisin' ourselves."

"I'd j'st as soon git me a couple Mexicans," declared McClung.

"Do as yuh like," gritted Essex. "All I want is Neilan—and I'll shore make that handsome road-runner wish he'd kept his hands off this outfit."

CHAPTER IX

THE FIGHT THAT FAILED

THE MORE THAT Henry Harrison Conroy thought about the Lazy R, the more curious he became. He got especially curious when he saw that Sam Hartridge, the lawyer, did not take his horse and buggy and go back to Scorpion Bend. Hartridge instead spent the day at the Tonto Saloon, drinking quite a lot.

Henry said nothing to Judge Van Treece, but watched Hartridge, who seemed to be merely waiting.

It was after dark when Henry saw Hartridge at last go to the livery stable. There the lawyer procured a saddle horse and moments later rode away in the direction of the Lazy R. Henry saddled his own horse and followed him. Evidently Hartridge had intentionally waited for dark before making the trip, and Henry was all the more curious to know his reason for the trip.

It was a long live miles over the old road. Henry rode slowly. There were no dogs at the Lazy R; so there was a possibility of his being able to get in close enough to hear something. There was a dim light in the main room, shining through flimsy curtains.

Henry dismounted before reaching the gate, and tied his horse off the road. There was not a sound to break the stillness as he walked carefully toward the house. His goal was a lighted window, but just before he reached there he heard the rattle of hoofs beyond the house. It was the Morgan outfit coming to visit Frank Neilan, but Henry did not know this.

He could see the milling horses, as the men dismounted, but it was too dark for identification. He crouched in near the window, unable to see the interior, but trusting that he might hear something.

There was nothing furtive about the Morgan men. Masked with handkerchiefs, and with guns in their hands, they came boldly to the door, yanked it open and strode into the first of the three rooms. Including Cal Essex, there were six masked men in the party.

There the six men hesitated. The door closed quietly behind them, and they heard the rasp of a fastener and the click of a padlock. They all looked quickly at each other.

"Somebody locked it!" whispered a cowboy.

"Look!" grunted Essex. He was pointing at the table, where a large square of cardboard had been propped in the light of the lamp. On it in bold black letters was printed this warning!

DON'T MOVE!
DON'T PULL YOUR GUNS!
WE'VE GOT YOU COVERED!

"What in the hell!" gasped Essex nervously. He jerked his head from side to side as he tried to puzzle out the warning.

"They locked the door behind us," whispered a cowboy.

"They've trapped us!" gasped another. "Listen! Horses runnin'!"

"Trapped—hell!" exploded Essex. He picked up a chair, ran across the room and flung it through a window. Essex was half-way through the window before the others realized what he intended doing.

Then, like five frightened rabbits, all trying to get into the same hole at the same time, the five cowboys made a dive for the smashed window.

Henry Harrison Conroy had no idea what was going on in the house—not even when a heavy chair smashed through the window, taking most of the window with it. A leg of the chair hit Henry on the head, knocking him flat on his back, while six galloping cowboys jumped, stepped and stumbled on him. As fast as he tried to lift his head, it was knocked back on the ground.

Dazed and bleeding he got to his feet, stumbled toward the corner of the house. At that point a man ran into him. But Henry did not go down this time; not Henry Harrison Conroy, the Sheriff of Wild Horse Valley.

His groping left hand hooked over a belt, and he began to belabor his victim with his right fist. Not with any science nor desire to reach a vital spot, because he was too dazed for that; but with an aroused fighting instinct, brought out from being battered around.

His victim was grunting, groaning and whimpering, but Henry was relentless. Smash... smash... smash, with the regularity of a ticking clock. Then he swayed back for a supreme effort, put every ounce of his weight and muscle in one mighty swing—and missed.

In fact, his miss was so mighty that he whirled himself around, caught his heel, stumbled wildly and went flat on his back, with an audible *woo-o-osh!* And for the next several moments, Henry was "out."

WHEN CONSCIOUSNESS returned he found himself gazing into the light of a lantern, held in the hand of Frank Neilan. A few feet away, propped up on one elbow, was a disheveled object. Henry now realized that this was what was left of Sam Hartridge, the attorney.

"It seems that you gentlemen might have selected a better place to fight," said Neilan soberly.

"Fight?" queried Henry huskily. "Was I fighting Mr. Hartridge?"

"It seems that you were, Mr. Conroy."

"Well," Henry blinked solemnly in the lantern light, "it—it was a nice night for it."

"Wh-what on earth hap-happened?" whispered Hartridge.

Hartridge had one eye swollen nearly shut, a split lip, a bruise on one cheek, and he had lost his collar and tie.

"Don't you know?" asked Henry.

"Certainly not!"

"Well, neither do I," said Henry. "I—I remember something about—well, something was thrown through a window—and hit me. Then I have a rather hazy remembrance of men jumping on me, kicking me. That," he squinted up at Neilan, "didn't happen to be you, did it, Mr. Neilan?"

"No, I had nothing to do with it."

Neilan placed the lantern on the ground and disappeared around the house in the darkness. Henry caressed his sore head and looked at Hartridge, who managed to get to his hands and knees.

"I—I feel awful bad," he told Henry. "Awful bad."

"I will match sore spots with you, sir," declared Henry. "If you—"

Henry hesitated. Several men had suddenly moved in close to them, and their faces were concealed with masks.

"That damn, fat-nosed sheriff!" snorted one man disgustedly.

"And that bat-eared lawyer from Scorpion Bend!" exclaimed another.

"Judging from the remarks, we are among friends," said Henry dryly.

"Yo're crazy, if yuh think so, feller!" snapped another. "Where are our horses?"

Henry felt in his pockets and shook his head.

"Think yo're damn funny, eh? Where didja put our horses?"

"Mr. Hartridge," said Henry, "have you misplaced the horses of these masqueraders?"

"I don't know what you are talking about."

The sheriff nodded with an appearance of deep concern.

"Well, neither do I; but there is no harm in asking."

His air of innocence, genuine as it was, seemed lost upon his masked and surly questioner.

"Where's Frank Neilan?" asked the man savagely.

"Great Heavens!" gasped Henry. "Is he missing, too?"

The man cursed bitterly and very profanely.

"Well," remarked Henry dryly, "after all that, there is little left for any ordinary curses."

"Some day," promised the man, "I'm goin' to tack yore ears on a fencepost."

Two of the men went around to the front of the house, but came back quickly. They were still cursing.

"The front door is still padlocked," one of them reported. "There ain't anybody in the house."

"Well, we won't do any good around here," decided the one who had filed a claim on Henry's ears. "No use huntin' for them broncs in the dark. C'mon."

They moved away in a body. Henry got to his feet, flexed his muscles and walked around in a circle.

"What outfit was that?" asked Hartridge painfully.

"I'm not even making a guess," sighed Henry. "If I wasn't sure that Jessie James and Billy the Kid were both dead—"

"They want your ears, Conroy."

"I vote unanimously with them, sir; I want them, too. Shall we ride back to Tonto City together—if we can bend ourselves to fit into a saddle?"

Hartridge tested his legs and arms painfully.

"I think we're a pair of fools, Conroy," he said.

"You merely *think* we are? Oh, yes I understand; a lawyer never commits himself. I do not mind stating that I know we are. And if it comes down to direct testimony, I'm sure I can prove it."

Groaning and grunting, Hartridge went down into the brush to get his horse, while Henry limped down the road and untied his steed.

"As I have often said," he remarked to the horse, "anything might happen in Arizona—and it did tonight."

Hartridge rode slowly out of the brush, and they moved off down the road to Tonto City.

"IT DOESN'T sound reasonable, Henry," declared Judge, as they sat in the office next morning. "Men jumping through windows onto you, masked men threatening to tack your ears to a post, when you would not tell them where you put their horses. Isn't it possible that you dreamed all of this, sir?"

Henry groaned and shifted in his chair.

"Does one dream bumps and bruises such as mine?" he countered. "Just in my middle is the perfect print of a high-heel boot sole, etched in a gorgeous purple. I know I couldn't have dreamed that; not even if I believed in dreams. Go to Scorpion Bend and take a look at the estimable Mr. Hartridge. If I dreamed mine, what sort of a nightmare did that man have?"

Judge nodded thoughtfully, his eyes closed.

"Henry," he said, "I have about come to the conclusion that there is some mystery connected with the Lazy R Ranch."

"Remarkable!" grunted Henry. "I congratulate you, sir."

"Yes," continued Judge, ignoring the sarcasm, "I believe there is. And I have a notion to go out there and sift it to the bottom."

"Very good," agreed Henry. He reached across his desk and picked up a pencil. "Your real name is Cornelius, isn't it, Judge?"

"Why, yes. But what—"

"Merely a peculiar kink in my make-up, Judge. I detest seeing nicknames on tombstones."

"Then you think they would resent investigation?"

"Look at me."

"You, sir, were snooping."

"I suppose there is a difference."

AT ABOUT the same time that morning, Sam Hartridge and Ira Hallam were in Hartridge's office at Scorpion Bend. Judging from the appearance of the lawyer's face, Henry did a fairly good job as a fighter. Hallam's fat face was the picture of deepest gloom.

"You didn't question Neilan at all, Sam?" he asked.

"How in the devil could I? The only time I saw him was when he came with that lantern. Even if I had been in shape to talk, you couldn't expect me to ask questions in front of the sheriff."

"You—you didn't see the four men—the ones that damn fool hired?"

"I didn't!" snapped Hartridge. "I crawled up to a window on the far side of the house, trying to hear something. I had been there a few minutes when I heard riders coming. They went into the house. Then I heard the horses running away.

"Then I heard a noise, which sounded as though a window had been smashed out, and men were running in the house. Well, I—I wanted to see what was going on; so I ran around the house, where at least six men attacked me. That was all I knew until I awoke and found—er—Neilan, standing there with a lantern, and the sheriff sitting on the ground."

"Then the men came back, Sam?"

"I suppose it was the same ones."

"What explanation did the sheriff offer, when you rode back to Tonto City together?"

"Not a damn one. All he said was that he believed he had discovered latent possibilities in himself."

"What did he mean by that, Sam?"

"I don't know, and I felt too miserable to ask him."

"Do you suppose he suspected you of something?"

"No more than I suspected him," growled Hartridge. "Damn it, Ira, that will can't be probated, unless we can prove that Bill Rose is dead. Not a thing on that ranch can be sold until after it is probated. I never thought about that."

"You're a hell of a lawyer, Sam!"

"We won't argue about that. But I am the administrator of the will, without bonds, and I believe the court will allow our man to occupy and operate the ranch, until everything is settled. It's a sure thing that Rose is at the bottom of Devil's Chimney; so we will eventually get that mine. In the meantime, I believe it can be discovered, and some ore dug out. How would that be?"

Ira Hallam shrugged his shoulders.

"You're supposed to know the law, Sam; I'm only an assayer."

FOR A young man, who should feel that he was between the devil and the deep sea, Frank Neilan seemed to be getting a lot of sober fun out of the situation. Lightning was doing the cooking, while Thunder waited on the table, and the four outlaws were really enjoying life at the Lazy R.

Pecos Charley Peters and Sody Slade were the ones who had fired the shots at the two Morgan cowboys at Outlaw Spring.

"We didn't aim to hurt 'em," chuckled Pecos.

"They blamed me for it," said Neilan.

"That's why they came here last night," laughed Sody. "I told yuh they would. They was all primed up to hurt somebody. That sign on the table was shore a great idea. You'll have to give me credit for that."

"It cost me a window," reminded Neilan.

"You got off cheap," declared Clovis. "If we hadn't been here to help yuh, they'd have killed you. Yo're green as hell, Neilan."

"Oh, I admit it," laughed Neilan. "But sooner or later they'll know you're here, and there'll be a pitched battle."

Pecos Charley hitched his gunbelt.

"Suits me," grinned Pecos. "I like trouble. But I'd shore like to know why that fat sheriff was here. Do yuh reckon he's lookin' for us?"

"I hope for his sake that he don't find us," remarked Zibe Tucker.

"Well, don't be a danged fool—and start shootin'," advised Pecos. "It's against the law to kill sheriffs in Arizona."

"And don't forget that my lawyer was here, too," said Neilan.

"You let us handle him," said Clovis. "We can't let that feller go too far."

"There is also Ira Hallam, the assayer," added Neilan.

"We'll handle him, too," stated Tucker.

Frank Neilan laughed quietly as he lighted a cigarette.

"Did somethin' strike you funny?" queried Pecos.

"It did," smiled Neilan. "I was thinking of an old, old proverb: Too many crooks spoil the broth."

"It was 'cooks,' wasn't it?" asked Sody Slade.

"Not in this case, Sody. Here is the situation: You fellows come in here, dodging the law, discover gold on Morgan's land, which you proceed to steal and hide in a tunnel on the Lazy R. Bill Rose dies and leaves the Lazy R to his nephew, which prevents you from realizing on your theft.

"A crooked lawyer and a crooked assayer, who know that Bill Rose discovered a rich vein on his property, pick me up, make me the legal heir, and plant me on this ranch. You gentlemen force me to hire you to help run the ranch, when everybody knows that the ranch is without any visible means of support. You have managed to continue Rose's feud with the Morgan outfit—and the sheriff's office is suspicious. Isn't that worth laughing about?"

"Do you weesh chili con carne for sopper?" asked Lightning, "or do you weesh chili con carne weeth frijole? Or maybe you weesh theese frijole weeth yourself."

"W'at he means," explained Thunder, "ees that you can have chili and beef by myself, or you can have frijole yourself and theese beef and chili together with eath other, and eef you do not weesh for these beef and frijole, you can have—I hope."

"That will be all right," nodded Neilan gravely, and added, "I hope so, too."

"Just what the heck are we goin' to have for supper?" asked Pecos Charley.

"Beef and beans, with a few chili peppers for seasoning," replied Neilan.

"Is that all?"

"That is all the ranch can afford," declared Neilan. "I have just a dollar and thirty cents left. If you gents expect to live here, you'll have to contribute to the larder."

"Yeah, I reckon that's right," agreed Pecos. "Well, we know how to get money, when we need some."

OVER AT the Quarter-Circle M, Cal Essex was assembling his information. Through a pair of field glasses he had watched the ranch house of the Lazy R, and had seen the four strangers. Essex knew every man in Wild Horse Valley, or thought he did, until he saw these four.

Thunder and Lightning, riding home from Tonto City next clay, were stopped by Essex and three of his cowboys. The two Mexicans were fairly well filled with tequila, and when they understood that it meant information or losing their ears, they became willing to talk.

Cal Essex wanted to know who the four strangers were. It

seemed a simple request, backed up by a sharp knife; so Lightning told Essex and his men all about Pecos Charley Peters, Sody Slade, Ed Clovis and Zibe Tucker.

"They was dodgin' the law, eh?" queried Essex.

"Theese law ees want to 'ang them," admitted Lightning.

"Murderers, eh?"

"Por Dios!" exclaimed Lightning. "They keel mos' everybodee een New Mejico."

"All right," nodded Essex. "That's fine. But remember—don't tell anybody that yuh told us—or I'll cut off yore ears."

"We cross my heart and hope you die," replied Lightning fervently.

"Well, that's fine," replied Essex. "Go home and shut up."

"Or lose your ears," added Thunder.

CHAPTER X

THE TWO-GUN GHOST

IT WAS SIESTA time in Tonto City, several days after the incident at the Lazy R, and everyone seemed to be enjoying it. Henry was asleep in his chair, feet on the table top. Judge, tilted against the wall, snored gently, his sombrero tilted over his eyes, while Oscar Johnson, stretched flat on the office cot, snored sonorously.

At the Tonto City Bank, George Reed, the cashier, yawned and looked at the big clock on the east wall of the bank. It showed five minutes until three o'clock—closing time. Further back in the room, Don Martin, the elderly bookkeeper, labored over his ledger.

There was rarely a customer in the bank at that time. In fact, there was little business in the afternoon, especially when the weather was as hot as it was this day. Reed turned and walked back to Martin, who glanced up from his work.

"Just about time to close the doors," the cashier said.

Martin glanced at the clock, nodded. Then his eyes shifted to the front doorway, and his mouth dropped open. Reed whirled when he saw the expression on Martin's face.

Three masked men were filing in, their guns trained on the two employees of the bank. Out in front another masked man sat on his horse, holding the tie-ropes on three other saddled horses. Reed saw all this in a glance; and he heard the leader of the trio say:

"No foolin' now—shell out the money. We're in a hurry, and unless yuh want hell to break loose—"

While Reed stood stockstill, one of the men stepped over the railing. He scooped all the loose money from the cashier's shelves.

"Get that safe open—we want real money!" snapped the spokesman.

"It's open," replied Reed. "If—"

"Back up ahead of me. You'll—"

From out in the street came the report of a shot. The man on the horse had fired that shot at Tom Rickey, proprietor of the hotel, who had just stepped outside. Rickey dived for cover.

The bandit turned then and sent a bullet toward the doorway of the Tonto Saloon. Several men who had stuck their heads out ducked back.

"C'mon!" snapped the spokesman of the hold-ups. "Hell will break loose pretty quick."

The three men started for the doorway. As they did so, Reed drew a gun from inside his coat. He didn't get to use it, though. One of the bandits, apparently expecting such a move, whirled and fired. Reed sprawled across a desk, shot through the heart.

The three ran out then, mounted their milling horses. Throwing a volley of shots toward the saloon and hotel, they galloped out of town.

In about three minutes they had entered the bank, taken less than two hundred dollars, killed George Reed, and were gone.

HENRY, JUDGE and Oscar awoke at the first shot, and were out on the street as the bandits departed, wondering what it was all about. They soon found out. George Reed had been instantly killed, and Martin was so shaken that he could hardly tell what had happened. They closed the bank and removed the body. Luckily George Reed was a single man.

After the coroner had gone, Tom Rickey came to Henry.

"They almost got me," he said nervously. "Didn't miss me an inch."

"Did you get a good look at them, Tom?"

"All masked in black, Henry. With all the confusion it's impossible to describe them singly—but I know those horses."

"You do?"

"Yes. There was a blue roan, a sorrel with four white stockings, a sorrel with white markings on its rump, and a tall black, with a blaze face. All four of those horses belong to the Lazy R outfit."

"Well, my goodness!" exclaimed Henry. "Are you sure of that, Tom?"

"I should be; I sold all of them to Roarin' Bill Rose about a year ago. If you remember, I collected four horses on a debt."

"Yes, yes, I remember that. Lazy R, eh? Hm-m-m. Well!"

Henry hurried back to the office, where he discussed it with Judge.

"Oscar said that the four new men up there were tough looking," reminded Judge. "They took a chance that the horses would not be recognized. What fools! Getting less than two hundred dollars—and killing a decent citizen. Hanging is too good for them."

Henry did not seem very enthusiastic.

"We can't go above the law, Judge," he said. "Hm-m-m. Four bad men. Well, it stands to reason that our force is not adequate to go to the Lazy R and make an arrest. At our age, no one could say that we filled an untimely grave; but I am thinking of Oscar."

Judge snorted. "I am thinking just like you are, Henry—and we are both liars. How would it be if I sent out to the Morgan ranch and secured several of their cowboys? We could add Danny Regan and Frijole Bill Cullison, if he should be sober. Say about six from the Morgan crew, with Danny and Frijole, Oscar Johnson, and us—that would make eleven men."

"Eight men," corrected Henry. "You can't count on Frijole—and there are you and me. Number, yes; men, decidedly not. But by all means, send a message to Miss Sally Morgan, asking the loan of six men. You might tell her, of course, what we wish to do with them, and that we do not agree to send them back in first-class condition. They might even come back in very bad order."

"Any special men you'd like to have, Henry?"

"Oh, no. She will likely send Cal Essex in charge of them. I am a bit curious to find out if he is as brave as he sounds."

IT WAS nearly sundown when Frank Neilan, alone in his ranch house, tossed aside an old magazine, yawned widely and got to his feet. He walked over to a front window and glanced out—just as Sally Morgan rode swiftly up to the front of the house and dismounted. With a gasp of surprise Frank Neilan flung open the door. Sally was hurrying up the steps, panting a little, and he followed her into the house.

"Why, Miss Morgan, this is a—" he began.

"Wait!" she interrupted. "Where are your men?"

"My men? Why, I'm sure I—"

"They're not here?"

"No. I expect them home at any time. But I don't see—"

Swiftly she told him what had happened in Tonto City that afternoon. She told him that the horses had been identified as belonging to the Lazy R, and that the sheriff had sent for her men to make up a posse.

"They're on their way to Tonto City now," she told him. "It won't take them long to come back here."

"Why—why, it's unbelievable!" he said huskily. "It's—"

Frank Neilan hesitated. Was it incredible? He remembered that Pecos Charley Peters had said, "Well, we know how to get money, when we need some." Could it be possible that this was how he meant?

"What do you *know* about those men?" asked Sally.

"Nothing," he replied miserably. "But why did you come here to warn them, if you felt that they were guilty?"

"I didn't come to warn them—I came to warn you. I didn't think you had anything to do with it. But when that posse comes, there will be a fight, if your men are here. Anything might happen, you see."

"Very nice," drawled a voice from the doorway. They turned to face Cal Essex. He stood there, covering Neilan with his gun.

"It was shore nice of the lady," sneered Essex, moving closer. "It will sound fine to Wild Horse Valley when I tell 'em that Sally Morgan sent her crew to help the sheriff capture four murderers, and then she went to warn the murderers herself."

"Where did you come from?" asked Sally.

"Me? Oh, I didn't go to Tonto. I sent the boys to join up with the sheriff, while I watched this place. I was goin' to join them when they got here. Good thing I did, too. How do you feel about it, Neilan?"

"Sort of numb," replied Neilan soberly.

Essex laughed nastily. "You was born thataway. I'll just hold you two here until the posse gets here. Mebbe the sheriff will want to know why yuh came to warn a murderer. As for you, Neilan—make one move to change the situation and I'll drill you full of holes. In fact, I'd like to have yuh make a break."

"I never carry a gun," replied Neilan. "But you're wrong about Miss Morgan coming to warn a murderer."

"Oh, I see—just a social call, eh? Well, it may mean a rope around your neck, feller. And it'll mean that Wild Horse Valley won't have much use for Sally Morgan."

"I wonder what will happen if my men get here ahead of the posse," remarked Neilan. "It would be interesting. If I thought—"

Just then he looked past Essex to the doorway, and his eyes opened wide. For a moment Essex forgot himself. He turned swiftly, and his gun hand jerked shoulder high.

At that moment Neilan sprang. His right hand grabbed Essex' wrist. With a quick jerk back, he twisted the gun away from the foreman, and as Essex turned he swung his left fist in a ripping uppercut that caught Essex under the chin. Essex went down, striking his head solidly on the floor.

Sally was leaning back against a table, breathing heavily, and Neilan had stepped back, was looking down at his fallen adversary, when a new voice spoke.

"I do not believe there is any use counting," said Henry Harrison Conroy. He stood in the doorway, calmly surveying the scene. "When they are hit in that manner, I do not believe a count is necessary."

"Mr. Conroy!" gasped Sally. "Where on earth did you come from?"

"Oh, here and there," smiled Henry. "As a matter of fact, I thought I would come ahead and look things over. Lovely afternoon, isn't it? Miss Morgan, I heard what Mr. Essex said. If I were you I would go home, before anyone else arrives. In that way, Mr. Essex would have difficulty in proving anything, especially when Mr. Neilan and I are willing to testify that he is a liar."

"Please go," added Neilan. "And don't forget that I'm very grateful for what you've done. It was mighty kind of you."

AT FIRST Sally hesitated; but she realized they were right. She went back to her horse, mounted and rode swiftly away.

"A wonderful woman," commented Henry. "Most wonderful, sir."

"In all the world," added Neilan.

Henry shot a sharp glance at the young man, then as quickly turned his attention to Cal Essex. The foreman was struggling to sit up. In a few moments he was able to shake the cobwebs from his brain and look around. He looked curiously at Henry, blinking rapidly.

"I hope you are sane again, Mr. Essex," said Henry.

"Sane? What do yuh mean?"

"You most certainly haven't been showing much sanity. By any remote chance, have you been smoking marijuana?"

"What do yuh mean?" growled Essex huskily.

"Mistaking me for a lady," smiled Henry. "Calling me Sally Morgan. Accusing me of coming here to warn a murderer. I hope that punch in the jaw I gave you has restored your sanity, sir."

"The—the punch *you* gave me? Why, you—you—" Essex struggled for words to express himself.

"Off again," sighed Henry. "Sad case. Must consult a doctor at once."

"Of all the damn fools!" choked Essex, blazing with wrath.

"I am afraid," said Henry, "that the responsibility of running a big cattle outfit has affected his mind, Mr. Neilan. I was told that he was acting in a peculiar manner several days ago. Visions of grandeur, and all that, if you know what I mean."

"I believe I do, Mr. Conroy," nodded Neilan soberly.

"You lyin', bat-eared, bug-headed sap-suckers!" howled Essex. He felt for his gun, but it was in Neilan's hand.

"Signs of violence," said Henry. "I suppose I shall have to take him to a doctor—a brain specialist, if we can locate one. Perhaps we had better—"

Essex started backing toward the doorway.

"You keep away from me!" he snapped. "Damn you and yore doctors! I'm as sane as you are. You try to touch me and I'll—"

He backed off the threshold, nearly fell down, and ran to his horse. He mounted it on the run, and went spurring away.

Henry and Neilan watched him from the doorway, and then looked at each other queerly.

"You're a genius, Sheriff," declared Neilan.

"I believe we have stilled the tongue of scandal, sir," replied Henry. "Now—where are your four cowboys, Neilan?"

"I haven't any idea, Mr. Conroy. Miss Morgan told me what happened in Tonto City. It was a terrible thing."

"The horses they rode belong to this ranch."

"That's what Miss Morgan said."

"Hm-m-m."

Henry leaned against the doorway and rubbed his nose.

"What are their names, Neilan?"

Neilan told him their names, and added that they were from Black River City. Henry wrote the names in his notebook.

"They rode over the hills from Black River Flats," he said.

"Presumably untrue," remarked Henry. "Few people know the trail, it is mighty dangerous, and ends long before reaching this valley."

"I believe they were in Black River Flats quite a while," offered Neilan.

"Punching cows?"

"Why, yes."

"That is queer, There isn't a cow in all that country, Neilan. Nothing but sheep."

"Here comes the posse," said Neilan thankfully. He was getting in over his head, trying to alibi the four outlaws.

THERE WERE five men from the Quarter-Circle M, and Oscar, Judge and Danny Regan. Frijole had just opened a new batch of prune whisky and was in no shape to ride. They approached carefully, until they saw Henry and Neilan.

"They flew the coop, eh?" queried Danny.

"I haven't determined," replied Henry. "Mr. Neilan says they haven't been here since this morning."

"Where's Essex?" asked Steve McClung.

"He left here a few minutes ago," replied Henry soberly. "What on earth is wrong with him? He mistook me for Miss Morgan, talked like a crazy man, threatening us with a revolver. I am worried about him."

"Why, I—I didn't notice anything," faltered McClung. "Yuh say he mistook yuh for Miss Morgan, Sheriff?"

"Wasn't that ridiculous?" queried Henry. "I'm afraid the man has lost his mind."

"He certainly isn't normal," agreed Neilan. "In fact, I would say he is decidedly crazy."

"I'll be danged!" whispered McClung. "That's funny."

"Decidedly," added Henry. "Well, I do not suppose there is any use of staying here longer. If they are guilty, I am very much afraid you will never see your crew again, Mr. Neilan. Sorry to have bothered you, and I wish you a very good evening, sir."

"It was a pleasure," replied Neilan.

"I suppose you boys from the Morgan ranch may as well go home for the night. Thank you for coming; and will you please convey my thanks to Miss Morgan—for allowing you to come. It was kind of her. Good night."

"Henry," said Judge, as, moments later, the four of them rode back toward Tonto City, "what sort of skulduggery are you concocting, anyway? Will you tell me?"

Henry looked injured. "My dear Judge! Skulduggery?"

"A robbery and a murder, sir! Circumstantial evidence points to the four men on the Lazy R, and you dismiss your posse. No wonder they call us the Shame of Arizona, sir! It—it smells!"

"You should mention smells to a man with a nose like mine."

"Free-holey brought in yug of prune yuice," said Oscar. "Yeeminee, das vars good liquor. Ay took von drink, turned my hurse loose, and sporred ha'al out of de hitch-rack."

"Officers of the law," sighed Judge. "No wonder the finger of scorn is pointed at us. It irks me sore, Henry."

"Try baking-soda in warm water," advised Henry.

SAM HARTRIDGE and Ira Hallam were awaiting the sheriff in Tonto City. That unscrupulous pair had heard about the suspicions against the Lazy R, and were anxious to hear what the posse had accomplished. They hung around, asking questions, until well after dark. Then they drove out of town, circled back and headed for the Lazy R. Hartridge did not want to go, but Hallam was insistent.

"I want to see that vein of ore," declared Hallam. "I'm taking long chances on being a party to a deception, and I want to see if the game is worth the candle."

"Maybe the ore never came from the tunnel," said Hartridge. "Maybe he found it on the ground somewhere."

"No, he didn't. That sample came from a depth, I tell you. We're going into that Two-Gun tunnel and take a look around."

They tied the buggy horse off the road and went stumbling across the hills in the darkness. Both men carried a candle. Hartridge complained all the way. "A fine job for a lawyer!" he grumbled. "Breaking my shins on boulders and ripping my legs to shreds on Spanish bayonet."

"Yes, and you're a hell of a lawyer," panted Hallam, "Don't know the difference between *corpus delicti* and *e pluribus unum*. A credit to the profession...."

Hallam knew the exact location of the tunnel. There were about two hundred feet of tunnel, which opened into a stope.

From there another tunnel angled to the left. About fifty feet back of this tunnel was where the cave-in had been made by the four outlaws.

Hartridge and Hallam climbed up on the old dump and went to the portal, where they lighted their candles.

"I feel like a burglar," whispered Hartridge.

"Well, you're not far from it," growled Hallam. "Come on."

Their feet made dull, booming noises, as they went slowly along. The candles flickered. The air was cool and dank. Hartridge shivered audibly.

"Like a grave," he muttered.

"Tomb," corrected Hallam.

"They're alike," growled Hartridge. "Smelly place, anyhow."

"Nice place for a murder, Sam."

"That's a pleasant thought."

They came into the stope, which was about twenty-five feet across, fifteen feet high at the dome, the floor a mass of broken rock. Hartridge, who had been behind, moved in beside Hallam. They lifted their candles high, surveying the place.

Suddenly they froze. Hartridge dropped his candle, grasping Hallam with both hands. Hallam whirled, accidentally knocking the candle out of his own hand, plunging the place into darkness.

Luckily they hit that tunnel dead center. It was hardly wide enough for a race, but it served nicely. Halfway to the portal of the tunnel, Hallam went down, but he bounced to his feet and kept on galloping.

Hartridge probably beat Hallam to the portal by twenty feet, but in the open country Hallam was the better at cross-country running. In fact, Hallam went so fast that he went past the horse and buggy, and had to come back; while Hartridge, almost in a state of collapse, got there in a dead heat with Hallam.

There were no questions asked. They tore the tie-rope loose, piled into that buggy and headed for Tonto City, with the horse at a gallop. Two miles from the spot where they had driven, Hallam said:

"Good Lord, Sam! Did you see what I saw?"

"If I—I didn't," countered Hartridge, "what do you suppose I ran for—to catch you?"

"Standing there—staring!" said Hallam. "Looking right at us, as though accusing us. Dead as hell—all but his eyes!"

"Good gosh!" exclaimed Hartridge. "We—we must be crazy, Ira. There are no ghosts. It's absurd, I tell you."

"Certainly," agreed Hallam. "I—I mean—there haven't been any—until tonight. I was afraid my heart would go bad on me, Sam."

"Well, we both saw it, Ira."

"Plain as the nose on—er—Henry Conroy's face. Should we stop in Tonto City and tell 'em about it?"

"Hell—no! They'd say we are crazy. We will just forget it."

"I guess that will he best. I—I wonder if it was our imagination?"

"Would two people imagine the same thing at the same time?"

"I don't know. I'm still as weak as though I had been sick for a week. Things like that are hard on a person—don't you know it?"

"That's a devil of a question to ask!" replied Hallam. "We will just drive straight through Tonto City, Sam; I want to get home."

"It's foolish," declared Hartridge. "Roarin' Bill Rose is dead—*but there was something that looked like him, Ira.*"

"Of course, he's dead. It—it just looked like Roarin' Bill—that's all."

"That's enough, isn't it?" whined Hartridge.

CHAPTER XI

EMPTY HOLSTER

DAN LEARY STOOD in the main room of the Morgan ranch house, hat in hand, rather apologetic in manner, as he faced Sally Morgan.

"We ain't said nothin' to Cal Essex," informed Dan. "He's down in the bunk-house, a-settin' on a bunk, actin' kinda dumpish. Yuh see, it was over at the Lazy R t'day, ma'am. We got there, findin' only Neilan and the sheriff. The sheriff said that Essex had gone crazy, mistook him for you, and—well, he said Essex—"

"Mistook the sheriff for me?" gasped Sally.

"That's right, ma'am. He said that Essex mistook him for you, and said he was goin' to tell that you went to warn a murderer. Essex wasn't there when we got there. They said he went out of there, heckity-blip. I dunno...."

Sally's mind was working swiftly. Cal Essex had been unconscious when she left. The sheriff, wanting to spare her, had managed to convince Essex that he had lost his mind, and mistook him for Sally Morgan.

"We don't know what t' do, ma'am," said Dan. "Yuh can't tell nothin' about a crazy feller. We don't know whether to hop onto him and tie him, or jist humor him."

Sally turned away, gritting her teeth to prevent laughter. Finally she turned, her eyes wet with tears of mirth—which Dan mistook for the opposite emotion.

"I—I would humor him," said Sally huskily. "Please go, Dan."

"I know jist how yuh feel, Miss Morgan," said Dan. "It's shore tough."

IN TONTO CITY next morning, Judge was still saying: "The question is, are you going out to the Lazy R and arrest those four strangers, Henry? Or are you going to stay here and polish a chair, adding to the shame of this already shameless office."

"Yes—and no," replied Henry. "I am thinking, Judge."

Judge sat down in his accustomed chair and tilted back against the wall. From this stance he looked balefully upon Henry Harrison Conroy.

"I expect they will impeach us—soon," said Judge.

"At least, it will be a diversion," murmured Henry.

"By the way," said Judge, "I was talking with a bartender from Scorpion Bend today. He asked me if I knew anything about the new strike Roarin' Bill had made on his ranch."

"Strike?" Henry lifted his head and squinted at Judge.

"Gold, I believe. The man said that Roarin' Bill had been in his saloon shortly before the tragedy, and imbibed freely. During this period of part-inebriation, Roarin' Bill intimated that he had brought in a sample of very rich gold ore for analysis and—"

"My goodness!" interrupted Henry. "Why, that is fine, Judge!"

"Are you trying to be funny, sir?" demanded Judge.

"You may cite me for contempt of valuable news, Judge, if I am. It is welcome information. Proceed."

"Well, that was about all. The man did not see the sample."

"An analysis would mean an assay, I presume, Judge."

"If you are interested—yes."

"As Danny Regan would say, 'I hope to tell yuh'," said Henry. "I am beginning to see a thin spot in the fog. Hm-m-m. And Mr. Hallam is an assayer, I believe."

"The only one in Scorpion Bend, Henry. Why—"Judge broke off short, stared at Henry for a moment, looked away and closed one eye. When Judge closed one eye, he was thinking deeply.

"Rich gold strike on the Lazy R—Hallam an assayer—and Hartridge contacted the heir...."

"Exactly," remarked Henry dryly. "It might put at value on the Lazy R far above the land and few livestock."

"I believe I have discovered something!" exclaimed Judge.

"Again, I hope to tell yuh, Judge. But where do the four men come in?"

"Merely incidental, I suppose—except for robbing banks and murdering folks."

"Merely inconsequential, Judge. What is robbery and murder!"

"I did not mean that, sir. What is our best move?"

"Tonight," replied Henry, "you and Oscar and I will go to the Lazy R. Unless I am mistaken, those four strangers are living in that old mine. We might leave fairly early, so as to have a little daylight in which to look over the situation. I do not believe they would chance living at the ranch house now. And with a modicum of luck, we might make a capture."

"And without said modicum of luck, we might get shot, Henry."

"Who knows their modicum until it has been tested, Judge?"

LATE THAT afternoon they rode out of town. They proceeded to a spot about a mile from the Lazy R ranch house, where they left the horses. With Henry in the lead, they shoved and stumbled their way through the brush to a point just across a small ravine from the old Two-Gun mine. They went into hiding to watch the place. There was no sign of life.

Darkness comes swiftly after sundown in the desert hills. They went at last quietly across the ravine and climbed through the brush near the portal of the tunnel.

As Henry climbed up to the dump level, he hunched down quickly, speaking a warning to the others. They drew back down into the brush.

"Four men coming," whispered Henry. "Our quarry, I think."

The four men came quietly to the portal, where they stopped. The light was very poor, but Cal Essex' voice was clear to the three officers, although he was speaking quietly.

"We know they ain't at the ranch house," he said. "This is the best bet. We can't all go in; so I'll go alone. I've got to go danged easy and not show a light; so don't get nervous. If they're in there, we'll get 'em cold, even if we have to cave this old tunnel in on 'em."

As Cal Essex disappeared into the tunnel the remaining three men hunched down. There was not a sound for sometime then except the calling of a mocking-bird. After about five minutes a coyote, far back in the hills, began his evening chattering howl.

Just then Henry pricked up his ears. In the air was a muffled drumming sound. Sort of a *thum-m-m, thum-m-m, thum-m-m,* growing louder.

Suddenly the three men up by the mouth sprang to their feet. Out of the tunnel shot Cal Essex, running at top speed. Nor did he stop. Ignoring the other three men, he swung left, a strangled yelp in his throat, and kept right on going.

After a moment of indecision, the other three took after him.

"Yumpin' Yudas!" exclaimed Oscar. "He ran like ha'al!"

"They all did," marveled Judge.

Henry climbed up to the portal of the tunnel, but it was too dark to see the disappearing cowboys from the Quarter-Circle M. Judge and Oscar joined him.

"I will just be damned!" blurted Henry weakly.

As they stood there the moon peeped over the hills, bathing the world in silver and blue.

"Pretty light here," muttered Judge. "If they should come back, we would make mighty fine targets."

"They did not seem to have a return ticket, Judge," said Henry.

"Yudas!" choked Oscar, his voice pitched nearly to High-C.

Judge and Henry turned. Standing full in the moonlight, bareheaded, clad in a hazy gray, stood Roarin' Bill Rose. There was no question of identity, because his face was full in the moonlight. There was not a quiver to his ghostly apparition.

"Good Lord!" gasped Henry, and stepped back—off the edge of the dump.

End over end he went to the bottom of the dump, landing

finally in the brush, without breath enough in his lungs to blow the dust out of his nose. Judge and Oscar did not stand upon the order of going—they merely went.

It was possibly ten minutes before Henry was able to get his head higher than his feet, after which he managed to stand up. Satisfied that no bones were broken, he clawed his way not too enthusiastically to the top of the dump, where he peered over toward the portal, But there was nothing in sight now, except the yawning, black mouth of the tunnel.

Henry slid back down the dump, and went ripping his way through the brush, back toward the horses.

He found Judge and Oscar waiting for him, with the horses untied.

"Where did you go, Henry?" asked Judge huskily, "When we looked around, it was as though the ground had swallowed you."

"I went backwards off that damnable dump."

"Do you suppose das prune yuice act like that, Hanry?" queried Oscar painfully.

"It might be the right solution, Oscar."

"Ay saw Roarin' Bill yust as plain. Yumpin' Yudas, das is first ghost Ay ever seen, and Ay hope it is de last vun."

"Amen," sighed Judge. "I guess I am getting old, Henry. I didn't do that last mile in less than a minute. I wonder if Cal Essex saw it, too."

"I only know what I saw," replied Henry. "It was gone, when I went back."

"You went back?" gasped Judge.

"Looking for you two," explained Henry. "It must have been a mirage. We both know that ghosts do not exist, Judge. It isn't scientific."

"Science be damned! I've got eyes."

"And very good legs for a man of your age, Judge. Suppose we go home. At last I am tired enough to enjoy riding a horse."

"Yudge can run like ha'al," declared Osmr. "Ay couldn't catch him, Hanry—and Ay vars yust as scared as he vars."

"Well," sighed Henry, as he hoisted his bulk into the saddle, "it is a phenomenon that is difficult to explain. Suppose we keep it to ourselves. No use having people laugh at us. We could not prove it, you must remember. They'll say—prune juice."

"I wish we had some, Henry; I feel the need of something."

"Ay have got quart inside my slicker roll," said Oscar.

"Thy name is Blessed, you wonderful Swede!" exclaimed Judge.

"My name is Oscar Yohnson, and Ay—Yeeminy! Das curk vorked out and de whole vest end of my hurse is prune yuice!"

"You negligent, half-witted, Vitrified Viking!" choked Judge. "You—it's all gone, Oscar?"

"Except de smell, Yudge."

"Probably paralyze the hind legs of the quadruped," said Henry.

"Let's go home, gentlemen. One evening like this is enough."

SO SWIFT of foot was Cal Essex that his three companions were outdistanced. They reached their horses, but Cal Essex was not there. Nor had he taken his horse.

"What the heck ailed him, anyway?" wondered Dan Leary. "My gosh, I never seen a man run that fast."

"Do yuh want to go back and see what it was?" asked McClung.

"I do not. We'll wait till Cal shows up. It might be that he's had a fall. This is mighty rough country for foot-racin'."

As a matter of fact, Cal Essex had had several falls, and his mind was altogether in a very bad condition, when he looked up from his one-man race to discover himself near the Lazy R ranch house. In his muddled condition he conceived an idea that Frank Neilan was at the bottom of his troubles; so he stumbled up to the front door of the ranch house, kicked it open and stepped into the main room.

Frank Neilan was standing at a table, trying to teach Lightning and Thunder the intricacies of seven-up, when Essex crashed in. Essex was hatless, his shirt torn, face bleeding from scratches. He stopped ten feet from Neilan, hunched forward, his lips drawn back in a snarl, an insane glitter in his eyes.

"You think you'll get her, do yuh?" he rasped. "You do, eh? Well, yuh won't, damn yuh, Neilan, I've come to kill you—now!"

His right hand, spread claw-like, flashed to his holster. For a moment Frank Neilan's heart stood still. He realized that he was nearer death than he had ever been in his life.

But the killer did not draw. The expression of bitter hate turned to one of blank amazement. His holster was empty!

Somewhere in his wild dash from the old tunnel he had lost his gun. Slowly his empty hand came away. He looked at it dumbly. Then he licked his lips, his eyes blinking slowly, as he backed away to the doorway. With a queer, strangled oath, he disappeared in the darkness.

Frank Neilan drew a deep breath. The two Mexicans were staring at the empty doorway.

"Madre de Dios!" whispered Lightning. "He say he's goin' keel you, and then he don't pull hees gon!"

"I'm theenk hees liar," remarked Thunder.

Neilan rubbed a hand across his eyes, shrugged his shoulders and went to close the door. He dropped the bar into place and came back to the table.

"I'm theenk thees man ees crazee," said Ligthning.

"Crazy?" queried Neilan. "By jove, I wonder if Henry Conroy was right, after all! I wonder if he meant that I wanted Sally Morgan."

"Don't you?" asked Lightning.

Neilan was suddenly thoughtful. "Maybe I do," he said.

"Eef you don'," remarked Lightning, as he shuffled the cards, "you are jus' as crazy as Cal Essex."

CHAPTER XII

THE GHOST WALKS AGAIN

IT WAS THE day after the ghost-hunt. Henry was sitting comfortably in Sam Hartridge's little office in Scorpion Bend.

"I swear that I don't know anything about those four men at the Lazy R," exploded the lawyer to his question. "Damn 'em, I—"

"Why damn them, if you know nothing about them?" queried Henry. "I ask you a simple question, and you—well, you blow up."

"I—I don't even know who they are," protested Hartridge.

"Haven't you asked Frank Neilan?"

"No, I—I haven't had an opportunity."

"By the way, Mr. Hartridge," Henry asked suddenly, "how do you *know* that this man is the real Frank Neilan?"

The lawyer could not hide his uneasiness at the question. He cleared his throat, shuffled some papers on his desk, before replying.

"Well, I wrote to him at his address," he said finally. "He wired that he was coming. He—he brought my letter—the one I wrote to him. Roarin' Bill told me that the young man was studying to be a mining expert, and—well, this young man seems to know something about mining. I really haven't any reason to doubt that he is Frank Neilan."

"I see…" nodded Henry. He leaned across the desk and continued, in a confidential tone. "Did William Rose ever mention to you that he had struck a rich vein of gold on his ranch, Hartridge?"

"No," replied Hartridge quickly. "No, he never mentioned it."

"I see. Well, he never mentioned it to me either."

"Then how did you know he struck it rich, Conroy?"

"Oh, merely a surmise on my part." Henry got to his feet. "Well, I must take the next stage back home. I thought you might possibly know something about those four men. I want them on suspicion of murder and robbery."

"Have you—er—looked for them at the Lazy R?"

"Yes, but they do not seem to be there any more."

"Good. I mean—it's a good thing for them, Sheriff."

"Yes, indeed. Well, I must be going, Mr. Hartridge." He strode out, leaving the lawyer to stare nervously after him.

It was still a half hour before the stage was due to leave for Tonto City; so Henry sauntered up to the depot. There he found Ben Conlan, the depot agent.

"Long time I no see yuh, Mr. Conroy," smiled the agent. "They tell me yuh had a bank robbery and murder down at Tonto."

"Yes, we did, Ben," admitted Henry. "A very bad thing."

"Any idea who done it?"

"Not the slightest. You haven't seen any suspicious characters around here, have you, Ben?"

The agent shook his head.

"I guess they keep me too busy to look for suspicious folks. Now, if it had happened earlier I might have helped yuh."

"How was that?"

"It was the night after Ab Morgan was killed. About nine o'clock, I'd say. I was in there, poundin' brass, when a man came up close to the window. I took one good look at him, but he turned away. I'll tell yuh he was a suspicious-lookin' feller. He looked as though his head and face had all been beaten up. You know what I mean—all swelled, and with discolored spots. I don't know where he went. Maybe he grabbed the freight that was just ready to pull out."

"Probably a tramp who had been in a fight, or fallen off a train," suggested Henry.

"I suppose it was. He looked pretty ragged and was bare-headed."

"It was the night after Ab Morgan was killed, eh?" Henry asked.

"That's right. I thought I'd help the feller if I could find him, but when I came out, he was gone. Prob'ly saved myself a couple dollars."

"Very likely. Ben," asked Henry soberly, "have you ever seen a ghost?"

"No," laughed the agent, "I never have. Don't believe in 'em."

"Neither do I," agreed Henry. "Well, thank you, Ben."

Ben looked at him in a slightly puzzled fashion.

"For what?"

"You think of something—I can't," smiled Henry. With that he walked away toward the stage depot, leaving the depot agent to scratch his head and wonder what Henry had meant about ghosts.

OSCAR AND Judge spent the morning in the hills at the Lazy R, trying to catch a glimpse of the four outlaws, but to no avail. Judge refused to discuss ghosts with Oscar, except to say:

"It is all poppycock, Oscar. There never was a ghost. If anyone asks my opinion, I shall say that the use of alcohol, derived from prunes, will cause severe hallucinations."

"Yah, su-ure," agreed Oscar. "It is oll coffeepot."

"Poppycock, you—you Swede. Poppycock!"

"De same to you, Yudge. But Ay still know what Ay seen. It might be poppycock to you but it su-u-ure look' like Roarin' Bill to me."

Henry, when he met them later in Tonto City, had nothing new to impart, except that he suspected Hartridge of knowing that Roarin' Bill had discovered a mine.

"What did he say about Neilan?" asked Judge.

"Rather vague, Judge. I have no doubt in my mind that the

young man is an impostor—but how can we prove it? And after all, it is none of our business."

"The breaking of a law is always our business, sir."

"Well, I am not going to lose any sleep over it. In fact, I like the young man. Unless I am mistaken, Miss Sally Morgan likes him, too."

"She does, eh? Would you let her marry an impostor—a liar, sir?"

"No-o-o, I would not like that, Judge. Perhaps it would not be fair to let her do a thing like that—if there was any danger of her ever finding out about it later."

"Why not make it a point to warn her?"

"We'd better find out—first."

"Yes, I guess that would be better, Henry. But how?"

"I wish I knew the answer to that one, Judge. In fact, there are many things that need answering. The ghost, for instance."

Judge nodded solemnly. "I was out there today—with Oscar. He is still shy about going near that tunnel."

"Aren't we all?" queried Henry.

"But we both know that such a thing as a ghost does not exist."

"Yust poppycock," declared Oscar.

"Is that all?" grinned Henry.

"Va'al, of course dere vars some of Roarin' Bill," admitted Oscar.

"Oscar has been adding to his vocabulary, Judge," laughed Henry.

"Ay found out Ay can run like ha'al, too," said Oscar soberly. "Last night Ay yumped over a cactus sax feet high."

"And Judge ran around it, eh?"

"No, by yiminy! Yudge yumped it first."

LATE THAT afternoon, while Judge and Oscar took a siesta, Henry saddled his horse and rode away from town. He rode straight toward the Lazy R, until he came to the spot where they had left their horses the night before. He paused there, thinking to leave his horse; then he decided to ride closer.

"If I feel like running," he told the horse, "I do not need to make it a marathon."

There was not a soul in sight when, a hundred yards from the old Two-Gun tunnel, he dismounted. Leaving his horse, he walked on, very quietly, to the mouth of the tunnel, There he sat down to ponder over the situation. The place did not seem spooky in daylight. In fact, it seemed ridiculous to think of a ghost standing in the mouth of that tunnel.

Henry was indulging in a quiet laugh over the episode of the night before, when the laugh froze on his lips. Footsteps were thudding softly in the tunnel, coming toward the entrance. Henry slid his gun loose from the holster and cocked it quietly. Slowly he elevated the muzzle to cover the opening.

Out walked Roarin' Bill Rose, hatless, wearing an old, wrinkled gray suit of clothes!

He stopped short at sight of Henry and his wobbling six-shooter.

"Don't shoot, Henry," he said. "I ain't heeled."

"My goodness!" gasped Henry, lowering the muzzle of his gun. "Amazing!"

Roarin' Bill scratched his matted hair and grinned foolishly.

"Well, yuh got me," he admitted. "Yuh would—sooner or later.".

"What is the idea of playing ghost?" queried Henry.

"I wasn't. Heck, I was only tryin' to keep out of sight. That danged fool lawyer and another feller came in here, and scared themselves into fits. Last night Cal Essex sneaked in on me— and went like hell. And what about you—last night. Wasn't the other two Judge and Oscar?"

"Well, Bill, you must admit that it was—er—ghastly. Do you not realize that you are supposed to be dead?"

"No, I didn't know that. I reckon I danged near did die. But what about me dyin'?"

Henry explained about the horse in Devil's Chimney, and how they decided that he had gone into it with the horse.

"I didn't know that," said the old man. "I don't even know where I fell off. Mebbe it was right near there, and I scared the horse over the edge."

"Did you walk to Scorpion Bend and take a freight train the next night?" asked Henry.

"Who told you?"

"Oh, I guessed it," smiled Henry.

"I'm not sure what I done. I was shot. Ab Morgan shot first. Gut me through the ribs. After I saw he was dead, I got scared. Nobody saw us. I reckon I could have proved self-defense, but right at that time I was scared and hurt. I don't remember what I done. Mebbe I went to Scorpion Bend. Guess I did, 'cause they took me off a freight train in Black River City, and doctored me up. My head was a sight. The hole in my ribs didn't amount to much, but they said I'd have to stay for a week or two more. But I swiped a suit of clothes and sneaked out.

"I thought I'd keep on goin', but dang it, I wanted to find out what was goin' on over here. I figured I could hide out and get information. But I can't find out a danged thing, except that them doggoned horse-thieves have moved into my place, along with some jigger I never met. They had some grub cached over in Ab Morgan's old mine; so I took it over here. Henry, what do you know?"

Henry told him some of the things that had happened. In the fading light of the evening, Roarin' Bill Rose sat there and cursed Sam Hartridge and Ira Hallam for a pair of liars and thieves.

"But you did make out that will," said Henry.

"Course I made it out, dang it! I got a look at that young crook through a winder last night, and I wondered where I'd seen him. Why, he was with Hallam, when I gave that sample to him. Nephew—hell!"

Henry smiled slowly. "I thought he located the heir too quickly."

"Yo're danged right! I'm goin' up there and kick him out."

"Not yet, William. I want Hartridge and Hallam here, before you do that. I've suspected them quite a while. But what about those four outlaws from New Mexico? Where are they?"

"They're around here some'eres, Henry. Yuh say they robbed the bank and killed George Reed? Doggone 'em, they can't behave a-tall."

"They will hang—if we catch them, William," declared Henry.

"Yeah, I reckon they will. But what about me, Henry?"

"I believe you can prove self-defense. You did not shoot first."

"How can I prove that?"

"By the simple fact that Ab Morgan could not have fired a shot, after you shot him. He was killed instantly."

"My gosh!" gasped Roarin' Bill. "Henry, you've got brains."

"I hope to tell yuh," replied Henry. "You stay right here, William—so I can find you, in case I need you."

"Anything yuh say, Henry; you've made me feel danged good."

"I do not feel badly about it myself, William the Ghost."

Henry went back to his horse, started toward Tonto City. On second thought, he turned his horse. He had decided to go and have a talk with Frank Neilan.

CHAPTER XIII

UNMASKING

IT WAS JUST getting dark when Sally Morgan limped up to the Lazy R ranch house. Frank Neilan, alone at the house, saw her and ran out to meet her. One glance at her and he swept her up in his arms and carried her into the house. She bit her lips to keep from crying.

"What is it?" he asked her. "Miss—Sally, why did you walk over here?"

"I—I was afraid to stay home," she said. "The cook is drunk, and Cal Essex is the only one of the boys at home. Cal acts so funny. We don't know what's wrong with him. He wouldn't go to town, but he let all the horses loose except his own; so I couldn't get away. Oh, he told me about it. I crawled through a window— and walked. I wanted to get you to take me to Tonto City."

"Why, my dear, of course I will. I'm glad you came to me. It makes me feel that you trust me—and I want to be trusted—by you, Sally. You don't mind if I call you Sally, do you?"

"No, Frank."

"Golly, that's great! I'll bet your feet are blistered."

She smiled ruefully. "I think they are. But can't we hurry? I'm afraid of Cal Essex. If he missed me, he might come here."

Frank nodded. "He came here last night, Sally. He kicked the door open and came in, acting like a crazy man. Swore he was going to kill me. Then he reached for his gun—but just as suddenly he turned and walked away. I don't understand what he was thinking about."

"I believe he is crazy, Frank; I really do."

From outside came the sound of a horse walking on the hard ground. Sally looked quickly at Frank, fearful that it was the Quarter-Circle M foreman.

He was thinking that too. "Get into that back room!" he whispered.

As Sally closed the connecting door, Frank Neilan took a gun from the fire-place mantle. A knock sounded.

"Come in," said Neilan tensely.

The door opened. It was Henry Harrison Conroy. Frank Neilan relaxed and placed the gun on the table.

"Good evening, Sheriff," he said.

Henry glanced at the gun. "Evidently you were not expecting me," he said dryly.

"One never knows whom to expect—in Arizona," Neilan answered.

"That is very true. Have your four friends been home lately?"
Neilan shook his head.

"I haven't seen them, Sheriff. Evidently they've left the valley."

"One never knows, does one?" queried Henry.

"You're riding late," observed Neilan.

"It seems," smiled Henry, "that we are fencing. Mr. Neilan, I have no weak spots in my armor tonight."

"I have no reason for fencing with you, Sheriff."

"Possibly not. However, I am asking you to do something for me."

"At your service, sir," smiled the young man. "Name it."

"Will you sit down at the table and write a note to Sam Hartridge, asking him and Ira Hallam to come here tomorrow night?"

"Why—" Neilan hesitated, looking curiously at Henry. "Why, that's a queer request. I don't understand the meaning of it, Sheriff."

"I merely want them here together tomorrow night, Neilan. I call you Neilan, because that is the name they gave you. What your right name is, I do not know—nor care. If you write the letter, saying that it is imperative that they come here. I'm very sure they will not ignore your summons."

"You say—*the name they gave me?*"

"Exactly," replied Henry firmly. "And do not edge toward that gun, sir. You are an imposter. Hartridge, Hallam and you, sir, conspired to take over this ranch, because of a rich gold vein discovered by Roarin' Bill Rose, just previous to the night he was—er—killed. You were substituted for a legal heir.

"Because you have not profited by this crooked move, nor have you been legally declared the heir to the Lazy R, I do not suppose the law can touch you. However, after the meeting here tomorrow night, I know of no reason why you should stay any longer in Wild Horse Valley, sir."

"I—I quite agree with you, Sheriff," nodded Neilan quietly.

The connecting door opened at that moment and Sally came out. She had heard all of the conversation. Henry looked at her in amazement.

"My dear Miss Sally!" he exclaimed.

"You see, Sheriff, it was—" began Neilan.

But Sally interrupted. "I believe it would be better if I told him the story, while he takes me to Tonto City," she said.

"Why, I was going—"

"Not now," said Sally coldly. "If Mr. Conroy doesn't mind…"

"My dear lady—it is an honor."

Neilan looked at Sally for a long moment. Then he turned to Henry. "There are horses and saddles in the stable, Sheriff," he said.

"Thank you, sir. If you will write that note—"

Neilan made no objection, but sat down at once and wrote the note. The sheriff pocketed it.

"May I saddle the horse?" asked Neilan.

Sally shook her head. "We can handle that nicely."

As they were going out, Neilan said:

"Sally, I'm sorry."

But she did not turn her head. Henry closed the door.

Neilan sat down in a rickety old chair, rolled and lighted a cigarette, his face grim. Then he laughed quietly.

"Well, you poor fool, you wanted adventure," he muttered half-aloud. "And if this isn't adventure—what is adventure?"

THIRTY MINUTES later Pecos Charley, Sody Slade, Ed Clovis and Zibe Tucker came filing in through the rear doorway of the Lazy R ranch house. Neilan was still sitting there.

"Saw the sheriff and a lady leave here a while ago," said Pecos.

Neilan nodded. "Yes, and you boys will keep fooling around until they hang all of you for that murder in Tonto City. Why didn't you leave the country?"

"Aw, we never killed that feller, Frank."

"You'd have a fine time proving it."

"You can't scare us away, feller," declared Ed Clovis. "There's too much of our money tied up in that old tunnel down there."

"It looks bad for all of us," remarked Neilan.

"How do yuh mean—bad?"

"If you're around here tomorrow night you will hear Hartridge, Hallam and myself denounced as crooks."

"Yuh mean—they're onto yuh?" asked Pecos quickly.

"Yes."

"Who the heck discovered that, Frank?"

"The sheriff."

"That pot-nose? Yuh don't mean it!"

"Sorry, Pecos; but he made me write a note to Hartridge and Hallam, asking them to be here tomorrow evening. If the law is obliged to take over this place, what chance have you fellows to ever dig out that gold?"

"By the horns on the moon, I believe we're sunk!" blurted Clovis.

"We might fix that sheriff t'night," suggested Tucker grimly.

"No killin', Zibe," warned Pecos. "We ain't killers—except to save our own lives. And you better remember that."

"What are you goin' to do?" asked Sody of Neilan. "Are you goin' to stay here and face the music?"

"Yes, I am," replied Neilan. "Because of the fact that I have never accepted this ranch as a legal heir, nor have I profited by any deals, the law can't touch me. I merely moved in here, under the name of Frank Neilan. I suppose there are a number of Frank Neilans in the world who aren't nephews of Roarin' Bill Rose."

"Yeah," sighed Sody, "I guess yo're in the clear; but we're sunk deeper than ever. I dunno what to do. I suppose, if we was wise, we'd hightail out of here right now."

"Let's go back to the hideout and talk it over," suggested Pecos. "I git nervous, settin' here in the house. They might move in on us at any old time." With the words, he got up. *"Adios,* Kid. If we don't come back—good luck to yuh."

"Same to you, boys," replied Neilan. "It's a great life."

"I wish I had mine to live over again," growled Ed Clovis. "I'd be a farmer."

"Yeah—and steal yore neighbors' spuds," laughed Pecos. *"Buenas noches, amigo."*

AS THEY rode back to Tonto City, Henry listened to Sally's story. The power of suggestion, he realized, must have affected Essex' mind. The subsequent ghost episode at the Two-Gun tunnel had not been exactly beneficial to him; and it was quite possible that the man, in his present mental state, might be very dangerous.

Sally had explained, of course, how she happened to be at the Lazy R ranch house. Neither she nor Henry referred to the exposé of Frank Neilan. It was evident to Henry that Sally's affections had received a rude jolt when she heard that the young man was an impostor.

"It is evident that something must be done about Mr. Essex," he told her. "You are in danger, as long as he is in his present mental state. You will stay at the hotel, until something is done."

"You know what he threatens to do," said Sally wearily.

"If he attempts it," declared Henry, "we will take him to court and prove that he is insane."

That night, Henry sent a man to Scorpion Bend with the message to Hartridge. It was to be dropped in the post office, so that Hartridge could not question the bearer. Back at his office, Henry said nothing to Judge about meeting Roarin' Bill Rose, nor of his conversation with the young man at the Lazy R.

CAL ESSEX came to town next afternoon. He rode in alone. He went to the Tonto Saloon, where he stayed about an hour. Then he went to the Tonto Hotel, where he talked with Tom Rickey. Rickey told him that Miss Morgan had come into town with Henry Conroy the night before, and was now in her room.

Henry had seen Essex ride in, and he had seen him go to the hotel. Judge was in the office, unaware that trouble might be brewing. Henry, from the doorway, saw Essex coming toward the office from the hotel. He himself went back to his desk and he sat down. He slid a six-shooter onto his lap and tried to appear indifferent. Judge was reading a newspaper and did not notice this.

Cal Essex stepped into the little office, his arms swinging at his sides, and stopped near Henry's desk. Judge glanced up.

"Good morning, Cal," he said pleasantly.

But Cal Essex was not interested in the morning nor in Judge; he was squinting at Henry.

"I just came to tell you," he said in a brittle voice, "that you better keep yore damn red nose out of my business, Conroy."

The muzzle of the big six-shooter jerked above the desk top, level with Essex' middle.

"Elevate them, Mr. Essex," said Henry calmly. "Higher, please—this gun has a soft trigger."

"Why—damn you… you…."

Essex might have been a trifle crazy, but he was no fool. His hands lifted above his head.

Judge dropped his paper. "Of all things!" he exclaimed.

"When you have recovered your equilibrium, Judge," said Henry, "you might remove Mr. Essex' gun."

Judge came forward, lifted the gun gingerly from the holster, and placed it carefully on Henry's desk.

"Now," said Henry, "you might prepare Room Number One for our guest."

"You—you are putting him in jail?"

"Like hell, you are!" yelled Essex.

"You will go to jail—or to the morgue," said Henry firmly.

"Why, I ain't done anything, damn yuh! You can't put a man in jail when he ain't done anything?

"I have often wondered if it could be done," said Henry. "A

little while ago I made a bet with myself that it couldn't be done. Now, I'm going to win that bet. Turn around and follow Judge."

Swearing impotently, Cal Essex entered the cell. Henry shot the bolts.

"Damn you, I'll get you for this, Conroy," declared Essex.

"Not until you get out," said Henry. "I shall do my worrying when you do get out."

Back in the office Judge turned to Henry.

"You cannot hold this man, Henry," he declared. "There is no charge against him."

"Disturbing the peace, Judge. He has been annoying Sally Morgan."

"Did she prefer charges?"

"All right, all right! Then he threatened me. You heard him."

"Yes, that is true. Well, a day or so in jail might cool him off."

Henry went to the hotel and told Sally what he had done.

"I am afraid it will only make him worse," said Sally. "If he would only agree to leave the country."

"Well," smiled Henry, "he is in a spot where it will be easy for you to discharge him. I will turn him loose, if he will agree to leave the country. Suppose you give me what wages he has coming, and I will do the rest."

Sally was agreeable to that. Henry went back to talk with Cal Essex. The foreman listened glumly to his offer.

"All right," agreed Essex finally. "Give me the money and I'll quit the damn outfit. I'll have to go to the ranch and pick up my war-sack and what few things I've got there. Then I'll come back here. How's that? Does it suit yuh, Fat Nose?"

"Perfectly," replied Henry. "You can have your gun, when you return to town."

"That's all right."

Henry unlocked the door. Essex walked out of the office and went straight to the hitch-rack. There he mounted his horse and rode swiftly out of town.

"I hope this is the end of Mr, Essex, as far as Wild Horse Valley is concerned," said Henry as he watched him go.

"I would not trust him very far," sighed Judge.

"By the way, Judge, we are holding a little party at the Lazy R this evening, and you will attend—you and Oscar."

"A little party at the Lazy R? What kind of a party?"

"I am not exactly sure—yet. Possibly a ghost party."

"Damn it, Henry, be explicit!"

"I can't, Judge; the entertainment hasn't been all arranged."

"Skulduggery?"

"Well, not exclusively, Judge. Perhaps a touch or two."

"Have you told Oscar?"

"Not yet. Always invite Oscar at the last moment—otherwise he might invite the rest of the town."

Henry left the office then, went down toward the hotel. About an hour later he came back.

"I left Cal Essex' gun with the bartender at the Tonto," he told Judge. "You and Oscar will secure a horse and buggy and take Sally Morgan home. Essex will likely be here, before you leave. I'm going for a little ride."

"Where?" asked Judge.

"Peddling invitations to the party at the Lazy R. You take Sally home, and then come to the Lazy R. You two might entertain some of the early guests—if there are any, Judge."

Judge shook his head wearily. "Henry, there are times when—"

"You have told me that same thing many times."

"Very well. If I must go blindly—I go blindly."

"Naturally," remarked Henry dryly. He went back to the stable to saddle his horse.

CHAPTER XIV

PARTY AT THE LAZY R

SALLY MORGAN WAS waiting in the doorway of the hotel, when Judge and Oscar drove up.

"Isn't Mr. Conroy going along?" she asked.

"Mr. Conroy, if I may say so, be damned," replied Judge quietly. "You do not mind the profanity, I hope."

"No, I am used to it," laughed Sally. "But why should he be damned?"

"Yudge is sore because Hanry don't tell him everything," stated Oscar.

"No one asked your opinion, Oscar," reminded Judge.

"Ay yust vant her to know de truth, Yudge."

Sally laughed at the lugubrious expression on Judge's face.

"I am sure that Mr. Conroy means well," she said.

"I suppose so," agreed Judge grudgingly.

"It is very kind of you to take me home."

"Hanry sent us," replied Oscar blandly. "He gives orders and ve take'm."

"Oh, shut up!" blurted Judge. "One would think we were slaves."

"Two," corrected Oscar. "Ay feel de same as you do, Yudge."

"And that, Miss Morgan, is a sample of the life I lead," sighed Judge.

About a mile out of Tonto City they met Cal Essex, his war-sack tied to his saddle. He merely reined off the road to let them pass, but did not speak.

"That takes a load off my mind," said Sally soberly. "I hope I never see him again."

"He will be obliged to leave the Valley, in order to get work," said Judge. "He is not very popular."

They were nearing where the road forked to the Lazy R, when they met Dan Leary. He waved wildly and reined up in a cloud of dust.

"I was just comin' in to get the sheriff," he told them. "Me and Steve McClung and Art Miller captured them four outlaws that have been hangin' around the Lazy R. They was livin' in an old prospector's shack on the Quarter-Circle M. We've got 'em hogtied at the Lazy R ranch house. There wasn't enough horses to bring 'em to town; so I came to get you fellers."

"Well my gracious!" exclaimed Judge. "You—you actually caught them, did you? Well, well!"

"We shore did. And we want yuh to take 'em off our hands."

"Why, yes, of course. I—I—Miss Morgan, do you mind riding up to the Lazy R? We can put Oscar in charge of the prisoners, and then I will take you home."

"That's perfectly all right," answered Sally.

"We ain't seen that Neilan hombre," informed Dan Leary. "Mebbe he seen us comin' and pulled out—I dunno."

"Why should he pull out?" queried Judge.

Dan Leary grinned. "I dunno. Feelin' guilty—mebbe."

Judge shot a quick glance at Sally. Her lips were tightly shut, and she was looking straight ahead.

"We will follow you up there, Leary," Judge said.

THEY DROVE up to the front of the ranch house. There two saddled horses were tied in the shade. Sally stayed in the buggy as Judge and Oscar went forward. Sitting along a wall, tied hand and foot, were Pecos Charley Peters, Sody Slade, Ed Clovis and Zibe Tucker. The four outlaws looked foolishly at Judge and Oscar.

"There's yore killers and robbers," said Steve McClung. "When the law can't get 'em—we can, eh, boys?"

"Any old time," agreed Dan Leary expansively. "Any reward, Judge?"

"I don't believe there is. They haven't been indicted yet."

"Ain't been what?"

"Charged legally with the crime."

"We never done it," growled Pecos Charley. "We ain't been near that town."

"Toff lookin' yiggers," declared Oscar.

"Very," agreed Judge. "Hm-m-m. I am wondering how to get them back to Tonto City. Perhaps we shall have to get some horses, or a wagon."

"Be dark pretty blamed soon," observed Leary. "Yuh better make up yore mind, Judge; we want to git home. Have yuh seen Cal Essex?"

"Mr. Essex quit the job, rolled up his blankets, and is now on his way out of the Valley."

"No."

"My statement is correct," said Judge stiffly. "I am not in the habit of lying, sir."

"I'll be a hen's offspring!" exclaimed Art Miller.

"Suit yourself," said Judge. He turned to Oscar. "I believe I shall leave you here to guard the prisoners, while I take Miss—"

"Here comes another horse and buggy," interrupted Leary. "Now, who in the devil is this?"

It proved to be Sam Hartridge and Ira Hallam, coming in answer to Neilan's note. They got gingerly out of their buggy. Hartridge spoke to Sally, looked around uneasily at the group of men. Then Judge walked over to him, told him about the four prisoners. After that Hallam and Hartridge seemed less nervous, and when Judge suggested that they all go into the house, they followed him. It was getting so dark that Judge lighted the lamp.

"Where is Frank Neilan?" asked Hartridge.

"Yeah—where is he?" replied Leary. "I reckon he pulled out."

"Why—why should he pull out?" asked Hallam weakly.

"Well, he's gone," laughed Leary.

"I—I think we ought to go back, Sam," said Hallam. "Neilan isn't here. No use of us staying."

"Well… yes… I guess…."

"What did you want Neilan for?" asked Judge.

"He sent for me," replied Hartridge. "I'm his lawyer."

"He'll prob'ly need one," laughed Leary. "If yuh ask—" He broke off, listening.

"What was that?" blurted Judge. "A woman's scream?"

He started toward the doorway, jerked back as two men stepped in. Judge's jaw sagged.

"Yudas!" gasped Oscar.

"Roarin' Bill Rose!" wheezed Pecos Charley Peters.

"Henry!" whispered Judge. "Henry Conroy!"

"Present," replied Henry. "Good evening, gentlemen. Ah, my friends from Scorpion Bend… Welcome to the party."

But no one was paying any attention to Henry—they were all watching Roarin' Bill Rose. Roarin' Bill looked grimly around. His eyes swept over the four captives, and he laughed harshly.

"They got yuh, eh?" he remarked. "Not a brain among yuh."

JUDGE TOOK a deep breath, realizing by now that it was actually Roarin' Bill Rose, in the flesh. Lightning and Thunder came in through the kitchen entrance, curious to know what was going on. They saw Roarin' Bill. Lightning swayed, threw both arms around Thunder, burying his head in Thunder's bosom, and they both fell down. And at that moment Sally stepped inside the doorway, her face a mixture of fright and astonishment.

"My—my dear Mr. Rose," gasped Hartridge.

"Don't talk to me, you—you crook!" roared Roarin' Bill. "You and that damn assayer! Yes, you—Hallam! I know what yuh done. The two of yuh thought I was dead; so yuh planned to steal this ranch. Don't you dare lie, or I'll crawl all over yuh."

"No… no," whispered the frightened Hallam. "We didn't know—"

"Yo're danged right, yuh didn't know *when you was well off*. You aimed to steal my ranch and git that gold mine. Well, you was wrong. That gold mine ain't on my land. It ain't on anybody's land; it's all dug out. I'll tell yuh where—"

"Bill!" blurted Pecos Charley.

"Shut up!" snapped Roarin' Bill. "I'm tellin' this. Them four tied-up badmen found the vein in Morgan's old mine; so they dug it out, packed the sacks of ore over to my old Two-Gun tunnel and cached all of it. It's right there now, and it belongs to Sally Morgan."

Everyone looked at Sally. She stepped closer to Roarin' Bill. He smiled at her and said:

"Howdy, Sally."

"We thought you were dead," she said.

"Well, I ain't. I reckon I'm awful tough. But," he looked around, "where is that danged young crook who claimed this ranch? I want to slap his ears off—the dirty snake."

"He's gone," said Leary. "I reckon he pulled out."

"Pulled out, eh? Lucky thing for him that he did. I'd show him how to dance."

"That will—" faltered Hartridge, and Roarin' Bill turned on him.

"Yea-a-ah! Exactly! I seen that young feller. I looked through a winder here and got a good look at him. Thought I'd seen him before. Damn you, Hallam, that young feller was with you the day I gave you that sample for assay. Yo're a fine pair of crooks, you and Hartridge."

"Go ahead," grinned Oscar. "Ay like it."

"Keep your nose out of it," ordered Judge.

"Yah, su-ure."

"I want to git my hands on that young crook," declared Roarin' Bill. "I'd like to make an example—"

A scraping noise at the doorway caused them to turn—and gasp at what they saw.

Standing there in the doorway, swaying on his feet, was Cal Essex—a double-barreled shotgun gripped in his hands, the twin muzzles covering the room. He was hatless, his face a bloody smear, his shirt in ribbons, one eye almost closed.

"Cal!" gasped Leary. "Cal—don't...."

"A fine pot-shot," laughed Essex huskily. "Damn yuh, I've got all of yuh together—even the woman. I'll show yuh. Fire me… put me in that damn jail. Crazy am I? Well, I'm sane enough to shoot straight. Don't move! Yo're all goin' to die; so yuh might as well take it right.

"I killed that damn Neilan. I told him I would. Now I'm goin' to make a clean sweep."

"Cal, you're—" began Leary fearfully.

"Shut up! Yo're goin' to take it, and yo're goin' to take it—"

BUT HE didn't finish. There was a *thud, thud* of running steps on the gravel just outside, and a dim form hurtled into Cal Essex. The shotgun flamed, but the muzzles were up, throwing the lethal charges of buckshot into the empty air. The two men crashed down in a snarling, cursing blur. Oscar Johnson dove through the doorway like a halfback tearing through the line with the ball, and went headlong into them.

"Oll right!" yelled Oscar. "Ay got him!"

The struggling mass disintegrated. Oscar had Cal Essex in his mighty hands, staggering toward the lighted doorway, while behind them came Frank Neilan. No one knew who he was until he staggered into the room. His face was bloody from a gash in his scalp. His lips were puffed, his eyes purple, but he was grinning foolishly.

Henry quickly handcuffed the unconscious Essex. Sally was staring at Neilan.

"Essex said he killed you," said Henry.

"It wasn't his fault that I'm not dead," panted Neilan. "I—I was over by the Morgan ranch, when Essex came there. He took his bedroll and rode away. I started back home and was on top of a hill, when I—I saw your buggy going toward this place.

"Then I saw Essex coming back. When your buggy was out of sight, he raced his horse back to the ranch; so I followed. I wondered what he was going to do. He went to an old dugout, got something out of there, and then came back to the end of the house. He crawled under.

"He—he was fixing a dynamite blast, when I surprised him. Luckily he had no gun, and so," Neilan laughed, "it was a good fight, until he hit me on the head with a rock. I guess he thought I was dead. When I regained consciousness I saw him come from the bunk-house with a shotgun, and go to his horse. So I—I followed him here."

"And just in time, too," said Henry. "That crazy fool might have murdered all of us."

"I hope t' tell yuh!" blurted Roarin' Bill.

"What the devil!" snorted Henry. For Frank Neilan had lifted the revolver from Henry's holster and stepped aside. Now he was covering Dan Leary, Steve McClung and Art Miller, who were standing together.

"Put bracelets on them, Sheriff," panted Neilan. "Those three and Cal Essex were the four masked men who held up the bank and killed the cashier. Essex told me all about it. He said Leary killed Reed, and—"

"That dirty liar!" cried Leary. "He shot Reed himself!"

"You can't prove it," snarled Essex.

"The hell he can't!" rasped Miller. "We all knew that."

Oscar and Judge quickly handcuffed the three men. Taking a deep breath, Neilan handed the gun back to Henry.

"Did Cal Essex confess to you?" asked Henry.

"Can you think of any reason for him to confess to me?" countered Neilan soberly. "Essex may be crazy, but he would be worse than crazy to confess a crime that would hang him."

"Wait a minute!" choked Roarin' Bill. "Who's this feller?"

"This feller," replied Henry, "is the young man who inherited the Lazy R, after you died. This young man, who seems to have been through a meat-grinder, is known as Frank Neilan, the heir to the Lazy R."

"He is, eh?" gritted Roarin' Bill. "You jist saved my life and a lot of other lives, but I jist want to tell yuh that—"

"Wait just a minute," interrupted the young man. "I am glad you came back, because I wanted to ask you a question."

"Of all the gall!" exploded Roarin' Bill. "You wanted to ask *me* a question? Well, you brass-faced young fool—go ahead and ask."

"Did you," asked the young man, "have a brother Albert, who became a preacher?"

"Yu—yes."

"And did you have a sister named Cora, who married a man named John Neilan?"

"Why—dang yuh—I did!"

"They were my father and my mother."

"Yo're father and—"

ROARIN' BILL came closer, staring into the battered features of the young man.

"Dug up some information, eh?" he said. "Smart, eh? Well, I'll bust yore smartness, you young pup. What was my sister's nickname? Answer that one—if yuh can."

"My father," replied the young man, "called her Happy."

And then—Roarin' Bill smiled. "Happy. That's what she was. Hell, I was the black sheep of the family; I lost track of 'em— mostly. I got a letter from Albert a couple years ago and he—wait a minute! Dang it, is yore name really Frank Neilan?"

"Absolutely," replied the young man.

"Then—then how in the devil did you happen—"

"It just happened. I studied mining, and drifted west. I was broke and down on my luck in Scorpion Bend, when I met Hallam. I didn't have a cent. Hallam fed me and when this deal came up—well, I needed money, and I scented adventure. When they mentioned the name of Frank Neilan, I—I thought it was only a coincidence, because I'd never heard of you. I didn't know I had an uncle out here."

"We are vindicated!" blurted Hartridge.

"You be damned!" snorted Roarin' Bill. "You ain't nothin' but a crooked lawyer—even if luck is with yuh."

Frank Neilan turned and walked over to Sally.

"I hope you forgive me, Sally," he said. "I'd hate to go away, knowing that you wouldn't forgive me for playing a crooked game."

"What do yuh mean—goin' away?" rasped Roarin' Bill. "You're a miner, ain't yuh? Sally might need a good man. I'll betcha you can uncover that vein again in her mine."

"After the crooked deal I pulled here?" queried Frank.

"Crooked? Hell's bells, kid, I got here jist ahead of the law. I'd be a fine whippoorwill to call anybody crooked."

"I'll need a foreman for the ranch, too," said Sally. "I—I seem to have lost all my hired hands."

Frank Neilan grinned. He looked at the four outlaws who had just been exonerated from any hand in the bank robbery and murder. His uncle's gaze followed his own.

"There's yore crew," laughed Roarin' Bill. "If it's all right with the law, I'll guarantee that they'll play straight."

"The law," declared Henry Harrison Conroy, "is satisfied. We have the men we wanted—thanks to Frank Neilan."

Frank turned and looked at Sally. She was smiling.

"You will need at least four men, Frank," she said. He smiled too, and he turned to Henry.

"If you'll release my four cowboys, Sheriff," he said, "we will be on our way to the ranch."

"My goodness!" exclaimed Henry. "You work fast, Neilan. This has been quite a party. But as I have always said—anything can happen in Arizona."

"That was said before you were born," remarked Judge.

"I but perpetuate the truth, sir," replied Henry.

"Ain't yuh goin' to arrest me?" asked Roarin' Bill.

"No," replied Henry. "Come in tomorrow and we will talk it over with Judge Myers. The plain facts will exonerate you, William. And to you,"—Henry held out his hand to Sally—"I wish all the luck in the world. We haven't had a wedding in Tonto City for ages—but it looks as though the drouth is about to be broken."

And judging by the glance that passed then between Frank and Sally, there seemed little doubt but that Henry's prophecy would be fulfilled.

AT THAT point Thunder and Lightning Mendoza stole out of the kitchen, where they had been listening all the while, and sat down on the back steps of the ranch house.

"W'at you theenk, eh?" whispered Thunder.

"W'at you mean—theenking?"

"W'at 'appen, which I am asking about?" explained Thunder.

"Leesten my leetle brodder," said Lightning, "sometime I'm theenk you haven't got a brain in my head for looking nor leestening."

"Sure," agreed Thunder. "But w'ut 'appen to everybodee?"

"In the firs' place," explained Lightning, "Onkle Beel ees not dead. He ees *tio* to thees yo'ng man, but I don' know it. You onnerstand?"

"You don' know eet. Sure. I onnerstand. But w'at 'appen?"

"I theenk that theese damn Morgan *vaqueros* do sometheeng wrong."

"W'at they do wrong?"

"Por Dios! You theenk I am jodge? Why you don' use my ear and eye for seeing theengs? You think I leesten for whole damn family?"

The cavalcade was leaving the Lazy R. Thunder and Lightning stood on the back steps and watched the string of buggies and riders grow dim, as they went toward Tonto City.

"I'm theenking that thees yo'ng man ees going to marry weeth Sally Morgan," remarked Lightning.

"Eet seem to me," observed Thunder, "that sometheeng 'appen to everybodee, but me and you."

From inside the ranch house came Roarin' Bill's voice.

"Thunder! Lightnin'! Where the devil are you—you colorado-maduro manhandlers of the King's English?"

"Don' be too sure," whispered Lightning. They went into the house.

Made in the USA
Middletown, DE
22 December 2020